SAAR'S LEGACY: BOOK ONE

Silk Over Razor Blades

by Ileandra Young

Saar's Legacy: Book One
Silk Over Razor Blades

Published in May 2015 by Little Vamp Press

ISBN: 978-0-9926995-5-0

Acknowledgements & Thanks

This page could be a mile long but I'd prefer that it isn't. There are so many people I need to thank I'm just going to rattle them all off. Here we go.

David Soden, Mum, Dad, 'Uncki' Charlie, Gemma Ward, Celine Connolly, Sally Edmans, Ava (Jordanna East)terby, Karen Perkins, Dave Johnson, Louise Burke, Lisa French, David Gilchrist, the writers of Leicester's Phoenix Writers Critique Group, Joseph Hitchman, Ian Fielding, Stephanie Fung, Victoria Plunkett and Rachel Phillips. All of you, in a way large or small, abstract or direct, have helped me get this work out into the open. It's taken me years (I'm not kidding, I'm talking YEARS!) but we're here. We've done it.

Thank you all so very, very much. This is a dream finally pulled from my mind and made real. It's your victory as much as mine.

Thank you for your support, help, readings, critiques, firm shoulders, listening ears and all the rest in times past and recent. You're all stars to me.

To my boys

This is what Mummy has been working on for so long. I hope you'll agree it was worth the perpetually grumpy face and occasional skipped trip to the park.

I love you.

Silk Over Razor Blades

DAY ONE

Chapter One

'That guy is staring at me,' said Lenina.

Abandoning her half-hearted perusal of a magazine, she pointed out the shop window to the figure in grey slouched against a lamp post on the far side of the road. He seemed to straighten as she looked, pulling a scruffy woollen hat further down over his shock of frizzy ginger hair.

Beside her, lost in the clutches of a generously stuffed leather armchair, Ramona looked up from her copy of *Brides Today*. 'What?'

'Outside by that bench. Some guy with a woolly hat.'

Her friend leaned forward and squinted through the window. 'You sure?' she said, her words heavy with Glaswegian overtones. 'He's just standing there.'

'For ten whole minutes. Just staring. It's creeping me out.'

'Maybe *he* thinks you should be wearing white, too.'

Lenina glared. 'Don't you start. Daddy already tried to talk me out of it. Even Nick wasn't sure when he heard.'

'Has he seen it yet?'

'No. He's not supposed to. Tradition.'

'You're wearing a wedding dress the colour of fresh blood. What the hell do you know about tradition?' Ramona's soft expression drained some of the sting from her words. 'It's beautiful, honey.'

'Really?'

'Aye, how many times do I have to say it?'

The door to the fitting suite opened, admitting a silver-haired stalk of a woman with short, rounded fingernails painted pale pink. She pressed one hand to her barely there breasts and gasped through carefully rouged lips. 'You're a vision, Miss Miller. Just look at you.'

'There's an old man lurking outside,' Lenina said. 'He's in grey. Shabby. Like a tramp. He's been watching me for ages.'

'Oh, is it Homeless Bob? Does he have a dog? This street is his favourite spot.'

'I didn't see any dog, but I'd say this guy is homeless.' Lenina turned to the window, meaning to point him out. 'Oh. He's gone.'

'Don't worry about it, Miss Miller, Bob is harmless. He loiters here because the bakery across the road gives him pastries at the end of the day. Now . . . let's have a look at you.' The woman tugged and tweaked at the dress. Twice she dabbed the hem with white pen and inserted a pin beside the mark. 'I wish more people would embrace bolder colours,' she said. 'I'm all for tradition, but white and ivory used to mean something. A woman should wear a dress that reflects her personality. Her inner fire.'

Lenina frowned. 'I just liked the cut.'

A nod. 'Yes, it does flatter you. Women with such lovely, strong hips should show them off.' The woman touched her own skinny frame. 'I had to pad my dress when I got married, just to prove I had a waist under all that fabric. But fashion was very different then. All shoulder pads and lace.'

Ignoring Ramona's giggles, Lenina smoothed the fabric over her ribs. 'It needs adjusting around the waist and across the shoulders.'

'Have you lost some weight?'

'Maybe.'

'You only have two more weeks.' The woman wagged her finger. 'No more or else I won't be able to help. Have you decided on hairstyles yet?'

'Loose, I guess.'

'Are you sure? We shouldn't hide those lovely high cheekbones under all those braids. No need for make-up either; you have beautiful dark skin. Show it off and have your hair off the neck.'

'I'll think about it.'

'Of course, Miss Miller. These adjustments will be done by Friday, I'll book you in for 4 p.m.'

'No, I'll be at the museum. Make it Saturday. I won't be working then.'

When the measuring, pinning and tucking was done, and the dress safely wrapped in plastic, Lenina turned back to her friend. 'You can stop laughing too. You should be protecting me. She practically said I'm fat.'

'What, when?'

'All that stuff about my hips.'

'Oh, Nina, stop it. You're not fat. The dress is gorgeous and so are you. She's just doing her job.'

Fifteen minutes later, in jogging bottoms and trainers, Lenina left the boutique with Ramona. As she walked, she tucked her mobile phone into the pocket of her sports armband.

'Sure you don't want a lift?' Ramona popped the boot of her scruffy 1960s Mini and shoved her own purple dress into it along with a pair of shoes. 'It's no trouble. Verni isn't home yet so I don't have to rush back.'

'No, no. I want the exercise.'

Ramona plucked a curl of ginger hair from her eyes and tucked it beneath her hat. 'Why? You heard the woman; don't lose any more weight.'

'I won't. But . . . I need the run. To clear my head, you know?'

'You're something else. Will I at least see you for lunch tomorrow?'

'Wouldn't miss it. You need to help me finalise the goodie bags.'

'Only if you promise to eat something.'

Lenina rolled her eyes. 'Fine. But no cake.'

'Deal.' Ramona climbed into her car and drove away, tooting the horn as she left the car park.

The car rumbled past a figure in grey, with a dirty denim jacket and a torn woollen hat. He turned to watch the car leave then looked straight at her.

She shivered.

His gaze stroked her body; a lurid, ethereal caress that made her stomach clench. His features were hidden by distance, but Lenina knew it was a man. No woman would look at her in such a way.

'I don't have anything, okay?' she called, wincing as the wind stole her words. 'Go bother someone else.'

He smiled, or seemed to, then walked towards her.

With a squeak, she turned and ran, forgetting her usual steady pace in favour of a full sprint. She left the line of shops that housed the boutique and bolted through the centre of town, fighting back the threat of tears.

Her route struck through the centre of town, taking her past bars, clubs and a few themed pubs with clusters of people gathered near the doors to enjoy their cigarettes.

Outside a pub she stopped long enough to draw several shuddering breaths. Her knees trembled and a fine sheen of sweat coated her forehead.

'You okay?' The voice came from her left. It belonged to a man wearing narrow black glasses and a concerned frown. The woman at his side tugged his arm, trying to turn him back to their conversation.

'Someone's following me,' cried Lenina.

'I can't see anybody. Do you need help?'

Lenina looked back over her shoulder. 'I— oh.'

'What did they look like?'

'I don't know.' She winced. 'I mean, he's gone now.'

The man raked a hand back through his hair, long dreadlocks each as thick as a finger. They curled over his face like ropes until he tugged them back. 'Do you want to stop for a second? I'll happily call someone. I don't mind.'

A chuckle bubbled from her lips. 'He's not there. Probably wasn't following me at all. I feel so silly.'

'It's okay.'

'No . . . I'm an idiot. Just highly strung I suppose. I'm so sorry.' She patted her braids, tried to neaten the rough ponytail that held them back. Lifting her shoulders a little higher, she smiled. 'I didn't mean to bother you.'

'It's no bother. It's my job. Are you sure you don't need help?'

'She's fine,' his companion snapped. 'Didn't she just say?' The woman, all red hair, glossy lipstick and tight clothing, gave Lenina a glare hot enough to melt steel. 'You're not even on duty tonight.'

Lenina backed off, hands raised. 'She's right. Sorry. I'll just go.'

She left before either of them could say more, careful not to look back as she jogged along the High Street. A safe distance away, she paused to tuck in her earphones and activate the media player on her phone. Though she often glanced over her shoulder, nothing followed her but the occasional scatter of leaves, chased by an empty crisp packet. Soon the lively voices and bright lights of the pedestrianized High Street chased away the fear, leaving behind the remnants of embarrassment.

As she left the outskirts of the city centre and began the winding path along backstreets she felt the wind snap more violently at her bare arms. She stepped up the pace again, regretting her decision to decline the warm interior of Ramona's car.

Her mobile rang.

'Heita, babe. All done at the boutique?' Nick's voice radiated excitement and reined-in curiosity, all laced with a faint South African twang.

'Yeah.' In that moment she forgot all about Homeless Bob. 'They think I'm fat.'

'What?'

'She says I have big hips.'

'You do. That doesn't mean you're fat. Where are you?'

'Nearly home, about to cut through Grick Park.'

He tsked; a soft, angry sound. 'Why didn't Ramona give you a lift?'

'I wanted a run. And before you start, I'm fine.'

'Babe, I've warned you about going through there alone. You heard what happened last week, didn't you? Some six-foot semi-pro wrestler got murdered on his way home.'

'Yeah, in London. This is Leicester.'

'It's still dangerous.'

She glanced over her shoulder. 'But there's no one else here.'

'Exactly.' He muttered something unintelligible in Afrikaans. 'Damn it . . . I'm coming to meet you.'

'You're not my dad, you know. I think I can make it home in one piece.'

'Keep to the path and go *around* the grass. I'll find you at the near end by the gate. Hurry up.' The phone buzzed then fell silent.

Lenina groaned, reactivated her music and turned off the path, on to the grass.

A line of trees surrounded the park and a gap directly opposite marked her destination. It led through a narrow alley and back on to the main road on the far side of the housing estate.

Her feet squelched on the damp grass. Twice, she narrowly avoided tripping on raised lumps and disguised holes forming the entrances to rabbit warrens. To guide the way, she followed the white paint marking the edges of the three football pitches, lined up side by side.

Halfway across she shivered, aware of the growing chill in the air. She paused the music and listened to the crushing silence of the park. Even the sound of passing cars couldn't reach this far.

A glance over her shoulder confirmed there was little point in backtracking, so she ducked her head, resumed her run, and fixed her gaze on the line of trees.

An especially savage gust whipped hair round into her eyes, temporarily blinding her. With the wind came a voice, low and soft. A whisper she felt more than heard.

Her shoulders tightened. Prickling, like the legs of invisible insects, crawling over her skin.

She reached the line of trees still staring over her shoulder, then slipped on a slick of brown leaf mulch. Skidding on her stomach, she came to a stop on the gnarled protrusions of a nearby tree root. The rough bark scraped her palms. Her phone sailed away through the darkness.

Panting, Lenina flipped on to her back.

'Hello?' Her voice quivered.

More whispering. This time mixed with laughter. She peered into the gloomy gaps between the trees. Swallowed hard. Held her breath. *There's nothing there*, she thought, *just the wind.* Cold moisture seeped through her joggers as she reached her knees.

'Damn it.' Lenina brushed the worst of it away and wiped her hands on her thighs.

'Don't fuss on my account, love. The baggy workout gear is gorgeous and so are you.' The low voice, with an East London drawl, spoke from the shadows. As it did, the whispering stopped.

Lenina scrambled to her feet, one hand fisted in her sports vest. 'Who's there?'

The tubby ginger tramp stepped out from behind a tree a couple of metres away. His hands curled around the trunk, filthy fingernails scraping the bark. He grinned, showing off crooked teeth.

'Bob?' She backed away. 'Homeless Bob from the High Street? The one who likes pastries?'

'My name ain't Bob.' His voice prickled down her spine like dabbling fingers.

Though her mouth opened no words came out. A quick shake of the head and another step back, wobbling on the uneven earth.

'Don't you talk?' He followed, hands sliding teasingly over the tree's trunk. One of them held a dagger with a savage looking blade, sharp with a double curved edge.

'Yes.' She swallowed and tried again. 'Of course I do. And . . . my boyfriend's coming.' She added that last part with a haughty toss of her head. 'He'll be here any second.'

He laughed, a sound like grinding metal. 'Good. I'm counting on it.'

Lenina pressed her shaking hands to her sides and glanced over her shoulder. The line of lights marking the path seemed a million miles away. Brighter lamps from the road beyond the tree line may well have been on the other side of the earth for the comfort they gave.

'You'll make a good starter.' The stranger smiled.

'Don't touch me. I'll scream.'

He glanced left and right. Broadened his smile. A trick of the light made his teeth long and sharp. 'Go ahead.'

Lenina ran. Her feet pounded the wet earth, each stride made awkward by damp, slippery grass. Her breath stuck in her throat, choking until she let it go in a rasping gasp. Muscles across her stomach and chest tightened. Her lungs ached.

Halfway back across the grass, she risked looking back.

A whimper broke free.

'Where . . . ?' Her stride slowed. Gaze darted left and right.

The park was empty. She faced forward and released a shriek when she saw the grubby stranger directly in front of her. Helpless to stop, she bounced off his chest, stumbled back, and hit the ground on her backside. More damp seeped through her clothes.

'Please don't hurt me!'

The man reached down, his chipped fingernails catching on her hair. He stroked her face with the flat of his dagger. The sharp point scratched her skin hard enough to break it. She felt its bite and bit her lip to keep from screaming. The smell of cigarettes, vodka and something older, meatier, assaulted her nostrils. She gagged.

It seemed a year and more since speaking to Nick, belittling his orders to stick to the path. It couldn't have been more than five minutes.

Please, she thought, *please come.*

The stranger knelt in the grass, tilting the edge of his weapon beneath her chin. With the other hand he gripped her face. 'Look at me,' he whispered. When she hesitated, he tilted her face to meet his. 'I said, *look.*'

The order beat Lenina's common sense like a ram. Her resistance splintered beneath it.

First she saw his lips. Thin. Pale. Surrounded by the shadow of short, coarse hairs. Nose: bulbous and red. A set of scars on his right cheek; four thin slashes like cat claws. Then, as the moon slipped from a scudding bank of cloud, she saw his eyes clearly for the first time . . . and gasped. Grey, like stormy seas. Or smoky diamonds. Gorgeous eyes framed by long, thick lashes which brushed his cheeks like delicate strands of lace. The man was beautiful and in that moment she wanted nothing more than to slide her arms around his neck and offer him everything.

Chapter Two

A wriggle of warmth pulsed through Lenina's belly as the stranger turned his smile on her. Warm and welcoming, it promised all manner of pleasures if only she would move closer. The band of fear around her chest loosened. She lowered her arms to her sides.

'That's right,' he murmured. 'Look at me.'

A straggle of ginger hair fell over his shoulder, not curly like Ramona's, just untidy.

She touched it. 'So soft.'

The man smiled. 'Come.'

Lenina leaned in, closing her eyes as the distance between them narrowed. She felt the hot rush of his breath slide over her forehead, tickle her nose, caress her jaw. Lower . . . to the side of her throat. She smiled. All fear gone.

Nick's voice pealed out of the dark. 'Get off her!'

Lenina hit the floor. She hadn't realised the stranger had her cradled to his chest until he let go.

Pressure built behind her eyes and made her head throb. Clutching the ache, she rolled over and saw Nick standing at the edge of the tree line, his mobile held out like a torch.

It lit the scene between them like a macabre shadow puppet show and she saw again the man to whom she so wanted to give herself.

Grey eyes, yes, but not the colour of diamonds. More like muddy snow. Thin lips surrounded by ugly salt-and-pepper stubble and four deep gouges in his cheek.

She heaved.

Nick lowered a trembling hand towards her but the hideous stranger slid between them with the grace of a figure skater.

'You must be the lucky boyfriend.' The man grinned. 'You took your sweet time.'

Nick stepped to the right, where his path was blocked yet again. 'Move!'

The stranger's feral smile flashed those yellow teeth again. 'Right looker, ain't you?' His voice resembled the brush of velvet, mixed oddly with that strong aura of East London. 'I like blonds.'

Lenina's stomach writhed. She swallowed the rising taste of bile and tried to stand, but her knees refused to hold her. 'Nick . . . ?'

'I'm here, babe.' Again he tried to reach her.

Once more the stranger blocked him, this time laying a hand on his shoulder.

Nick smacked it away. 'What the hell's wrong with you? I've called the police.'

'Liar.' The low voice held smug confidence.

'How would you know?'

'I know you . . . Nicholas Harrison.'

Nick flinched. 'How do you know my name?'

A mocking smile in answer.

'Have we met?'

The man shrugged. It meant everything and nothing.

Hands shaking, Nick put his mobile away. Never once taking his eyes off the stranger and his weapon, he extended his hand. 'Nina?'

When the man advanced again, Nick spun about and shoved him in the chest. He might as well have pushed a brick wall.

The stranger cocked his head to the side, tangling grubby fingers in his knotty ginger hair. 'That was rude.'

'Yeah? Get the fuck out of my way. How's that for rude?'

The man snarled. There was no other word for it.

Then Nick screamed.

Lenina blinked – she must have – because when she next looked, Nick lay prone, the man on top of him, both hands circling his throat. The dagger lay forgotten on the ground.

Nick struck out with his fist but the blow swung wide and caught nothing but air.

Braying laughter, loud and gravelly, filled the night air.

The sound shivered all the way through Lenina's body and left her trembling.

Nick strained to bring his legs up and lever the clawing stranger away from his face. Lenina watched him flail and urged her leaden limbs to move.

'Run, Nina!' he cried. 'Run away.'

She hugged herself. Shook her head. Fought to block out the screams ringing in her ears. Her aching throat and rasping breath made clear who the screams belonged to.

She peered through her fingers.

Nick's arms flailed. His back arched off the ground. Gold hair fanned across the dirt, a pale splash in the darkness.

Lenina scrambled to her feet and rushed at the shabby stranger. 'You're hurting him. Please, let go.'

The man ignored her, leaning over Nick's face and shoulders. He gave a low moan and opened his mouth.

'Get off him.' She grabbed his face from behind and dug in. Her sharp, polished fingernails found the soft orbs of his eyes.

The stranger reared up with a shriek. Lenina realised she was airborne a split second before her back hit the tree. Stars of purple and gold danced before her closed eyelids and cold numbness crawled down her back and shoulder. She bounced and hit the ground on her face. Grass tickled her nose, its fresh scent a stark contrast to the festering reek of the man above her. He flipped her over and straddled her hips. Blood trickled down his cheeks.

'You first, love,' he snarled. 'Then him.' He bent close, wrenched her head to one side and fastened his lips to the side of her throat.

An instant later his teeth sank in. White hot. Piercing. Burning. Different descriptions whirled through Lenina's mind but none matched what she felt. The teeth tore through her skin with a wet, meaty crunch. An eager tongue swirled over her earlobe, then hot drool dribbled over her skin, mixed with something smoother and thicker.

The world dipped in and out of focus. Low buzzing filled her ears. Time stood still, one eternal moment stretched out into forever. Then sound came rushing back; the greedy gulp of a parched man slurping water on the banks of earth's last oasis. Feral grunting. Moans of pleasure.

Lenina whimpered and pushed at the stranger's chest.

He responded by tightening his thighs on her hips. His body pressed flush to hers. Both hands tangled in her hair and pinned her in place. Without lifting his face, he rolled his hips, pressing an unmistakable bulge against her hip. The sensation sent fresh tears rolling down her cheeks.

Familiar images danced before her mind's eye. She saw her father, gaping at the second adjustment to the wedding quote; her brother glaring at a suit hanging in the bridal boutique, shaking his head; her mother fingering the delicate lace of a traditional ivory wedding dress while sneaking covert glances at tiny christening robes.

Fresh moans from the stranger broke the procession of memories. He pressed his erection harder against her body and mumbled. Lenina thought she heard the word 'tribute', but the rest drowned beneath the sounds of her pain-wracked sobs. The coppery scent of blood overpowered every other, even the stranger's mouldy meat smell. It slid down her neck and pooled in the hollow of skin between her neck and shoulder. More gathered in the curve of her ear. The scratchy wool of his hat grazed her chin. She saw a beetle crawling across it, shiny carapace glinting in the moonlight. It paused then crawled back the other way, ambling away from the scene of agony with an ease Lenina envied.

She blinked. When her eyes next opened she saw clouds over the moon again and knew, in a distant way, that time had escaped her. Her hands stopped shoving. She lowered them to the grass.

A fresh image filled her mind. Nick dropping his shopping bags to kneel in the middle of the High Street. He ignored her embarrassed protests and held up a purple jewellery box, teasing it open while watching her face. The ring inside glittered in the watery sunlight, the diamond at its apex gleaming with star-like brilliance.

'Marry me,' he said.

No more than an arm's length away, the present-day Nick sprawled on his back, eyes closed, breathing shallow.

'Nick, help me.'

He moaned and clutched his head. His hands shook.

'Please.'

The man sucking her throat laughed through his pursed lips. Renewed ferocity made Lenina shriek and grind her heels into the grass.

He jabbed his free hand between her lips. 'Shut up.'

His hairy skin tasted foul, but the intimacy of this intrusion brought life back to Lenina. She bit down and ground her teeth together until fluid burst on to her tongue with the taste and smell of old pennies.

The pleasured moans turned into a yelp of surprise. He punched her, hard enough to rattle her skull and Lenina slackened her jaw. Pain exploded across her face. Blood ran down her lips and chin. Some touched the back of her throat and kept going, burning a trail down her throat and beyond. She felt every drop as it went and each one sent a fresh line of fiery pain coursing through her body.

Her heart beat harder, hammering her ribs with such force that she jerked forward. A tingling sensation prickled at the ends of her toes and travelled through her body like the march of tiny ants. With it came a rush of agony that bunched her muscles into painful knots before letting go. She threw herself to the side, gripping her stomach as it fought to eject every piece of food it contained.

'Bitch!' The man cradled his hand to his chest. 'You'll regret that.'

Lenina had just the time to realise that she already did, before vomit clawed free of her mouth. Blood-streaked ribbons of bile and food splashed the grass. Some caught her hands and knees, but violent convulsions rendered her prone and helpless. A sensation like the prick of a thousand hot needles pierced a trail down her spine. It continued along each limb and billowed out until even the tips of her fingers felt ready to burst. Tears streamed down her cheeks. Wiping them away left pale smears of pink against her fingers and palms.

At her side, Nick finally sat up. He swayed and faced her. 'Nina?'

The man chuckled, shaking his injured hand. 'You're both gonna die.'

The words barely left his mouth before Nick lurched across the grass like a drunken rugby player. He caught the stranger around the knees and pulled him down to the ground. 'Nina, run,' he begged.

She longed to do as he asked. But cold now replaced the heat in her body and dark mist crawled across the edges of her vision. She shivered. 'Help me . . .'

Though not a wrestler by any means, Nick used his broad shoulders and strong hands to good effect. His crooked nose told the story of past fights and he wasted no time in taking charge of this one, pounding his fists into the stranger's mid-section. 'Can you hear me, babe? Stand up. Please.'

She reached towards him, but her vision clouded with more featureless darkness that finally obscured him and everything else. Her hand fell on something long and hard. Something sharp that pricked her fingers and added fresh pain to the growing catalogue.

When the cloudiness cleared, what Lenina saw made her heart make one last desperate bid to beat free of her chest cavity. Instead of the park she saw stone statues. Long corridors filled with golden sunlight. In place of grass and the stranger's sickening scent, Lenina smelled blood laced with the sweet tang of cinnamon and cumin. Sand compacted beneath her feet: hot, dry and coarse. Replacing the taste of blood, there was beer, strong and yeasty. The imagined taste washed down her throat but couldn't begin to touch the roaring thirst she felt.

Loud voices took over from the wind in the park, clear and jubilant, raised in song and prayer. All of them spoke a language utterly foreign, though strangely comforting to the ear.

Weary, confused, Lenina tried to touch one of the statues. When she raised her hand, she saw not her own familiar fingers but a square, thick-fingered, scarred hand. A hand with chipped fingernails caked with dirt and sand. A hand with dark hairs bristling from the knuckles. The hand wore no engagement ring.

From behind a stone statue with a carved falcon's head, a woman approached, dressed in white. She had large eyes, ringed with thick, black make-up and full, pouting lips. 'Good to see you, Saar,' whispered the ghostly form.

No sooner had the woman spoken than the images vanished.

The park returned with a rush like howling wind, and Lenina felt the ginger stranger sprawl beside her, crushing her extended hand. Dark smudges ringed his thin lips which hung open in a silent 'O' of surprise.

Lenina heaved again, scrubbing at her eyes. With effort she pulled free and scrabbled away from him.

Nick stood two steps away, his chest heaving, hands bunched into fists. A lump of blood dribbled from his left nostril. His clothes hung off his body, ripped and bloody. 'Get lost,' he hissed. 'I've got more where that came from, I swear to you. Touch her again and I'll break your legs instead of your nose.'

The stranger narrowed his eyes. Snapped his mouth shut. 'Fine,' he grunted. The word emerged thick and laboured. 'Fine!' He scooped his dagger from the grass and leapt to his feet in a move so fast and smooth it might have belonged to a dancer. He rushed forward, slashing with the weapon.

Lenina screamed, curling her hands over her head even as Nick dived towards her. He crashed against her, shielding her body with his own as he took them both to the ground.

Pounding footsteps reverberated through the grass.

Silence.

It seemed like hours before Nick allowed her to sit up. He gazed at her, blinking away the blood dripping into his eyes from a cut on his forehead. A swelling on his cheek signalled the start of a bruise. His lower lip swelled.

'You okay?' He touched her cheek.

She whimpered.

Her last clear thought before unconsciousness claimed her, was that neither of them would be in any state to pose for wedding photos.

Maybe she would wear make-up after all.

Chapter Three

31 July 30 BC

Screams of wounded and dying men rang out across the sand.

Golden grains, once dry and loose underfoot, clumped into red-soaked clods, as if the earth itself wept tears of blood. Beyond, shrouded by clouds of dust, a shape hundreds of cubits tall stabbed into the air like an accusing finger.

Saar wiped blood from his eyes and cleaned his sword on the body of the dead man at his feet. 'Forward,' he cried. 'Drive them back to the river.'

As if his voice gave strength to those still standing, he watched his men pierce the Roman forces and continue until the first line broke and scattered.

'Use your gifts, blessed sons and daughters. Show them the true power of we who are god-touched. Offer mighty Set his rightful tribute.'

The change in atmosphere was palpable. The excited energy of his soldiers lifted the hairs on his arms and neck. A prickle of warmth rushed over his skin. Fangs lengthened from his gum line to brush his tongue.

Many of his men tucked their swords away. Others tossed down their weapons and formed tight fists. None stopped fighting.

Stares and whispers among the enemy quickly changed to screams as Saar's chosen soldiers exposed their deadly fangs. Men and women alike attacked like animals: biting, scratching, pulling, kicking.

Saar threw down his own sword, flexed his fingers and attacked. His first victim shrieked as he gripped the man's head, yanking it to one side. A quivering expanse of naked flesh showed above his breastplate.

In that straining throat, Saar saw a pulse, beating against the skin like a trapped butterfly. Hunger swelled within him, moistening his tongue. With effort he tamped it back and closed his lips over the jumping flesh. He bit down in one smooth move.

Blood spurted into his mouth, hot and smooth, tinged with a sweet edge that characterised the taste of fear.

Two swallows later he let the man fall, unwilling to let the pleasure of feeding distract him. Instead, he moved on and saw, all around him, others of his men performing similar savage acts.

Even Kiya, after hurling her daggers into the back of a fleeing soldier, leapt on his flailing body and rode it to the ground. She bent over his throat and bit deep to access the blood beneath.

A rush of pride tingled through him as he watched her. Her beauty, her skill, her deadly accuracy. Never before had women fought at his side, but today, he could think of nothing better.

Despite the change in hand-to-hand tactics, Octavian's men displayed an impressive level of discipline. After recovering from the initial shock they resumed their attack and several Alexandrian soldiers fell.

Saar smiled.

Those soldiers unmarked by his blood fell and quickly died. Others touched by the power of the mighty god Set, healed within moments. Though they bled and screamed like all others, they resumed battle after a brief rest, most of them as if untouched and often with renewed ferocity.

Through the heat of battle Saar felt a new tug on his senses. He had no other way to describe it. Deep inside, where he felt the minds of all of his God-Touched children, he recognised the touch of one he feared he'd never feel again. Hope soared within him.

His lungs tightened. 'Mosi? As he spoke the name he saw the man approaching from the city, sword in hand. He laughed. 'Mosi! In my hour of greatest need you return to my side.'

Anger crackled across the bond between them, stinging his skin like insect bites. Hot enough to steal his breath. He stumbled on the sand. Stared. 'Why, Mosi?'

The answer became clear as he looked.

Mosi wore unfamiliar armour, his dark hair hidden beneath an ugly plumed helmet. He carried a Roman sword.

The hairs on Saar's neck and arms snapped to attention. His innards tensed into painful knots. 'No. You wouldn't. Please, no.'

Their gazes locked.

Mosi smiled. A cold smile, the like of which Saar had never seen on his face before.

His sometime friend pointed with his sword and began to run. With him came a fresh unit of Roman soldiers, charging down the slope in tight formation. They sliced through the unprepared Alexandrian forces, scattering them into smaller, vulnerable groups.

Kiya screamed, her voice shrill with panic as the enemy charge washed over her. When Saar saw her again, she lay pinned to the sand by a heavy wooden spear.

Saar forgot the battle. Forgot Mosi. Forgot everything.

He dashed towards Kiya with single-minded purpose, beating or kicking those who strayed across his path. Before he could reach her, arrows filled the sky, temporarily blocking the sun like a flock of birds. Though they came from the direction of the city, they had nothing to do with his men. He barely had time to bellow a warning before the first arrow struck his shoulder. The impact spun him around. Pain robbed his breath. The next rain of arrows landed with deadly accuracy, peppering the Alexandrian forces until they resembled porcupines.

First to fall was a tall, thin man with eyes the colour of charred wood. Distantly, Saar recalled his name to be Aswad. Six arrows sprouted from his chest, neck and shoulder, their shafts shuddering in the dying sunlight. He held out his hands, screaming, then fell into the sand on his back. Aswad's skin paled to the colour of faded parchment. His flesh withered, drying like an animal carcass left too long in the desert sun. Then the limbs began to crumble.

Saar froze, fingers slack on the arrow shaft protruding from his left shoulder. His heartbeat filled his ears like a steady drum until he could hear nothing else.

'What—'

An explosion of pain cut him short. Searing agony as though he'd been dipped in hot tar. But not his pain. Saar gazed at Aswad and knew it was *his* pain. Knew that the younger man was going to die. With that knowledge, the rock of Saar's mind cracked and a fragment broke free, like a piece of amber beneath a clumsy hammer.

He could hear it, the shattering of that secret place in his head which housed the connection to each of his children. Though he fought to gather the pieces, the act resembled futile attempts to repair broken pottery without clay.

Saar dropped to his knees. Sweat coursed down his back. It burned in his wounds and mixed with the blood before running down his skin like crimson tears. His exposed fangs lengthened from his gum line and slashed his lips and tongue.

Aswad's body crumbled like an aged statue. Dust gathered beneath his writhing limbs until nothing remained but a large pile of golden sand, encased in bloodied clothes.

He gaped. Stared. Brushed his hand through the warm sand. It couldn't be real. His eyes . . . perhaps an illusion. A trick of the fatigued mind.

Pain winked out, taking all sensation of Aswad with it. The place he once inhabited in Saar's mind ached like a raw wound; a deep gouge in the mountain face of his senses.

Saar clenched his fists to stop them shaking. A deep breath in, then out again, but the drums in his head intensified. He couldn't stop them. More arrows rained from the sky. Fresh screams rent the air as the deadly projectiles met their targets.

To his left, another of his children screamed and grasped her stomach. Eyes bulging, body shaking, Moswen stared at her belly where the same terrifying decay consumed her flesh. Sand cascaded from the tips of her fingers, climbing both arms and meeting at her chest. Her legs collapsed beneath the weight of her trunk and spilled sand across the ground.

Saar gasped as the pain began anew along his abdomen.

Another fragment chipped free in his mind, the piece called 'Moswen.'

Her screams cut short as the decay claimed her face, and Saar felt the loss like a deep pit in his head. He shrieked and gnashed his teeth until blood filled his mouth. It seemed to take hours, though he knew mere moments had passed.

Battle raged around him, a roaring, shrieking, thunderous clash of determined forces vying for supremacy and control of the field. No time to sit. To lie still. Fight, fight, always fight, pushing forward, attacking, driving the enemy back.

When Saar eventually scrambled to his feet, a sea of panicked faces stared back, a small circle of calm in the midst of the swirling storm of fighting.

Nobody spoke.

For long moments Saar could think of nothing to say. Shock, fear and anger stoppered his voice. Then the sounds of continued battle returned him to his senses.

'I—' he licked his lips. 'Those unworthy of our gift will return to the sand. Look, I stand. You stand. Set blesses only those worthy and destroys the weak. Take heart in your strength and fight on.'

It worked. For a short time. Then Mosi's archers recovered from their own shock and fired another volley. Three more arrows punctured Saar's body; spine, thigh and buttocks.

He stumbled. Fell again. Saw every god-touched soldier within two hundred yards do the same. Even those beyond the line of fire pitched to the ground with agonised howls and shrieks, all of them clutching at buttocks, spine or thigh.

Close by, a soldier almost as old as himself crashed to the ground. Blood poured from the side of his mouth. 'Help me!'

'Adofo, are you hurt?' Saar demanded.

'No.' The other man clutched his thigh. 'I've taken no arrow, nor felt any sword's bite.' Yet florets of glistening red formed beneath his clothing, spreading from three distinct and familiar points.

Victory and the chances of attaining it visibly slipped from Saar's grasp. Over his shoulder, he saw the enemy forces form two groups. One broke off to march on the city whilst the other stayed to deal with the flagging Alexandrian men. The few still standing either dropped their weapons or fled towards the river.

'Fight. Stay and fight, you craven beasts.' Saar yanked the arrow from his thigh. Blood jetted into the air.

The battlefield dipped in and out of focus. Cold crawled through Saar's limbs. His leaden legs dragged beneath him, demanding a brief pause while his god-touched body handled the blood loss.

'We heal,' he cried, though his voice trembled. 'Warriors touched by Set are blessed with his strength and resilience. His blood gives us unending life.'

Adofo's body exploded in a skin-shearing blast of desert sand.

Saar's words morphed into a scream. His back arched. He felt pain like thousands of claws pulling his skin, shredding it from his flesh one agonising scrap at a time.

It took seconds. Felt like hours.

The drum-like thud of his heartbeat reached a fevered pitch and when he next opened his eyes, Saar realised he was lying on his face. The moisture on his cheeks was not blood or sweat.

Staring at the darkening sky, Saar fought to catch his breath. He felt the dry caress of the wind on his cheek and the tickle of sand on his neck and shoulders. He wondered why he could still feel them. Why the sting of sweat in his cuts and scrapes burned in the heat of the sun. As blood pulsed from the wound in his thigh he realised that the flow remained steady.

He was no longer healing.

Saar turned his head and sought his immediate children; the seven men and seven women touched directly by his gift.

He found them one by one and realised that with Adofo, Aswad and Moswen already gone, the others might soon follow. Hasina, Ife, Faki, Jamila, Jafari, Kakra, Atsu, Musa, Nubia, Kiya and Mosi.

Mosi . . .

'You betrayed us.' Saar saw him lying on the sand close by, cupping both hands around a wound on his thigh. He felt a burning desire to touch the other man's cheek, to brush away the blood and tears on his smooth skin. Instead he spat in his face. 'You betrayed me.'

'I had to correct your mistake,' said Mosi.

'Saving our home from Antony's idiocy is no mistake.'

'Are you so blinded by your hate of the man? He loves Cleopatra.'

'His love brings ruin to the rest of us.' Blinking away tears, Saar tried to stand. On the fourth failure he lay still. 'If we lose this battle Octavian will add us to his growing pile of toys. But I could stop him. I could save us all if you would let me.'

Mosi sighed and lay back. He took his hands from his thigh and let the blood flow free, a slow pulse that would surely kill him.

Saar growled through his teeth. 'Alexandria will fall because of your weakness. Our queen. Our home. Our families.'

'I have no family.'

'You have me. Your god-touched brothers and sisters. Was I not good to you?'

'You were. Once.'

'Yet you reject my gift and kill us all.'

'Believe what you will but I won't share your illusions. This is no gift. We're dying.' Mosi heaved himself into a sitting position long enough to point across the battlefield. The gesture encompassed the hundreds of men dying from three distinct arrow wounds. Wounds from arrows still embedded in Saar's body.

'Your wounds destroy all of us. Our bodies are linked to yours. Your gift becomes weaker with every child, and our every breath, thought and desire rides on your whim.'

Mosi's insight startled Saar into sullen silence.

'And with every death of a man or woman "blessed" with Set's black blood, a piece of you dies too.'

Across the battlefield more god-touched soldiers succumbed to Saar's injuries and to some extent he felt them all.

Saar scrunched his eyes shut, clenched his fists and squeezed down on each connection. He began his own battle to shut down his senses and keep them out as he'd learnt to do years ago.

But it was all too much. Too close. Too many.

'We're dying, Saar. All of us. Accept it.' Mosi's gaze met his, all soft browns and flecks of gold. He smiled and, despite his impending death, peace filled his features.

'All of us . . .' Saar sat up. 'All of us.'

Panic seized him.

Scrambling away on his hands and knees, he made his painful way across the sand, mindless of the decaying bodies he crushed on the way.

'All of us,' he said again, swallowing the bitter rush of bile at the back of his throat.

Kiya lay a short distance away, still pinned fast by the spear shaft through her abdomen.

Tears trickled down her cheeks, stained red. Blood pumped from her thigh and more oozed into the sand beneath her. 'My love . . . why? How?'

'Be still.' He touched her face. 'I'll save you.'

'You told me we would live together forever.'

Tears dampened his own cheeks. 'We will. I promise.'

She held out her hand. Sand slid from her fingertips.

Saar moaned and grasped his head with both hands. 'No. Not you too.'

She smiled, even as the terrible decay consumed her arms and legs. 'My love, you must win. Show them what it means to be god-touched.'

'I can't do this without you.'

'Kiss me, dear love.'

Saar leaned forward, eyes closed, eager to enjoy one last taste of her lips. His mouth brushed the dry coarseness of desert sand. When he looked again, all that remained of Kiya were the clothes she once wore, and the spear shaft which then fell flat to the ground.

Physical pain meant nothing any more. Cramps and convulsions rocked Saar's body but he barely felt them. Numbed to it all, he stirred his fingers through the sand that once made his lover's body and felt . . .

'I'm done,' he whispered.

As he spoke the words, the last traces of Kiya's presence cracked free from his mind and crumbled away.

The sole survivor of his fourteen children sighed and touched his shoulder. 'It's over. This curse of yours isn't the future. Human men and women must rule.'

Saar gripped the bloodied linen of Kiya's dress. The lingering warmth mocked his pain. He held it to his face, inhaling the sweet, familiar scent of figs and cumin. 'I love like a man,' he whispered. 'I fight like a man. I'm as human as any other.'

'You stopped being human the day you first drank blood to pay your debt to Set. It ends now. Here. With us.'

Saar gagged as Mosi's hands wrapped around his throat, once so warm and loving, now hard and cruel. The last rays of the dying sun caught the edge of a bronze dagger with a double curved blade. The gems in the hilt sparkled like tiny red eyes.

Mosi wept as he plunged it home.

Saar screamed, writhing as the deadly weapon pierced his chest and sank into his heart.

Chapter Four

The bright light made Lenina wince. She squeezed her eyes shut. Cried out. Rolled left and, just before toppling, felt hands around her waist, pulling her back from the edge.

She struck out with both fists, flailing and kicking. 'No, let go!'

'Nina, whoa. Stop, it's me!'

Several seconds passed before Lenina recognised the voice. When she did, she froze and peered over her shoulder.

Nick lay on the bed beside her, wrinkles of worry slashed across his forehead. The bruise forming on his left cheek gave him the appearance of a blond, lopsided Quasimodo.

'What happened? Where did the guy go?'

'Shh.' He pressed her shoulders against the sheets. 'Calm down. Sit for a second. We're home.'

'But how? We were in the park. That guy— he attacked you. You were screaming.'

'Me? No, babe. Not me.'

'*Someone* was screaming.' Lenina put her hands to her head, picking at the tattered shreds of her memory.

There was no battle. No sandy city covered by a pallor of smoke.

Instead a familiar room, filled with the comforting scents of deodorant and cocoa butter. Soft ticking from the Dali-style clock above the bed. CDs on shelves. Clothes on the floor. A wine glass with a ruby red smudge around the rim. Soft sheets of Egyptian cotton rustled beneath her hands. She clutched them, rubbed the softness between her fingers.

Nick watched. 'Better?'

'There was a man. I saw him— no, I *was* him. He was looking for Cleopatra. Or I was.'

He sighed. 'I'm calling the hospital. I think you hit your head. Wait here.'

'Don't leave me!' She grabbed his arm, burying her head against his chest, fighting for the familiar smell of his body. Instead she found cold patches of damp, sticky blood. She shrank back with a cry.

'Babe, calm down.'

'Blood. It's all over you. You're bleeding.'

'I'm not, promise. It got on my clothes when I carried you home.'

'I'm bleeding?' She tensed.

'You were. Please sit still. I don't know how much blood you lost, but you need to calm down. Now you're awake I can get the first aid kit.'

She grasped his hand. Hers trembled. 'Don't go.'

He hugged her. 'I won't. Never. You're safe now. I've got you.'

Lenina clutched him, listening to the steady thud of his heartbeat through the warmth of his chest. When she pulled back, his shirt stuck to her cheek. Pulling it free brought a hiss from her lips. 'He cut my face,' she whispered.

'And your neck. You sure you don't want the hospital?'

'I don't want to, Nick. They'll keep me in and I won't be able to see you. I want to stay with you. What happened?'

'When I found you on the park that guy was—' he gritted his teeth. 'It's really muddled. You were lying there, staring at the sky like you were hypnotised. I punched him. He hit me back. I blacked out. I think.' He ruffled a hand through his hair. 'When I woke up there was blood everywhere and he was lying on you. Kissing your neck. I thought—' he lowered his head.

Lenina saw tears shining in his eyes. 'Nick . . .'

'I told you not to go through the park. Why did you do that?'

Lenina hugged herself. 'I didn't know he followed me.'

Nick's eyes narrowed. 'You'd seen him before? Christ, babe, what is it with you? What are you trying to prove?'

'Nothing. I didn't want you to worry. I thought he was gone.'

'So you thought you'd sweep it under the carpet and it would all go away?'

Her eyes burned with the threat of tears. 'Please don't shout at me.'

The frown deepened, lit by angry fire. 'He tried to rape you.'

Though the word 'rape' made her stomach writhe, it didn't feel right. Memories of the last few hours returned in snatches but in none of them did she fear for anything but her life. And perhaps her sanity.

Then she remembered the solid press of an erection against her leg.

She chewed her bottom lip to stop it wobbling. 'I'm sorry.'

He stroked her face. 'I was so scared. What if he'd really hurt you?'

'You got there in time.'

'Barely.' He leaned over, tugging her into a hug and burying his face in her hair. 'Ek het jou lief,' he whispered. 'So much.'

Lenina gave a tiny smile. 'I love you too.'

Nick kissed her forehead. Glanced at his watch. 'The police said they'd send someone over half an hour ago. Where are they?'

'You didn't need to call them.'

'Of course I did. What about everyone else? What if this guy kills someone?'

Lenina gazed at her fingers, noting her nail varnish had chipped in several places. 'I just want to forget about it.'

'We can't do that. You must realise that. The guy knew my name. What if he's been watching us? What if he comes back?'

Her fingers trembled. 'But won't they want to talk to me? Like an interview? I'm not up to that– I'm a mess. My hair is a wreck. I need a shower. I stink–'

'They don't care how you look, babe. They'll want to know what happened. Let me check the front door.' He walked out.

Lenina leaned back on the bed, gnawing the end of her thumbnail.

Alone, she had time to take stock of her body. The mirror above the dresser helped her do so.

Blood formed crusty patches on her face and neck. The right side of her throat bulged with thick layers of crimson, still wet in places. Knowing her manicure was ruined, she scraped at her cheek, picking until she found the skin beneath. Red raw and ugly, the slender scratch started near her ear and ended in the crease of her nostril.

She whimpered and closed her eyes.

The ginger stranger flashed beneath her closed lids, face pinched with pleasure. She heard the grunt from deep in his throat and the stench of stale cigarettes clinging to his filthy clothes.

Her eyes flashed open. 'Nick!'

'What? What's wrong?' He dashed back into the room still holding his mobile.

Lenina sagged against the dresser. Her knees trembled. A great weight filled her chest as she remembered. As the true horror of that night penetrated her shock. 'He attacked me,' she whispered. 'I could have died.'

'It's okay, babe.' Nick dropped the phone and pulled her against him.

'What if he'd hurt you? It would be my fault. I can't even remember what he did. Everything's foggy and distant. What if he *did* do something to me? What if he—?'

'You had all your clothes on. I arrived in time, remember?'

Lenina couldn't shake the nagging sensation that Nick was wrong. She stared into his eyes, seeking comfort in the familiar blue.

'The police told me since we're home and no one was hurt, it isn't an urgent case. Someone will be over to take a statement soon.' The tight emphasis on 'soon' made clear how he felt.

She picked at her clothes. Ran her fingers through her bloodied braids. 'I'm gross. Blood . . . grass . . . I need a shower. Come with me?'

He arched an eyebrow.

'It's faster together. And I don't want to be alone. Please, Nick.'

'Sure.' He took her hand and towed her into the bathroom.

Standing in the shower, water drumming her back, Lenina shuddered beneath Nick's hands as he stroked her shoulders with slippery hands.

Lenina wriggled away. 'You're slimy.'

'It's gel.'

'Wash it off.'

'You don't like it?'

Staring at the tiles on the opposite wall, Lenina brooded on how much the slick glide of gel on his fingers resembled the sensation of fresh blood against her skin.

She remembered the stranger as he'd gripped her shoulders, and the way his mouth dragged down the side of her face to reach her throat. The warm lap of his tongue. For a moment she returned to the park, pinned beneath a cruel, foreign weight.

Even with the blood swirled away down the plug hole the smell lingered, clogging her nostrils like wads of cotton wool. Her face stung and, despite her best efforts, water slowly soaked the bandage against the side of her throat.

She jerked free and stood directly under the shower head, letting the water pound her skull and paste her braids against her face and back.

Hot water sluiced over her neck and she caged a groan behind her teeth. 'Damn it.'

'Don't get any more water on it, babe. If you really don't want to go to the hospital we have to make sure it doesn't get infected.'

'It hurts.'

'I've got painkillers downstairs.'

'No good down there, are they?' Lenina snapped. A sigh followed. 'Sorry. This isn't your fault.'

Nick touched her shoulder. 'Please let me take you to hospital.'

'No.'

'Can I hug you at least?' He stepped forward to wrap his arms around her, but the slick of shower gel on his hands took Lenina back to the park.

She shoved him away. He slipped on the bottom of the bath. Fell. Swore, a rough burst of Afrikaans.

'Sorry! But I can still feel his mouth and his breath in my ear . . . that horrible smell . . . when you touch me with that stuff on your hands I feel it all again.'

The water plastered his blond hair flat to his head. 'Nina . . .'

'I'm so sorry.' She clutched her face.

Nick's lips compressed into a tight, thin line. 'Tell me what to do. I don't know how to help you, but if you tell me . . . I could make some tea?'

That brought a faint smile to her lips. 'That's probably the most English thing you've ever said to me.'

'I have my moments, né? *Do* you want one?'

The mere thought of drinking made Lenina's stomach cramp but the helpless look on Nick's face was far worse. 'I guess.'

His shoulders relaxed. 'Kwaai. I'll do that now. Shout if you need me.'

She nodded, hugging herself beneath the shower jets until he climbed out and vanished from sight. Only when the bathroom door closed did she release the breath she held.

Minutes later she exited the shower, skin tingling from the harsh scrubbing. Wrapping her hair in one towel and her body in another, she stepped over the pile of bloody clothes and returned to the bedroom.

The first thing she saw was the bed, dotted with leaves and flakes of dried blood.

A scream bubbled in her throat, but she held it back and channelled the nervous energy into her breathing.

Slowly in. Slowly out.

Again and again she repeated the exercise and then stripped the bed.

She did so faster than ever before, handling only the edges of the sheets where blood couldn't touch her fingers. Wadding the whole thing into a ball, she dragged it to the bathroom and left it with her clothes.

With the sheets gone and a clean body, Lenina immediately felt better. Even the room smelled better.

She closed her eyes to enjoy the silence.

Darkness consumed her mind's eye, filled with jagged shadows thrown by the branches of bare skeletal trees. Terrible laughter rang in her ears. In the dark she saw steel-grey eyes, ginger hair and yellow teeth. Fruity shower gel gave way to the scent of old cigarettes and mouldy meat. Almost strong enough to taste.

She opened her eyes with a gasp. Her heart's thudding seemed louder in her ears than ever before. She could feel it in the side of her neck. Her fingertips. The back of her throat. She swallowed and took a deep breath through her mouth, to cleanse the scent of old smoke.

'Smoke and blood,' she murmured. 'Alexandria burns.'

Lenina slapped her hands over her mouth.

The memory came crashing back like slap to the face: sand, swords, bodies strewn across the ground like so much waste. Blood everywhere. She saw it all through the eyes of a man with strong square fingers, a deep, rumbling voice and a lingering ache in his chest. She felt the grit of sand through his sandals as he walked back towards a city slowly burning to the ground.

'Nick . . . ?' Her voice barely carried.

Charred flesh; its reek filled her nostrils.

Lenina lurched forward, stumbling against the dresser. Pots of moisturiser and make-up hit the floor. She clutched her stomach as the vision returned, playing bright and clear, using the back of her eyelids like a projection screen.

Smoke hung low over a city composed of golds and browns. No cars. No street lamps. No greens but for the occasional flower display, trampled by dozens of marching feet.

'Nick, help me!'

A girl, no more than six, crouched behind the body of a woman, clearly dead from a savage slash to the throat. She cried and held out her hands as Lenina came closer. Cried out for *Captain Saar*.

Lenina came to herself with her head cupped in her hands, her body bent double against the floor.

Through the carpet, she heard the doorbell ring and knew the police had finally arrived.

Chapter Five

Lenina tugged a dressing gown over her chosen pyjamas before trudging downstairs. She kept the towel wrapped around her damp hair. On reaching the living room, she saw two strangers standing over Nick. He sat on the sofa, cradling his head in his hands.

She crept into the room and hugged herself, flinching when three pairs of eyes turned towards her.

'Nina . . . this is Inspector Brad Thorne.' Nick pointed to an older balding man whose stomach hung out over his belt and strained his shirt buttons. His tie dangled at half-mast.

'*Detective* Inspector.' The man spoke with the faint wheeze of a long-term smoker. His narrow eyes, the colour of grave dirt, scanned the room from top to bottom, taking in everything from the cobwebs in the far corner, to the mismatched shoes beneath the radiator.

'Sorry. *Detective* Inspector Thorne. This is Detective Sergeant Tristen Blake.' Nick gestured to a younger man, nearer her age, with lively green eyes and a tailored suit.

He smiled. 'Nice to meet you. Sorry it's in such unpleasant circumstances.' He held out his hand.

She took it and watched his fingers envelop her own. A plain silver ring circled his smallest finger. An expensive watch nestled beneath his sleeve, exposed as the fabric slipped back over his wrist. When he pulled back, his fingertips trailed over the back of her hand.

'And you.' She spoke automatically, wiping her damp palm against her thigh.

Sergeant Blake nodded and pulled a new notebook from his pocket. He removed the wrapper as he spoke. 'I understand you were the unfortunate victim of an attack in Grick Park. Tell us what happened.' His gaze travelled over her face, sweeping down then up before returning to her eyes. His smile broadened. He took a step closer.

Lenina perched on the end of the sofa. Nick reached for her, but quickly retreated when she flinched away. She gave him an apologetic glance then relayed her story, from leaving the bridal boutique to reaching the park.

As she remembered the chill in the air and the whispers on the wind she saw Sergeant Blake lean closer. Only then did she realise her voice had fallen to a whisper.

When she reached the reappearance of *Not-Homeless-Bob*, Inspector Thorne stopped reading titles on the book shelves and yanked a notebook from his own pocket. The dog-eared corners and grubby cover matched his look perfectly. So did the tiny nub of pencil he tugged from the spirals. 'What did he look like?'

'Not-Bob?'

He sighed and tapped his foot. 'The attacker, yes.'

'It was dark,' she murmured, casting another glance at Nick. 'But . . . he was shorter than me. Tubby. Gross clothes. Smelly. He looked like a tramp.'

Thorne peered over the top of his notebook. 'Can you be more specific?'

'More than tramp?'

'My colleague means can you describe his clothes? Did he have any distinguishing marks? Anything to narrow down his identity.' Sergeant Blake glared at his partner.

Lenina frowned, captured by the sudden impression of two wolves about to fight for the position of alpha.

She raised her voice. 'He was ginger, I think. Maybe grey clothes? And there were scratches on his face.'

'New?' Sergeant Blake flipped to a fresh page.

'I'm not sure. One second they looked small, the next they were huge.' She gnawed her bottom lip.

His face was right there, swimming before her eyes like a mirage. Why then were the details so hazy, as though obscured by mist? She tightened her jaw.

Blake tucked a wisp of hair behind his ear. 'What did this man do?'

Lenina hesitated. She looked down at Nick and saw the worry in his face. She clasped his hand.

His gaze snapped up, locking on hers. He squeezed her fingers. 'It's been a traumatic night, Sergeant. She doesn't remember much.'

'Fine. What do *you* remember, Mr Harrison?'

Nick straightened his shoulders. 'When I arrived they were on the floor. He was touching her.'

'Miss Miller?'

She gathered herself. 'He tackled me. I fell over. I tried to get him off, but he was so heavy. Then Nick came and he left me alone. I guess Nick was the bigger threat.'

'I see.' Blake didn't look up from the notebook. 'What then?'

Nick swallowed audibly. 'I fought him. But he was strong for an old guy.'

'How old?'

'Early fifties, late forties.'

Thorne sniffed. 'That's not so old.'

Blake shot him a withering look. 'Then?'

'He dazed me. When I could see straight he was lying on Lenina again. I didn't know what he was trying to do, at the time it looked like he was kissing her.'

The younger detective glanced at her. She met his gaze, surprised to see genuine pity there. The expression warmed her. Gave hope and peace where, moments ago she felt nothing.

'Miss Miller?'

'He lay on me and pinned me in the grass.' As she spoke, more memories hurtled back, strong and swift, like a punch to the gut.

His lips on her throat and the wet flick of his tongue. Unspeakable pain as his teeth broke flesh. She heard it; a dull crunch like snapping celery.

Lenina looked at the floor. 'He bit me. On the neck.'

Thorne frowned. 'Like a dog?'

'Sort of.' She touched her shoulder, near the edge of the bandages beneath her dressing gown. 'And there was blood everywhere.'

'What happened to it?'

Nick took over. 'You guys took so long, we couldn't sit around covered in blood. We've had a shower since then.'

'The world doesn't revolve around you and your girlfriend, Mr Harrison.' Ignoring Nick's glare, Thorne pressed on, addressing himself to Lenina again. 'So, you remember nothing, then all of a sudden this guy bit you. And there was blood everywhere but you've conveniently had a shower, washing away all the evidence.'

She bit her lip. Frustration bubbled through her calm. 'There *is* evidence. Look at my face. He had a knife— no a dagger or something.'

'Now there's a weapon? This story keeps getting better.'

'Brad . . .' Blake made a 'steady' gesture with his free hand. 'We're here to investigate.'

'How can we investigate if the story keeps changing?'

Nick bunched his hands into fists. 'It's not a story. Look at us. We're cleaned up but look at my face. How else would I get bruises like this?'

Thorne didn't speak, but Lenina saw his gaze flick towards her.

'It's the truth,' she said. 'He really did bite me. He said something about a tribute.'

With every word she spoke more details returned.

'Tribute? Meaning?'

'I have no idea. It's just what I remember.'

'Right. Okay.'

Nick surged to his feet. 'I don't think I like your attitude, Detective Thorne.' The South African traces in his accent strengthened, a sure sign that anger had mastered his reason.

'And I *know* I don't like yours, Mr Harrison.'

'We're victims, né? You should be protecting us. How about doing your job?'

Thorne swelled like a rotting fruit. 'I'm a detective inspector of the law. Watch your mouth.'

'You watch yours.'

Lenina watched the play-off between Thorne and her fiancé for a moment or two before covering her face with her hands.

When a gentle hand touched her shoulder she almost cried aloud, but it was only Sergeant Blake. His fingers were warm through the layers of clothing, the weight of his grip a gentle comfort.

'You okay?' he whispered.

She stared into his eyes, caught up by the strange sensation of reassurance she got from doing so. Slowly she shrugged his hand away. 'Why doesn't he believe me?'

He cleared his throat and leaned back, clasping both hands before him. 'We're forced to look at our cases from every possible angle, but that's no excuse for him to make you feel like the bad guy. Tell *me* what you remember.'

'You believe me?'

'I believe that *you* believe it. That's plenty for me.' He smiled, showing off the straight white lines of his teeth. That same curl of hair fell into his eyes and he flicked it back again, an unconscious gesture as distracting as it was endearing.

'Miss Miller?'

She stopped staring, and clasped her hands to avoid touching her flushed cheeks. 'Sorry, what?' When she realised that her gesture mirrored his, she tucked both hands beneath her on the sofa.

His gaze made her stomach squirm, her palms sweat. Like the nights spent gazing at the posters of pop stars plastering the walls of her bedroom during her teenage years.

She wiped the hands on her dressing gown again and winced when her engagement ring caught her eye with a glimmer of reflected light. A rush of guilt flooded her stomach.

'You need to tell me what you remember. If we plan to catch this man, I must know everything. Can you help me with that?' The low undertones in Blake's voice seemed to suggest more.

Lenina watched his face, searching for a hint of playfulness to match what she heard in his voice. Or thought she heard.

'He bit me,' she whispered. 'On the neck.'

'Show me.'

She turned her head and tilted her chin, tugging at her dressing gown. Blake's hands nudged at her pyjama top then peeled the bandage down.

As the sticky edges tugged her skin, fresh pain shot through her neck and shoulder.

'Sorry,' he murmured, still pulling.

Removing the bandage completely, he hovered his fingers over the area. 'Not much bruising. More than one set of marks, overlapping. He really *did* bite you, didn't he?'

The last fragment of memory clunked into place. The stranger's hands on her neck, her ribs, her face. The loud gulps as he swallowed. Moans of pleasure. Blood trickling down her chin. Pooling in her ear.

'Yes. He was drinking the blood.'

Blake gazed at her, his green eyes calm. Serious. Accepting. 'Really?'

'Yes. Please, I know it sounds crazy, but he did. He got off on it.'

'It's okay, Miss Miller. I believe you.' Though he never once touched her, muscles low in Lenina's body clenched in response. He pulled away after too short a moment. Her gaze followed his fingers.

'It's not too bad, quite neat despite the overlapping marks. You should still get it looked at.'

'That's what Nick said.'

'Go to your GP. You may need antibiotics to be sure it doesn't get infected.' He stepped back. 'You said you had a shower; I assume there was blood on your clothes too?'

'Yes, they're upstairs.'

'I'll need to take them. Grappling with this man should have left some trace of him. Be right back.'

Lenina watched him leave and return thirty seconds later wearing thin latex gloves. He carried a handful of large paper bags, a camera and a small metal ruler.

He took several pictures of the marks on her throat and the scratch on her face before measuring both with the ruler. All the results he jotted in his notebook.

His actions interrupted the stand-off between Nick and Inspector Thorne.

'What are you doing?' snapped Thorne.

Blake gave his partner a steady look. 'Miss Miller mentioned blood on her clothing, I'm going to bag it. Problem?'

Thorne looked stunned. 'No, but—'

'Good.' He didn't wait for the rest, instead gestured to the stairs. 'Lead the way, Miss Miller.'

Lenina bit back a smile at Thorne's dressing down and walked past Blake's outstretched arm to ascend the stairs.

She pushed open the bathroom door and pointed to the pile of clothes and bed sheets nearby. She loitered in the doorway and watched Blake bend down and lift the stained workout vest with the tip of his pencil. Her bra caught in one of the arm holes and dangled in the air.

He cleared his throat. Dropped it quickly. Moved on. 'We'll need to take all of these clothes. Is that okay?'

'Yes, of course. I want them out of this house. I don't need the reminder. I just want . . .' she sighed, hugging herself. 'I don't want to think about it any more.'

'I appreciate that, Miss Miller but I'm afraid I have more questions.'

When she tensed he stood straight and moved closer. The hot rush of his breath billowed over her cheeks as he moved in. Near enough to pick out individual hairs in the faint shadow of stubble about his jaw.

'Tell me more. Have you seen him before?'

'Not before the boutique. But he knew Nick's name. What does that mean? I'd never notice him normally— what if he's been following me?'

Blake placed a hand on her arm. Warm and strong, his fingers flexed against her dressing gown. She didn't pull away.

'We'll catch him. I promise.'

'Thanks. And thank you for not dismissing me. I know your partner thinks I'm nuts or just looking for attention.' She swallowed and tore her gaze free of his, looking instead at the shiny toes of his shoes.

'No one should dismiss you.' Another flex of his fingers. 'Everything you say has value.'

Her gaze snapped up. 'Excuse me?'

'In the case, I mean. This man could be very ill.'

'Oh.' Despite herself, Lenina's shoulders sank with disappointment. She stepped back. 'I never thought of that.'

'I have to explore every avenue.' Blake bent to the pile of bloody clothes and placed them, one by one, into the bags. He sealed each one and wrote the date and time across the top. 'Can you remember anything else?'

She cast back, searching the tattered scraps of memory. 'I bit him.' The remembered taste of blood and skin made her heave. She clapped a hand to her mouth and tried to ignore the tingling in her gums. 'I wasn't trying to hurt him— I was scared.'

'Given the circumstances, I think you can be forgiven.'

'But I got skin in my mouth. And blood.'

Sergeant Blake became very still.

'Am I in trouble? Is that bad?'

'Don't be alarmed, Miss Miller, but you must visit your GP. Let them assess if you need counselling and take the necessary blood tests.'

'Blood tests?' Her voice jumped several octaves.

'It's a small risk, but if you did ingest some blood you should get checked for all the blood-borne diseases. Particularly HIV and hepatitis.'

Lenina leaned in the doorway and sniffed back tears. 'This can't be happening. I'm getting married in two weeks. I have a dress. I have flowers. Doves. Catering. This can't be real.' Tears trickled down her cheeks.

The detective moved closer. His hand touched her shoulder again. 'You'll be okay.'

'You don't know that.'

'Have faith. We'll catch this guy and lock him up, then we can all move on. Get those tests. If they come to anything I have the numbers of some excellent counsellors. You're not alone.'

She sniffed. 'Thanks.'

His hand squeezed her shoulder.

Lenina leaned against him and caught the scent of peppermint on his breath, clean and fresh. It reminded her of home and the garden in which her mother also grew basil, thyme and sage. Safety and comfort all wrapped up in a single familiar scent.

The tears dried. She stepped back. 'You must think I'm an idiot.'

'Not at all. You've been very strong about all of this.'

She opened her mouth to say something self-deprecating, but the words melted on her tongue. She gazed into the sergeant's eyes and lingered there, wallowing in a green so deep it reminded her of forests and exotic oceans. Heat crept up her face and neck, forcing her to look away.

'Sorry,' he frowned. 'I don't mean to embarrass you, but Mr Harrison is a lucky man.'

'Excuse me?'

'You said you were getting married I just assumed . . . my mistake.'

'No, you're right.'

'Then he *is* a lucky man. Shall we go back down?'

In that moment Lenina could have stayed in that bathroom for the rest of her life, enjoying the scent of mint and Sergeant Blake's warmth. Then she saw the smears of blood on the sink and shuddered.

'Okay. I think they've stopped shouting now.' She took the lead back to the living room, relieved to find everything in one piece when she got there.

Nick sat on the sofa with his hands clenched in his lap, watching Thorne who glared studiously at the framed photos above the fireplace.

Neither of them spoke.

'We're done here,' Blake broke the brittle silence. 'Unless there's anything else to add, I think we've taken enough of your time.'

Nick stood and held out his hand for a shake. 'No, that's everything, Detective. Thanks.'

When Lenina's turn came she slipped her hand into his and held tight. His skin was warm, dry and smooth. Large and powerful, his hands closed over hers and squeezed firmly. The contact sent a little wriggle of warmth rushing up and down her arm. She heard the sigh of soft voices in her ear and the scent of peppermint threatened to choke her. Though she looked around she saw no one speaking. Then the voices faded away, leaving behind a low buzzing like TV static. The whole time he stared into her eyes.

By the time the handshake broke, Lenina felt naked. She stepped back, cradling her hand to her chest. Nick came up behind her and hugged her. She didn't pull away.

'Thank you, Sergeant Blake.'

His gaze lingered on hers. 'My pleasure,' he whispered. Then, turning to Thorne, he added, 'We'll see ourselves out. Come on, Brad.'

The pair slipped into the hallway and were gone.

DAY TWO

Chapter Six

Next morning Lenina woke to a sensation like fire writhing through her gut. She lurched out of Nick's arms and stumbled into the bathroom just in time to lift the seat off the toilet and hang her head over it. Her heaving stomach strained to return its contents, but there were none.

Dry-retching, tears streaming down her face, Lenina clung to the bowl and waited for the spasms to pass.

An eternity later, she flushed the toilet and sat back on her heels, wiping drool from her mouth.

Nick appeared in the doorway, his hair sleep tousled. 'What's wrong?'

She shook her head.

'I heard you puking.'

'Nothing came up,' she gasped. 'Get me some water please?'

He passed her a plastic cup.

Sipping the water eased her throat somewhat, but the pain continued. 'God . . .' she murmured.

'You okay?'

'Stomach ache. Headache.' She touched each location in turn. 'Even my teeth hurt.'

'Maybe you should stay off today.'

Lenina sighed. 'I can't. The samples from Cairo arrive this afternoon. I've got to log them.'

'Someone else can do it. You're not the only curator in the place.'

'I'm the only one who knows anything about Egypt.' She tried to stand but her knees wobbled before she made it halfway. Tumbling down, she sat on the mat, legs akimbo. 'What's wrong with me?'

'Rough night. It's catching up with you. Come on.' Nick tucked his hands beneath her arms and pulled.

She swayed, but eventually managed to stand without help. 'Thanks. Let me clean my teeth.'

'Go ahead. Don't mind me.' Grinning, he stepped past her and fumbled with his boxers. Seconds later, as she squirted toothpaste on to her brush, she heard the thunderous gush of his morning relief.

'Aaaah,' he moaned.

'Gross.'

'You love me anyway, né?'

Shaking her head, she noted that she did. Playful banter like this was one of the many reasons she'd agreed to married him.

Lenina watched her reflection as she cleaned her teeth. She spat and watched pink-tinged froth slide down the plug hole. 'My mouth is bleeding.'

'Don't brush so hard.' Nick planted a kiss on her cheek and washed his hands. 'See you downstairs.'

His reflection vanished from the mirror.

Lenina looked at her face again.

Her features remained the same, despite the horrific events of the night before. Somehow, she expected that her experience would stain her but the only visible change was the scratch on her cheek. And the bite marks between her neck and shoulder.

She touched the fresh bandage, wincing as the light contact sent an ache racing up and down her throat. For the first time she considered that the hospital might not be such a bad idea.

A phone rang, making her jump. Leaving her reflection behind, Lenina ran back to the bedroom and snagged her mobile from the dresser. 'Hello?'

'Hey, chuck,' the bright voice echoed against a backdrop of road noise.

'Daddy?'

'Yeah, how are you?'

She glanced at the clock. 'Do you know what time it is?'

'Sorry, did I wake you?'

'No.' She froze. 'Is everything okay? Mum? Jordan . . . ?'

'They're fine. Don't worry.'

She exhaled. A long breath she hadn't been aware of holding. 'Not that

I don't love hearing from you, but why the early morning wake-up call?'

'I'm in the neighbourhood. Can I stop by?'

'Now?'

'Sure.'

She carried the phone downstairs. 'What are you doing in Leicester?'

'Work meeting. I had to stay over.'

'You drive buses.' She chuckled. 'What sort of meeting brings you all the way up here?'

'Important ones.' His voice became guarded. 'If you don't want to see me, just say so.'

'Don't be silly. It's just early. I'm tired.'

'You don't sound yourself. Everything okay?'

She paused. Her breathing quickened. 'What do you mean?'

'You sound different. Stressed.'

'Switch off your radar, Daddy. I'm fine.'

'Can I come over? I'm ten minutes away.'

Lenina caught up to Nick in the kitchen. She smiled her thanks as he handed her a mug of tea. 'Seriously?'

'I'm at the Holiday Inn.'

Nick raised a questioning eyebrow.

'Dad,' she mouthed at him.

He nodded and returned his attention to the toaster, snatching the slices from the air as they popped up. He took a large bite from one before adding a generous slather of honey.

'You can if you want, I suppose.' She glanced at Nick. He shrugged.

'Becalm your enthusiasm, chuck. You'll bowl me over.'

'Funny. See you soon.'

He hung up.

Lenina put the phone beside her mug and ran her hands through her hair. 'Bloody hell.'

'What, babe?'

'Don't know. I feel weird. And now Daddy's coming. He'll freak out.'

'About last night?' Toast crumbs flew. 'Don't tell him.'

She pointed to her neck.

He shrugged. 'Like you've never had to hide a love bite before.'

Anger surged through her. 'This isn't a love bite.'

'Sorry, sorry, I know. Calm down. Look, you don't have to tell him anything you don't want, but it would help, né? And how do you think he'll feel if he finds out another way? You know how he gets.'

'That's exactly why I don't want to tell him.'

'Your choice, babe, but he'll know for sure if stay I home.'

She stared at him.

'You really think I'd leave you after last night? They can manage without me for one day. Just like the museum can manage without you. We'll skive off together.'

'I don't want to stay off work. It's important to me.'

'They're just bits of broken pottery.'

She scowled. 'It's not *just* broken pottery. It's my career. Don't dismiss it. I don't do that with your stupid interviews or sports commentary.'

'Dismiss— what?' He put down the toast. 'Where's this coming from?'

'You! Making jokes . . . this is a big deal. What if that guy is outside our house? What if he's following me around? What if I'm sick?'

He looked vague.

'Weren't you listening? I told Tristen that the guy bit me.'

'Who?'

'The detective! The homeless guy bit me, but then I bit him back and got blood in my mouth. What if I caught some horrible disease?'

Nick swore, another of the few phrases in Afrikaans she really recognised. He continued in English, speaking as he might to a petulant two-year-old. 'You had a whole conversation with the detective upstairs, remember? While I was down here defending you to his domkop partner. I didn't know about the blood. We'll go to the hospital—' she stamped her foot. 'Fine – the GP – and get all the tests you want. But you need to calm down.'

'I am calm.'

'Then why are you shaking?'

Lenina looked down at her hands. A tear slipped free and traced a stinging path along the scratch on her cheek. 'I'm sorry. I know this isn't your fault. I feel so . . . and the wedding . . . look at me! I'm a mess. All this won't heal before the ceremony. And *you* look like you've been in a boxing ring. It's a complete disaster.'

'It's not. We just have to take things one step at a time. We'll go to the GP. We'll talk to the make-up artists. Both of us can wear make-up if we have to. Your bridal consultant will be thrilled.'

'You'd wear make-up for me?'

'I'd do anything for you. You must know that.'

She stared at him, drinking in the softness in his eyes, the downward tilt of his lips. 'I do. I'm sorry.'

'Come here.'

Lenina ran to him and let him put his arms around her.

For the first time since the attack it felt right to be there. His warmth, his strength, even the shape of his muscles beneath his dressing gown.

'Let me call Donna,' he whispered. 'I'll tell her you threw up this morning.'

'Don't you dare. She'll be picking out cots and babygrows before you know it.'

A smile further brightened Nick's features. He pressed a light kiss to her uninjured cheek. 'Would that be so bad?' he whispered. 'Pregnant? A baby? You wouldn't like that?'

'It would ruin our honeymoon.'

Nick's laughter filled the kitchen. He kissed her again, harder this time. 'Is that all you think about?'

'Yes. And my dress.'

'Bimbo.' After one last squeeze he left her. 'Don't forget to call the doctor. I need the appointment time if I'm coming with you.'

She hesitated, toying with the rim of her mug. 'No, you go. Daddy can come instead.'

'I thought you didn't want him to worry.'

'He doesn't have to know *why* I'm going.'

'Your funeral.' He carried his plate, toast and all, into the living room. Moments later, Lenina heard the sound of the local news from the TV.

In the still of the kitchen she sipped her tea, thinking back over the night before. The pain in her stomach had subsided somewhat, but the headache remained. Sharp. Piercing. Each time she glanced through the window to the garden outside, bright shafts of watery sunlight made the feeling still worse. Squinting against the glare, she stood and pulled the blinds down. As artificial twilight fell on the room, the pain receded slightly.

'Great,' she murmured.

Fishing in a drawer unearthed a blister pack of ibuprofen and she swallowed two with another glug of tea.

While waiting for the drug to kick in she heard the trill of the doorbell. Nick grumbled from the other room. Seconds later, two voices floated through, one light and playful, the other deep and strong, like a drill sergeant. The second voice came closer.

A quick swivel on the chair had Lenina facing the door in time to see her father plough into the room. Tall, broad and dark in faded black trousers, and a battered leather jacket. His white shirt was open at the neck, framing a flash of gold jewellery against his hairy chest.

For all that his clothing was neat and tidy, his face didn't match. A worn, tired look lived in his eyes and his forehead showcased a liberal collection of wrinkles. More so than the last time she saw him.

He shrugged off the jacket, wiped both hands over his shiny bald head then swept her up. His massive arms curled around her body, lifting her off the floor. Her toes scraped the tops of his shoes.

Gasping, she turned her face sideways to free it from his chest. 'Daddy?' she wheezed, 'put me down.'

He squeezed harder. 'I heard what happened. I'm so sorry.'

Lenina groaned, making a mental note to flay Nick for his wagging tongue. 'I'm fine. I'm not hurt.'

'Hurt? Why would you be hurt?'

Her feet hit the ground so hard her teeth knocked together. 'What? What are you talking about?'

'The wedding caterers? They pulled out.'

She stumbled then righted herself, tilting her head to get a proper look at her father's face. 'When?'

'They didn't tell you? They phoned me yesterday because the company's gone into administration.'

The sick sensation returned to Lenina's stomach. 'How am I going to get new caterers at this point? I knew this would be a disaster!' She gnawed her thumbnail. 'Maybe I can go back to that place on Harrow Road. If we offer them extra they might be able to squeeze us in . . .'

'I'll handle it, chuck.'

'But we were going to have vol-au-vents and canapés.'

He chuckled. 'Any caterer in the East Midlands can handle that.'

'But they need to be gluten free. And what about the main course? I'll have to go through all the allergy details again. There's no time.'

'I said I'll handle it. Why don't you tell me what *you* were talking about?'

Lenina returned to the table and hid behind her tea. 'Don't worry about it.'

'Chuck . . .' His voice deepened. Took on that warning edge she remembered from her childhood years.

'Honest, Daddy, it's nothing. You're going to make me late for work.'

The doorbell rang again.

'Is this a morning tea party or something?' Nick's agitated voice carried over the low drone of the breakfast news. Lenina glanced towards the living room then back to her father. She opened her mouth, ready to speak again, when Nick put his head around the door.

'Nina, the detective is here again.'

She looked at her father. Saw the frown on his face deepen.

'What detective? What's he talking about?'

She sighed. 'Coming . . .'

Chapter Seven

Lenina sat on the sofa beside her father while Sergeant Blake stood close by. She held her mug with both hands, sipping slowly as if that might steady the race of her heart. It didn't, but the show of calm made the reality easier to attain.

Nick, after glancing at his watch, sprinted upstairs to get dressed. She heard him banging drawers and slamming cupboards, searching for a shirt that didn't need ironing.

'Good morning,' the voice came from her left. Low. Soft. Smooth like the sweet silk of expensive chocolate. 'I'm Detective Sergeant Tristen Blake.' He extended his hand. 'You look very familiar; have we met before?'

After a glance at the proffered hand, Ray folded his own in his lap. 'I'm Raymond Miller and no we haven't. What do you want?'

Blake retracted his hand, eyebrows arched towards his hairline. He glanced at Lenina, then adjusted his tie, running a finger along the inside of his collar. 'I'm following up last night's attack. I'm sure you already know the details from Lenina?'

Ray pursed his lips. 'No, my daughter hasn't told me anything of the sort. Though I'm sure she was planning to.'

Leaning further over the mug of tea seemed safer than answering.

Tristen cleared his throat, 'I'm sorry to come unannounced, but I need to ask Lenina— Miss Miller— more questions.'

She glanced up, surprised by the correction. He caught her gaze and widened his eyes before looking past her. When she followed his line of sight she realised her father was staring at them with pursed lips and a wrinkled brow.

Freeing one hand from the mug, she placed it on his knee. 'It sounds worse than it was, Daddy. Some madman attacked me in the park last night.'

Ray gnawed his bottom lip. 'I assumed you were hiding a love bite.'

Lenina flashed back on the sensation of blood dripping down the side of her neck. The wet crunch as the ginger stranger plunged his teeth into the side of her throat. 'No,' she whispered.

'Did you get an appointment for those blood tests?' Sergeant Blake spoke softly.

Ray frowned. 'What blood tests?'

The look in the detective's eye showed he realised his mistake. Little spots of pink formed on his cheeks. 'I suggested that Miss Miller book in for some blood tests against blood-borne diseases.'

'He bit me, Daddy.' Lenina spoke to the floor. 'And I bit his hand.'

'This was last night. Why didn't you tell me?'

'Because I knew you'd freak out.'

'Am I not allowed to worry about my daughter?' He turned away, rubbing his mouth with the tips of his fingers. Fine tremors rippled over his shoulders, tension singing through every limb.

As she stared at his distraught expression, Lenina's shoulders slumped. She touched his knee. 'I'm sorry, Daddy . . . I should have said something.'

Ray's eyes glimmered with the unmistakable shine of unshed tears. 'You could have died.'

'I wouldn't go that far, sir.' Blake fussed with the cuffs of his suit jacket. 'The individual Miss Miller described is dangerous, but I don't think he's capable of killing anybody.'

'You know that for sure?'

Lenina jerked away from her father's knee. She recognised the icy stab of Ray's tone and prepared to weather the inevitable storm. Though she longed to warn the detective of the danger, he spoke before she could catch his eye.

'We have profilers. I also have some experience in the area.'

'Really? How old are you?'

'I fail to see how that's relevant.'

'Experience is relevant, Detective. You seem young. I want to know how your *experience* is going to help my daughter.'

Sergeant Blake tucked a curl of hair behind his ear. 'I'm thirty, Mr Miller. And I'm a trained detective, this is my job.'

'Then do it properly. This crazy person attacked my daughter in public and you tell me he's not dangerous? Where was Nick through all this?'

'Coming to get me.' Lenina re-entered the conversation with a whisper. 'It's my fault. I took a short cut across the park. He told me not to but I did anyway. If he hadn't come to get me . . .'

Ray gathered her into another of those rib-crunching hugs. 'You should be able to go wherever you want without worrying. This isn't your fault. And you,' Ray glared at the detective over the top of her head. 'What are you going to do about it? Why are you here instead of looking for this man?'

'I have some follow-up questions. If you don't mind, I'll ask them, then get out of your hair.'

'Fine.' Uncurling his arms from around Lenina's shoulders, the bigger man leaned back on the sofa and folded his arms. 'Well?'

Sergeant Blake straightened his shoulders and took a deep breath. 'Lenina,' he began.

Ray cleared his throat.

'Miss Miller, what you told us yesterday was very helpful but—'

'Us?'

Blake's hands clenched briefly. 'My partner, Mr Miller. Detective Inspector Brad Thorne. He accompanied me last night.'

'Where is he now?'

Though irritated by her father's tone, Lenina silently echoed the question. She looked at Blake – really *looked* at him – and felt a little flutter in the pit of her stomach. The detective's hair gleamed as if professionally treated. She could smell it; some expensive shampoo and conditioner that brought to mind apple orchards and yellow meadows. His royal-blue suit fitted his body with the same hints of tailoring as the first and clearly cost as much. Beneath it he wore a green shirt that matched his eyes so well, the choice couldn't be anything but deliberate. His tie, narrow and black, had complementing stripes of the same emerald green.

As if he'd dressed for a date, Lenina thought. The pleasant flutter of butterflies became the writhing ache of embarrassment as she took in her own pyjamas and dressing gown. She longed for a dash of lipstick, a flick of mascara or foundation, anything to counter the naked sensation of inadequacy she felt in that moment. Blake stared at her and his gaze caressed her skin like the brush of warm fur, something she could roll in or cuddle. Lenina felt a mad urge to giggle. Or sing. She did neither, merely stood and crossed to the other side of the room, under the pretence of placing her empty mug on the fireplace. Her shoulders itched and she knew Blake watched her every move.

How can he make me feel like this?

'Miss Miller. I need to show you some pictures.' Sergeant Blake pulled a small envelope from his pocket. Shaking the contents on to his hand, he held out a stack of five photos. 'Do any of these faces look familiar?'

Her fingers brushed his as she took the photos. Instead of the faint excitement she experienced the day before, Lenina felt the vibrant pulse of life within his skin. The ebb and flow of hot blood coursing through his veins. Lenina licked her lips, eyeing the single track of a pale blue vein along the inside of his wrist. She traced it all the way into the cuff of his jacket.

'Miss Miller?'

She cleared her throat and busied herself with the photos. As she skimmed through, she heard her father speak again.

'Sergeant, you never did say where your partner was.'

His voice chilled the room. 'Brad's in the office working a separate case.'

'Oh?'

'Unfortunately yours isn't the only case we're handling right now.'

'And who decides the priority?' Ray leaned forward.

'The Chief Inspector.'

'I see. But shouldn't you be working together?'

'Daddy, stop it. Please.' Lenina returned the photos, shaking her head. 'Sorry, none of these is the guy.'

She'd barely looked at them, instead watching the sergeant move from beneath the thin veil of her eyelashes.

Blake tucked the photos away and stepped back. Lenina followed him, fighting an inexplicable urge to close the distance between them. She thrust her hands into her dressing gown pockets to prevent them wandering. 'It doesn't feel like I've helped.'

He smiled. 'Now I know who *not* to look for. That's useful, Lenina. I promise. I'll get out of your way now.'

The way he said her name sent a delicious shiver rippling down her spine.

'Thanks.' She touched her cheeks, aware of the heat there. Not wanting to be obvious by fanning her face, she turned away and took a few deep breaths. 'I'll show you to the door. Daddy, can you put the kettle on, please?'

From the corner of her eye she saw Ray glare at her, but her persistent blushes took precedence over his resentment. She dashed for the hallway and heard the detective follow.

Reaching the door, she pressed her forehead to the cool glass and tried to think. What was wrong with her? How could a few smiles and a smart suit reduce her to a giddy, senseless wreck? She wasn't a teenager any more. And what about Nick, the man she intended to marry?

The hand on her shoulder made her yelp. Lenina spun around so fast that her dressing gown swirled around Blake's knees. She stumbled and his hand steadied her, also sweeping her close enough to smell the mint on his breath.

'You okay?' he whispered. 'Do you need to sit down?'

'No, you made me jump.' She tilted her head back, gazing into his eyes and all the shades of the forest they held. 'And I'm stressed.'

'I'm not surprised. But I want you to know that you've really helped me today.'

A warm, fuzzy tingle ran from her head to her toes. 'Really?'

'Oh, yes.' He grinned. It felt like watching the sun peep out from behind clouds. 'Really.' His voice dropped an octave. 'Sorry if I got you in trouble with your dad. He didn't look happy.'

She nodded, startled by how difficult it was to think with his hand on her shoulder. 'He worries about me. More than he needs to. That's not your fault.'

'Good. Because I didn't come here just to show you photos.'

She licked her lips and tried to back up. The door blocked her retreat.

'I wanted to check on you.'

'Oh.'

Another smile and a flash of white teeth. 'I wanted to see you. Be sure you're okay. You've been through a lot.'

Her heart hammered her ribs. Sweat broke out on her palms. 'That's sweet.'

'It's my job.'

Every sensible part of Lenina's rational mind told her this visit was far above and beyond the call of duty.

She stared into his intense green eyes and inhaled until the smell of peppermint saturated her nostrils. His lips parted and between them she saw the pale tip of his tongue.

Wild thoughts of kissing raced through her mind. 'Thank you.'

'No problem, Lenina.' The syllables of her name lingered on his lips before hitting the air, giving the impression that he tasted each one before letting it go. She shivered so hard that his hand slipped off her shoulder and down her bicep. He held her elbow gently and leaned forward again. His breath whispered over her face, hot and sweet. His eyes widened, pupils growing large and dark.

'Nothing you want or need will ever be a problem, understand?' He didn't wait for an answer. Instead, he released her elbow and reached into his pocket. The loss of his touch made her gasp.

'Take this.' Blake pushed a small white card into her shaking hands. 'My office number. And mobile. Just in case.' At last, he backed away.

Ray chose that exact moment to stick his head around the doorway. 'Everything okay out here?'

She shoved the business card into her pocket.

'Yes, thanks.' Blake held her gaze for a fraction longer before glancing over his shoulder. 'I was telling Miss Miller how to reach me if she remembers anything else.'

If his earlier actions hadn't been clue enough, the blatant lie cinched it. Lenina felt the hairs on the back of her neck stand to rigid attention. She felt light-headed. Warm. Her skin tingled with a need to be touched and she took several deep breaths through her nose.

Averting her gaze, she stepped to one side and opened the front door. 'Thank you, Detective. I appreciate your help.' He stared at her, she could feel it, but nothing short of open threats could have made her look up in that moment.

Before he could speak, Nick thundered down the stairs in his motorbike leathers, the huge round helmet dangling from the bend of his elbow. 'You still here, Detective?'

His appearance broke the spell. Lenina felt Blake look away like a prickly blanket lifting off her shoulders. She gazed at her fiancé. Her chest tightened. Did he know? Could he tell how her body responded to the proximity and scent of another man?

She made several attempts to swallow the growing lump at the back of her throat. 'He's leaving now,' she said.

'Yes, I have what I need. Bye, Mr Harrison.'

'Yeah, bye.' Nick gave the detective an absent wave and stopped before Lenina. He placed his hands on her shoulders. Kissed her cheek. 'You okay, babe? You're all flushed.'

She looked at his chin, not daring to meet his eyes. 'I'm fine.'

'Remember to call the doctor. Let me know if Ray is staying or if I need to ride back from the office.'

'Sure.'

Another kiss. 'Thanks. Bye, Ray. Good to see you.'

'You too.' Ray inclined his head.

Nick swept out the door, taking the detective with him. They shook hands on the drive and Nick leapt on to his bike, wedging his helmet on to his head and riding away. Blake climbed into his own car and drove away. Only after both men cleared her line of sight did Lenina close the door.

Ray loomed behind her, arms folded tight across his broad chest.

'We need to talk,' he said.

Chapter Eight

Lenina paused en route to the kitchen, drawing a deep breath through her nose. She could still smell Tristen on the air; his peppermint breath and a trace of his spicy aftershave. It brought to mind his smile and gentle hand on her arm. Her cheeks warmed.

Armed with the pleasant memory, she entered the kitchen. Ray waited for her at the table, massive hands wrapped around a mug of tar-like coffee. The bitter scent warred with the peppermint and chased it away, as if even her father's beverage wanted the detective gone. Opposite him was another mug, again of coffee. A pot of sugar stood beside it, spoon sticking out to one side.

'I don't like coffee,' she whispered.

Ray pursed his lips. 'Then I'll drink it. But you should lay off food this morning.'

'Why?'

'Stress and shock can do funny things to your insides. Make sure you're settled before you try anything solid.'

She sat down. Picked up the mug. Put it down without drinking. 'I'm sorry, Daddy.'

'What for?'

Though she opened her mouth, the response refused to surface.

He snorted. 'You don't even know why.'

His words cut like razor blades. 'For not telling you what happened. I didn't plan to.'

'I know. But I worry about you.'

She gripped the edge of the table. 'I'm twenty seven, not a little girl. I can cope.'

'Can you?'

Glaring into his calm, steady face, she saw the question in his arched eyebrows. 'What's that supposed to mean?'

He sighed. 'Sometimes things happen that you can't help. But they change you. I want to be sure you're ready for whatever comes next.'

'There is no 'next,' it was just a crazy, homeless man. I want to move on and forget the creepy guy even exists. I'm more concerned about this horrible scratch on my face and what to do about the catering. Two weeks really isn't very long.'

Ray leaned back in his seat. He tucked his thumb into his mouth and gnawed the nail. 'You and Jordan are everything to me. If anything happened . . .'

'It didn't. I'm hurt, but okay.'

'You don't feel weird? Ill? Tense?' His gaze strayed to the bandage on her neck.

'Of course I'm tense; you haven't stopped nagging me since you arrived. I thought Mum was supposed to do that.'

'We swapped, I'm better at it than she is.'

It took Lenina several seconds to realise he'd made a joke.

Ray sighed. 'Would you tell me if something was wrong?'

She thought back to earlier that morning and the excruciating pain in her midsection. Dry heaving over the toilet bowl. Bizarre and full sensory dreams about soldiers in ancient battles.

Lenina nodded. 'Of course I would.'

He stared. She gazed back, giving him bland, innocent eyes.

'What's all this about the doctor?'

'Tristen suggested it.'

The guarded look returned to Ray's eyes. 'Did he?'

'He thought it would be a good idea if I had blood tests and some counselling.'

'I get the counselling. Though he should have offered you an in-house doctor. You said the man bit you.'

'Yes. And I bit back.' She frowned. 'You okay?'

He gazed at his hands. 'I'm so sorry this happened to you.'

'It's not your fault.'

'I'm your father. I'm supposed to protect you.'

'How? You were miles away. Please don't get weird over this. It's why I didn't want to tell you.'

He nodded, but his eyes gave away his pain. 'Let me call the doctor. You lie down.'

Lenina nodded, not knowing what else to do. After planting a kiss on his cheek she returned to her room. Shucking the dressing gown, she crawled beneath the duvet and snuggled down. When the floor boards creaked a short while later, she considered faking sleep.

'Chuck? They didn't have any appointments for today so you're booked in for Monday.'

She uncovered her head. 'Not even emergency ones?'

'I tried to explain but the receptionist said the risks of blood-borne diseases is pretty low.'

'The receptionist? What does she know?'

'That's what I said. So I talked to a doctor. She said the same thing.' Ray sniffed. 'So did the other three.'

'Daddy . . .'

'If they're not even going to look at you today I want to be sure they know what they're talking about. The last one gave me a list of counsellors though. I stuck it to the fridge.'

'Thanks, but Tristen already offered me one.'

The bed springs squealed and compressed on one side. Lenina peeped out of the duvet to watch her father sit beside her.

'Tristen?'

Too late she realised the error. 'Sergeant Blake.'

He started chewing his thumbnail again.

'What's wrong, Daddy?'

'Am I that transparent?' Ray folded his hands in his lap and swivelled to face her. 'Don't you think it's odd that he came here alone?'

A creeping warmth crawled up Lenina's neck. She raised the duvet to her chin. 'No.'

'I do. Police aren't supposed to do that. Something about safety.'

'Like I'd beat him up?'

'*You* wouldn't, chuck, but yours isn't his only case. Policemen work in pairs to protect themselves and the people they see.'

'Why would *I* need protection?'

'Ever heard of police brutality?'

'Of course, but he was nothing but nice to me.'

'Too nice.' Ray leaned over the bed, causing the mattress to complain even more.

The warmth progressed to her cheeks. 'He was just doing his job.'

'Girls like you don't see it; you're too—' he waved his hand around, as if to pluck a word from the air, 'naive.'

'I'm not.'

'Men like him prey on girls like you, taking advantage of their position of power. I've seen predators like him before. He practically licked his lips when he looked at you.'

Lenina searched for the right words to disagree. Then she remembered the soft touch of his hand, the sound of her name falling from his lips. In her mind's eye, Lenina saw the deep intensity of Tristen's gaze as it followed her through the room. The sexy twist of his smile. She heard the low rumble of his voice and felt her lower body heat up enough to match her face. He'd stopped being *Sergeant Blake* some time ago. She shook her head, fighting to push it all away. The struggle resembled trying to shift a house from its foundations with her bare hands, exhausting and impossible.

'He's a policeman,' she said, hoping her voice didn't sound as weak as she felt.

'I don't care.' Ray's hands made fists on the bed, scrunching up the duvet. 'Don't see him by yourself.'

'Don't you trust me? I'm getting married, remember?'

'How could I forget?' He cocked an eyebrow. 'My savings account is still screaming for mercy. But, it's not you I distrust.'

'What could he possibly do to me?'

'Wouldn't you prefer not to find out?'

Another shiver rippled down her spine, this one like the tickle of a warm, teasing finger. She bit her lip.

Mistaking the gesture, Ray grasped her shoulder. 'I don't want to frighten you, but that man is trouble. Good men go bad all the time. It doesn't take much. All the goodwill and morals in the world mean nothing in the face of something you really want.'

She smiled. 'Some bus drivers can't be saved, right?'

'I wasn't always a bus driver. Please be careful.'

Lenina nodded; she'd seen the medals and heard the stories enough times. 'I will.'

Ray's shoulders relaxed. A smile returned to his lips. 'Thank you.' He kissed her forehead, stood and walked to the door. 'Do you want me to stick around for when you wake up?'

'Don't you have work?'

'Not today.'

She considered asking him to stay. The idea that he might be around to hug her when she woke, appealed more than felt comfortable to her grown-up self. It took her back to her childhood days and the dark, winter nights in which he'd told her fun stories to protect her from monsters beneath the bed. The days in which she was still his *Little Woodchuck.*

Then she thought of Tristen and the greedy way his eyes drank in the features of her face. She pressed her thighs together and moistened her lips with the tip of her tongue. Lenina found herself wondering what it might be like to feel those eyes caress the rest of her body. To feel his hands stroke her bare skin. To feel his lips against her ear as he whispered her name.

'I'll be fine. Go home.'

'Call me when you wake up.' Ray's voice saved her from the fantasy. 'I'll answer, even if I'm driving.'

She took a deep breath. 'I will. Promise.'

He loitered long enough to give her a tight smile. 'Bye, chuck.'

Chapter Nine

28 January 31 BC

Saar finished drinking and let the body slide to the ground. He wiped a hand across his mouth and allowed himself a few moments to acclimatise to the new memories. They came in a colourful blur. A shady mud hut surrounded by flowers. A smiling woman with short, silver hair. Three naked children. The market place in Rhakotis. The limestone quarries.

Each memory of the dead man transferred to Saar through the drinking of blood and he collected them, piling the stranger's life into the growing store belonging to dead men and women.

He sat in one of the low wooden chairs around a cloth-covered table. A cool breeze whispered through the chamber, product of the incredible design employed by the palace engineers. High arches, open windows and long corridors funnelled the north wind through the building where it spiralled into each room bringing with it the cleanliness of the breeze and, on some days, the salt of the sea. *One day*, Saar mused, *I'll see the sea properly. Sail on it. Visit distant lands.*

The room, given over to entertaining important guests, had several terracotta pots mounted on gate-legged stands. They formed a uniform row along one wall above which were several shelves housing linen, rolls of papyri and jewellery. Opposite, four lamps set on pedestals awaited the coming of night.

All quite different to the memories of the man on the ground. His home comprised two rooms, built with plain mud brick and floored with rushes. A single set of steps afforded entry to the roof and the second room housed two clay ovens, three chairs and a rickety table of rotting wood.

Saar shook himself and pushed the memories aside.

Beside him, Kiya leaned over the cooling body, eyes closed. 'You have an amazing skill, dear love. I envy it. You could learn anything about anyone.'

He rubbed the back of his neck. 'Perhaps, but there is only so much space within me for all these lives. I can't keep collecting them.'

Opening her eyes, she smiled, stood and tugged at one of the wooden chests between the oil lamp pedestals. 'You can do anything.' Her delicate fingers picked out the paintings on the lid, vivid depictions of the sun god and his consorts.

'You think so?'

'I know. You prove it daily.'

Her pride warmed Saar's heart. Leaving the chair, he scooped up the dead body, slung it over his shoulder and carried it to the waiting chest. 'I'm but a man.'

'A great one. Your plans will see our city safe, our people protected. The gods did well in choosing you.'

He grinned, bending long enough to kiss her upturned lips. She reached up, trying to pull him closer, but he slithered free and gestured to the dead man on his shoulder. 'First this.'

Kiya dropped her gaze, an exaggerated display of coquettish innocence that only a fool would believe. She opened the chest with a flourish and removed the rolls of cloth from inside. When Saar placed the body within, she spread the cloth on top and closed the lid.

'Now may I distract you?'

'Of course.' He caught her as she flung herself into his arms and whirled them both in a tight circle. She clung to him, giggling, long hair flying behind her.

When he stopped, she leaned close, breathing hard against his nose and jaw. This close he could see the streaks within the blue paint around her eyes, the shadow of her long lashes on her cheeks.

'You're so beautiful,' he whispered.

She kissed his forehead, stroking both hands through his shaggy dark hair. 'Now *you* distract me.'

'From?'

'You promised we would visit Panya.'

Saar thought of the shabby mud hut in which his ageing mother lived, and sighed. He chewed his thumbnail. 'Why will she not come here? She has permission, she would be safer. Cared for.'

'Pride, dear love. You're the same.'

He opened his mouth to answer, but the sound of approaching footsteps stole the words. A glance at Kiya conveyed his need and she bent to the chest, shoving it with such force that it shot across the tiled floor and back into place against the wall. Not a moment too soon.

The owner of those steps appeared in the arched doorway. 'I'm sorry to disturb you at rest, Saar, but we must speak.'

Saar grinned, forgetting worry for his mother, the dead man in the chest and even Kiya. He rushed to the doorway and embraced the newcomer. 'Mosi, it's good to see you.'

Mosi remained stiff, his shoulders and spine locked against the hug. Though he didn't fight the embrace, neither did he return it. He gazed at the floor without speaking.

Never before has he refused my touch.

Saar let his hands slide free of his second lover's shoulders. He felt the strong, subtle muscles and battle-roughened skin and likened it to his own.

When Mosi refused to speak, Saar gazed at the younger man and reached out along the invisible line that linked their minds together. Though he flinched, Mosi lowered his mental shield, apparently ready to endure the invasion of his thoughts rather than speak them aloud.

What Saar found at the end of that line made him cold all over. He stared, watching the other man shift his weight from foot to foot. 'Kiya,' he said, without looking away. 'Please leave us.'

She rushed forward and clung to his arm. 'No. I would stay with you.'

He pulled away, still staring at Mosi.

Kiya's gaze bored into his back. Her fury rushed along the similar invisible bond they shared and hit his senses like a chariot charge. He stumbled and, finally, looked away from Mosi to search her face.

Anger bled into her features, twisting her lips, furrowing her brow. Traces of black, like ink, crept into her eyes and swallowed the brown colour he loved so much. And the white around them. Soon her eyes resembled two empty pits, wells into the depth of her fury.

'Anything you would to say to him, you may say to me. Are we not equal in your love?'

Saar took a deep breath. He felt the familiar tingle across his skin and beneath his eyelids which told him that his own eyes had made the same transformation, filling with black until the whites were all enveloped. 'I won't pander to your jealousy today, Kiya. Do as I say.'

'This isn't jealousy, this is right and wrong. Why should I be shunned whenever he sees fit to visit?'

Gripping her shoulders, Saar spun her around and shoved her towards the painted archway. She stumbled and only a snatching grasp at the wall saved her from falling.

'Saar—'

'Get out,' he hissed.

Kiya paled from her chin to the top of her forehead. With a final glare at Mosi, she spun on her heel and stalked away.

Only when her rapid footsteps faded from even the range of his incredible hearing did Saar relax. He puffed a heavy breath through his nose and returned to the wooden chair, slumping down, head cupped in his hands.

A bitter taste filled his mouth at the thought of his foul treatment.

Mosi followed, standing before the chair with his hands clasped behind his back. His young face was pinched with distaste. 'You didn't have to do that.'

'I did.'

'She'll hate me more than ever.'

He nodded. 'Perhaps. But you could be nicer to her. Include her. Don't taunt her with our time together while she is busy with the queen. She's right; you're equal in my love.'

'I know.'

Saar rubbed his fingers through his hair again, frustration causing his fingers to shake. It wasn't Mosi's uncertainty and anger that robbed him of sleep night after night. Made every moment with either of his lovers fraught with emotional pitfalls.

'Explain yourself,' he murmured.

'May I sit?'

'Of course.' Saar scooted his chair closer to the table and gestured to another close by. 'Join me for some bread. Or beer, if you prefer.'

'I still can't eat or drink, Saar. You alone have that pleasure.'

'You've tried?'

'Every day. My body continues to reject food. It's increasingly painful and I have more important ways to spend my days. Set has no desire to accept mere food as tribute.'

Saar frowned but let the matter lie. 'Leave the bread. Speak your troubles.'

Mosi sat. Back rigid, hands on his knees, he stared at the opposite wall before speaking. 'You cannot read them from my thoughts?'

'You know I don't do that. Not to you.'

Pink splotches coloured Mosi's cheeks. 'Forgive me. I'm nervous.'

'You may say anything to me. We have no secrets.' Saar leaned forward in his chair.

Several more seconds of shuffling his fingers, then Mosi looked up. 'You must not kill the king. Antony may be weak, stubborn and foolish, but he is king. Destroying him will cause more trouble than it saves.'

Saar frowned. 'You know Octavian moves against us?'

'Rumours, Saar.'

'Fact.' Saar pounded his thigh with his fist. 'Antony's insult cannot be ignored any longer. We must prepare ourselves for the next strike of Rome's hammer.'

'Then why can you not do that *with* Antony?'

His upper lip curled. 'Because *his* actions brought us into danger. I want nothing more to do with him.'

'So you'll kill him?'

Saar shrugged, toying with a piece of flaking paint on the arm of his chair. 'He's but one man.'

'You'll kill dozens, if not hundreds if you pursue this plan.'

'Octavian will be here within months and Antony is too weak to lead us. Continuing to build Red Fang with god-touched warriors is the only way we'll survive.'

Mosi touched the sides of his head. 'Shouldn't we use our strength and power to help him? Talk to Antony. Arrange negotiations with Octavian before he attacks with the might of Rome at his back. You're wise. They'll heed you.'

'I'm a soldier, nothing to them. Nor will I be until I have power among them.' Head cocked to one side, Saar gazed at his lover. 'Why are you saying this? Where have these thoughts come from?'

Irritation flickered through Mosi's gaze. He stood and began to pace. 'I'm not a child, though you treat me like one. I have thoughts and opinions of my own.'

'I never disputed that.'

'No?' He snorted. 'You say we've been blessed by Set and our task is to pass on the gift. But you keep your powers secret. You bless only a select few of your deliberate choosing. You plan revolution and revolt against our god-picked rulers. You don't act like the gods' messenger.'

'What do I act like?'

Mosi had the good grace to hesitate before he answered. 'A madman.'

'Madman?' The word punched Saar like a fist. He flinched.

'You asked. I've always been honest with you.'

Whilst true, that didn't stop the words hurting. Reaching out, Saar trailed his fingers down Mosi's cheek. He smiled when the other man turned his face, allowing those fingers to brush his mouth.

'Your honesty drew me to you. One of the many reasons I love you.' Following his hand, he stepped close and kissed Mosi on the lips. A chaste touch but the smaller man shuddered beneath him.

'Don't. I can't think when you touch me.'

'Perhaps you've thought enough.'

'No, Saar. I've not.' He took a step back and held his hands before him like a shield. 'You must hear me. Your plans are wrong. *You* are wrong.'

'If you would just think on what I propose you would see it's the only way. When we kill Antony—'

'No! No "we". I won't be part of your plans for murder.'

'What would you have me do?'

'Leave Antony alone. Leave the army alone. Let Cleopatra rule as the gods dictated. To the rest . . . let change come as is natural.'

'And bend before Rome? You know I can't do that.'

'You must, or else . . .' He looked at the floor.

Saar waited. A gust through the narrow corridors lifted his shendyt about his legs and blew loose sand across his feet. He remembered then that this was royal property and that shouting of his plans to kill the king was unforgivably foolish.

'Or else what?' he whispered.

'I'll leave.' Mosi's lower lip quivered as he spoke. A wisp of hair fluttered on the breeze and though he tucked it behind his ear, the strand was too short to stay in place. Remnants of an unconscious gesture years old and long redundant.

Standing almost toe to toe, Saar gazed at his lover and felt a pang in his chest.

The pain wasn't his. In the back of his mind he felt Mosi's anguish, his indecision. Faint imprints of his emotions lived in that secret place within Saar's head, put aside for the thoughts and feelings of all his god-touched children. Mosi, the first of those fourteen children, had the strongest signature.

Again he reached out, but Mosi leapt back. He stumbled over the chair and sprawled on the floor, his usual grace and calm vanished.

Scrambling upright, he fled to the archway, turning right into the space beyond.

Saar followed, dashing into the columned passageway filled with statues, paintings and high ceilings decorated with large squares of blue, red and gold.

On other days he walked slowly through this space, taking the time to appreciate the beauty of it compared to his own modest home. Not today. Today he ran after Mosi and grabbed his retreating arm, spinning him around.

Grunting, Mosi hit a column and Saar pressed against him, pinning his lover's hands to the cold carved stone.

'Don't leave me,' he begged.

Mosi closed his eyes. He didn't struggle, but his arms sang with tension. 'Don't touch me. Please. I can feel you in my head. I can't get away.'

His words made plain something Saar had stubbornly resisted until now. He swallowed a painful lump at the back of his throat and tightened his grip on Mosi's wrists. 'I don't want you to. I love you.'

'Then change your plans. It's evil. *We* are evil.'

'How can men touched by the gods be evil?'

'We sacrifice others so that we may live.'

Saar growled at a return to this irritating recurring argument. 'Tribute. Men and women should be honoured to give their blood to the gods. We take only those who deserve to die.'

'What gives you the right to make that decision? Why should you be special?'

'Because I was marked to lead. Me, no one else.' Saar squeezed until Mosi's wrist bones crunched.

'You called it a curse once.'

'I was too afraid to see at first but this is no curse. This is a blessing from Set himself. A gift. Given to me.'

The other man struggled, but not with his full strength, still showing signs of wanting. He looked up.

Like Kiya minutes before, Mosi's eyes changed to reflect his heightened emotion. But rather than black, his eyes filled with glowing white.

'Power isn't how a man is measured, Saar. It's not having power but how that power is used which makes a man special. Actions make a man great.'

Saar let go. He heard the faint pop as Mosi's bones clicked back into place. Leaning against another of the pillars he wiped his face with both hands. Sweat gathered on his forehead, beading on his skin to roll down his cheeks and neck.

'My plan will protect us all,' he whispered. 'You must see that. But if you're not with me, you're against me.'

'I'm against your plan, not you. I love you.'

'They're one and the same. Join me.'

Mosi rolled his wrists. His chin trembled. A slump to his shoulders made him appear old and frail. At last, he looked up and as he did, the white glow faded from his eyes. 'No.'

The word struck like a punch to the ribs. Saar sagged against the pillar and tamped down a sickness in his stomach. 'Mosi—'

'I said "no", Saar.'

The silence between them was brittle and cold.

'Then leave.' Saar sniffed, conscious of a growing burn behind his eyelids. The ache in his heart threatened to knock him flat. He pointed along the length of the passageway, between the double rows of pillars, to the exit doors at the end. 'Go, before I forget I love you.'

Mosi bit his lip. Shiny tears filled his eyes and gathered in the corners before falling. With heavy steps, he walked away.

Saar watched him go then slumped to the ground, head resting against the pillar.

Though the passageway formed a link to the rest of the palace complex, he couldn't move. Not yet. Not even the thought of Cleopatra herself happening upon him in such a state could move him.

Instead, as tears streamed down his face, he watched the first of his god-touched children step through the doors and vanish from sight.

Chapter Ten

Lenina woke sobbing, cradling her face against folded arms. She kicked out but something held her legs, both ankles bound together by something warm and fluffy.

A cold shard of fear pierced her chest, dragging a scream from her mouth.

Wrenching sideways, arms flailing, she tumbled off the bed and hit the floor on her face. Seconds later the duvet followed, freeing her feet. Gasping, tingling with pain, she lay still, rubbing her cheek against the scratchy carpet. Somehow feeling something so normal helped numb the fear.

Her heart continued to race, hammering so hard it made her ribs jump. She opened her eyes. Beneath the bed she saw a pair of Nick's old socks. Beside them, an earring, two mugs and a pile of empty chocolate wrappers.

She sat up. Pulled her knees to her chest. Gazed at the room. *Her* bedroom. Not a palace. Not an ancient room filled with treasures the like of which she had only ever seen behind glass at the museum. Not a battlefield soaked with the blood of dying men.

She saw drawers, clothes spilling out like cotton innards. The mirror above the unit of drawers, a selection of make-up, moisturisers and cleansers lined up in front of it.

All so normal.

Sunlight streamed through the window, lighting the whirling motes of dust until they glinted like airborne diamonds. Beautiful if not for the distracting headache pounding the base of her skull. She turned her back on the light, shielding her eyes with a curtain of hair.

The dream rushed back, crashing in on her senses and rolling her under.

A fading sun, warm breezes and the sadness in one man's face. A pang in her chest as he stepped away, the rush of anger from the one named Kiya. Anger followed by Mosi's immeasurable sadness. Her own anguish. She relived his betrayal and clutched her chest as the pain of it speared her lungs. Her damp cheeks tingled.

'Just a dream,' she whispered, as if to make the statement aloud would prove it true. 'A stress nightmare.'

A lively, hip-hop jingle made her jump and she spun around, trying to locate the mobile.

She found it inside her dressing gown pocket. 'What?'

'Where are you?'

It took Lenina several seconds to identify the chirpy Scottish voice. She sighed and perched on the end of the bed, clutching the phone with both hands. 'Ramona?'

'I'm in the coffee shop but I can't see you. Are you even here?'

'No, I'm at home.'

'Why? What's wrong? You ill? Should I come over?'

Lenina held the phone away from her ear. After a deep breath, she brought it close again to interrupt the exuberant flow. 'I'm okay, just sick.' She touched her chest again, aware of how flushed she felt. How sweaty.

'Sick how? Vomit sick? Lady sick? Virus sick? Hangover sick?'

'I threw up this morning.'

'Oh, aye? Right, we can handle that.' A rustling sound came over the phone, followed by the quick tap of feet on the pavement. 'I'm coming over via the chemist's.'

'Why?'

'Pregnancy test.' She hung up.

Head buzzing from the whirlwind that was conversation with Ramona, Lenina pulled her dressing gown back on before trudging downstairs.

The air swirled around her as she disturbed it with her movement, reviving the scents of old coffee, toast and peppermint. The smells soothed her and she paused to drink them in, sighing as the minty scent flooded her nostrils. With it came a thought of green eyes, long hair and a white smile.

Through the thin walls Lenina heard the soft murmurs of the neighbour's television and the barks of an excited dog. She paused in the living room, gazing at the off-white walls and the pattern of light falling on them from the bay window. Squinting against the brightness, she crossed to it and pulled the curtains closed, plunging the room into comforting twilight.

Hugging herself, she entered the kitchen. Completed washing up and a note stuck to the fridge reminded her that her father had been there.

WASHED UP.
CALLED WORK FOR YOU; DONNA SAID DON'T WORRY.
CALL ME WHEN YOU WAKE UP.

DAD x

Letters in the note blurred beneath the appearance of tears. She filled a glass with water and carried it back to the living room, wiping her face the whole time. Her own thoughts broke the peaceful silence, thoughts of screams, shouts and the clash of weapons. Voices, some fearful, some desperate, others hot with anger.

Water slopped over her hands. While her fingers clutched the glass and her body trembled, Lenina tried to think about something else. Anything else. Shoes. Dresses. The wedding. Catering.

Each time she managed to steer herself away from the horrors of her dreams, they returned with a stinging snap, filling her mind with horrific detail.

More sips water. A quick flick through a magazine. Day time talk shows and local news. None of it helped.

Lenina sat on the sofa and curled her knees up to her chest, hugging her shins. Long moments she sat that way, stubbornly resisting the wild, peculiar urge to think.

'Why is this happening to me?' she murmured, brushing tears from her cheeks.

The images flashed across her eyes again. The tall, slender man with choppy dark hair and serious eyes. Something troubled her about his expression, his words, his manner but what bothered her more was the chest-tightening sensation of longing each time she pictured his face. The sense of loss mingled with raw, white-hot anger.

It had to mean something. Dreams often linked to the unconscious mind as it tried to work through a problem. Everyone knew that.

But two men arguing over whether or not to kill the king had nothing to do with anything happening in her life. Not even if the king happened to be one her job required her to specialise in.

She thought again of the palace, the names, the clothes. Then further back, to the first dream and the tower in the distance, half-shrouded from view by clouds of dust. Enough historical and archaeological texts discussed that incredible building to make it instantly recognisable. At least to her.

The Pharos of Alexandria; one of the world's first lighthouses which once stood at the end of a mile-long stretch of sand and silt connecting the coastline to the island of Pharos upon which it sat.

But even that made no sense. Work at the museum hadn't touched on that part of Egypt for very many months, focused instead on the Incan Empire and new finds from South America.

Lenina lowered her legs and took a deep breath.

The presence of the Pharos dated her dream at no earlier than 293 BC and pinned it inescapably in Egypt. Talk of Cleopatra, Octavian and Antony narrowed the range still further; close to the end of the Ptolemaic Dynasty, before Egypt became part of Rome's republic in 30 BC.

Another deep breath.

Thinking about the dreams in those terms steadied her heart rate. She risked another sip of water, pleased when her hands successfully brought the glass to her lips and back again without spillage.

Leaving it behind, she approached the bookcase near the TV and skimmed the contents. The top two shelves held Nick's books: westerns, science fiction epics and the occasional piece of horror. The next two, an explosion of pink and purple spines, held Lenina's preferred reading material: general romance, fantasy and a huge section dedicated to Mills and Boon. The last shelf held old textbooks, notes and journals from her archaeology degree.

From there she pulled down *Ptolemaic Egypt: End of the Hellenistic Period* and flipped it open to the index.

No entry for Saar. While Romans, Antony, Octavian and Cleopatra featured heavily, she saw nothing directly related to the man in her dream. She left the book and selected three others. Fifteen minutes later Lenina closed *Cleopatra: Queen of Kings* and exhaled a long, slow breath through her nose.

Again, nothing. Saar wasn't real.

As she returned her text books she stared at Nick's collection of ugly black, brown and grey covers. Towards the middle, the words 'Bram Stoker' beckoned. On the cover she saw a man in a black suit, with pale skin, dark hair and a pronounced widow's peak. Dracula of course.

Lenina scoffed, prepared to tuck the book back into place when she noticed the small white fangs peeping from between his stylised lips. Her right brain, fuelled by sudden terror, raced through different scenarios in which the word 'vampire' featured prominently. Despite that, her left brain growled and insisted on a more rational explanation that didn't involve fantasy and make-believe.

But hadn't the stranger bitten her throat? Sucked at the blood? What else could that be if not—

The doorbell rang.

Lenina screamed, spinning on the spot to face the unexpected sound.

'Nina? You okay?' Ramona's voice floated through, muffled by the door between them.

Rushing to the door, Lenina flung it open. 'I'm so glad you're here.'

'Aye, I heard about the caterers. Bummer.' Ramona flounced into the living room like a bubbly red-haired puppy. She dropped a carrier bag near the sofa and crossed the room to fling open the curtains. 'Don't sit around in the dark moping. It's bad for you.'

Lenina flinched beneath the sudden stab of sunlight.

Ramona gasped. 'What happened to your face? And your neck— is that a bandage? What happened to you?'

Lenina slumped on to the sofa and cradled her head in her hands. 'It's a long story.'

'Aye, then make it short. I'm listening.'

But Lenina had no idea what to say. Her recent revelation about vampires skimmed across the surface of her thoughts like a drop of fat on a skillet. Her tongue felt thick and refused to form the words she wanted.

'Come on, you can tell me anything. Were you shaving? Do you have a hair problem? My aunt has the same thing. Nobody knew until I caught her stealing razors from the supermarket.'

'I don't have a hair problem,' she snapped.

Ramona gave her a pointed look.

Lenina launched into her story, starting at the boutique car park, through to that morning when her father had left her in bed. Despite ample opportunity, she couldn't bring herself to mention the dreams. Or Tristen's solo visit.

Ramona listened in uncharacteristic silence, her eyes widening with every word. When the tale finished, she scratched the trail of freckles across her nose and cheeks and closed her mouth. 'And you say nothing ever happens to you. You okay? Need a hug?'

Surprisingly, the offer was exactly what Lenina needed. She leaned over and wrapped her arms around Ramona's shoulders. The balm of physical touch soothed instantly and in the wake of that hug she gathered the last traces of her dreams and packed them away at the back of her mind. Instead she closed her eyes and enjoyed the tickle of Ramona's hair against her nose. The red strands curled all over the place, carrying the scent of pencil shavings and fresh paper run through a photocopier.

Ramona patted her back. 'Are you crying, honey? Lots of sniffing going on.'

'No.'

'Maybe you have a cold?'

'I'm fine.' But Lenina kept sniffing, focused on something beneath the familiar natural perfume of her friend's clothes and skin. Something sweeter. Warmer.

When she buried her face in the space between Ramona's neck and shoulders she saw the source. A vein pulsing gently behind her ear.

Blood.

A fine tingling spread through Lenina's gums. Sharp points scratched her tongue.

How she knew, Lenina couldn't be sure, but the fact remained the same; Ramona smelled like blood and the blood smelled like . . .

She clung tighter and sniffed again, this time to snort back tears.

Another pat on back. 'Don't worry, honey, it's over now. Let's get you something to eat.'

'I'm not hungry,' she murmured.

As if to prove the lie, her stomach gurgled. Saliva flooded her mouth and she thought again of the blood rushing hot and sweet beneath the flimsy protection of Ramona's skin.

She jerked free and put her hands in her lap.

'When did you last eat?'

'Last night.'

'Then you threw up this morning. There's the test by the way.' Ramona nudged the bag with her toe. 'Of course you're hungry. You pee on that there stick. I'll make sandwiches.'

'No.' She could think of nothing worse.

'That thing about ignorance being bliss is a lie, Nina. Believe me.' She tipped her head and narrowed her eyes, adopting her 'teacher face.' It worked on sixteen- and seventeen-year-olds and Lenina flinched beneath it too. But it did offer the chance to escape and catch her stampeding imagination before it carried her straight into a psychiatric facility.

In the bathroom, she dropped everything and focused on the mirror. Her wide, startled eyes gazed back at her, pupils dilated to huge black pools, lower lip quivering. She caught a flash of something white and opened her mouth to get a better look.

Fangs. Six of them; sharp, bright and white.

She touched one and an unmistakable bead of blood at the end of the finger dissolved any doubts.

Definitely real.

Lenina turned her back on the mirror, aware her chest was heaving again. She heard blood rushing in her ears and the pound of her pulse in every sensitive spot from her throat to her wrists. The lights seemed suddenly far too bright and she yanked the cord near the door, plunging the room into darkness. Perching on the toilet she buried her face in her hands and hugged herself. Rocking back and forth, she did her best to focus on her breathing. To slow it down.

Though her breathing took time to steady, the fangs in her mouth did recede. The sharp points shrank down to the straight edges of her teeth that eighteen months of braces and retainers gifted her during her teenage years.

Ramona knocked the door some minutes later. 'Nina, honey? Can I come in?'

'No.'

'Are you crying? Is it the test? Did you do it? Can I see?'

'No.'

'It can't be that bad. Let me help.'

Lenina fought the urge to pound her fists on the door shrieking. *No, you can't! No one can!*

Instead she made a show of using the toilet and flushing it. She even dribbled a little urine on the test stick, fumbling with the packet while she sat.

Wiping her eyes on her sleeve she opened the door and pressed the stick into Ramona's hands.

Her friend frowned past her shoulder. 'Why were you sitting in the dark?'

Only then did Lenina realise that she'd performed a handful of complex motions in the pitch dark. Repressing a shudder she switched the light back on and opted not to answer.

Ramona stared at the white stick of plastic. Seconds later her shoulders slumped. She let out a huge sigh. 'Not pregnant. Thank God. Not that you wouldn't make a great mum,' she hastened to add. 'But if you got pregnant now, I'd never hear the end of it from Verni. You're already getting married, she hasn't stopped pestering me.'

Lenina thought again of the fangs in her mouth and the horrible bruises on Nick's face. She even thought of Tristen and the gorgeous twist of his smile. His peppermint breath. His warm, soft hands on hers and her heart's flutter each time he looked her way.

'I can't get married,' she whispered.

Ramona cocked an eyebrow.

'I mean— I can't— like this. I'm a mess. The caterers pulled out, I hate my dress, Nick looks like a boxer, and we still haven't decided on goodie bags for the guests.'

'Calm down. Don't let this,' she waved the stick, 'worry you. Nick won't mind waiting. And you'll have fun trying, aye?'

Lenina shook her head.

How could she possibly explain that babies were the last thing on her mind? Especially without mentioning the dreams?

Ramona tossed the test stick in the bin. 'Come have a sandwich. I made loads: tuna, ham or cheese.'

Once again Lenina opened her mouth to decline, but her stomach clenched tight and gurgled so loudly that it seemed churlish to do so.

Back in the living room, now lit by the overhead lights, Ramona lifted the plate of sandwiches and held it across her palm like a waitress. 'Madam?'

Lenina selected a tuna sandwich and nibbled from the one corner while listening to Ramona talk about her latest batch of maths students. Halfway into an explanation about the changing curriculum for A-level, Lenina zoned out and focused instead on what she'd seen in the mirror.

It isn't possible, she thought, still munching. How could it be? Perhaps a trick of the light or a result of the stress?

People couldn't just spontaneously grow fangs like a sabre-tooth. And then shrink them again . . .

She lowered her hand to the plate again, but found only crumbs. 'Wow, Ramona, don't I get any?'

Her friend stopped mid-flow. She glanced at the plate. Her eyes popped. 'Me? This is my first one.' She waved the remaining corner of a cheese sandwich. 'What did you do, inhale them?'

Lenina stared. 'I didn't. I can't have.'

'And you said you weren't hungry. Aye . . . maybe we should do another test. I did buy two.'

'I'm not pregnant.'

'But with an appetite like that—'

'Romey, I'm not pregnant. Stop badgering me.'

The smile faded from Ramona's face. She shuffled in her seat while avoiding Lenina's gaze then finished the last of her sandwich. 'I'm just worried.'

So was Lenina. Aloud she said, 'Sorry. I'm a bit tense.'

'I'll say.' Ramona brushed crumbs from her hands. 'Let's go for a walk then.'

'Now?'

'Aye. It's gorgeous out there, blue skies, gold leaves. Fresh air will do you good.' Enlivened and comforted by her new role of mother hen, she stood and clapped her hands. 'Chop, chop. Get dressed. We'll talk about why you suddenly hate your beautiful dress.'

All the talk in the world couldn't fix Lenina's real problem. Just the same she sighed, turned and trudged up the stairs.

Chapter Eleven

Lenina kicked a pine cone. It skidded across the pavement before balancing on the edge of the kerb. The slipstream from a passing car dragged it into the road where a second car crushed it. She felt much like the pine cone.

'Isn't this nice?' Ramona clung to her arm like a limpet, chubby cheeks rosy in the cold. She wore a woolly hat crammed over her red curls, giving her the look of a fluffy, upside-down ice-cream cone.

'It's okay.'

'Moody,' she chided. 'It's good to be out of the house. Stop whining.'

'I'm not whining; I'm tired. I have a headache.'

Squeezing her arm in what she probably thought was a comforting way, Ramona pointed to the coffee shop across the road. 'Let's get a latte.'

'I don't want a latte.'

'I do.'

Narrowing her eyes against the watery sunlight, Lenina slouched through the doors and searched for a seat away from the windows.

She reached a seat near the back half a pace behind another woman who was balancing a cappuccino in one hand and a laptop in the other. With a defiant tilt of her head, the woman sat, opened her laptop and took a sip of coffee. Lenina closed her fingers over her palms. They felt itchy but she knew the urge to slap this woman was merely a reflection of her poor mood.

Another search revealed a table near the front, still littered with debris from the last user. It faced the window, but the outside awning offered shade. She raced towards it, weaving around tables, knocking her hips against chairs to slam her rear into the nearest seat just as a weary-looking man with a mullet and a stack of folders approached from the right.

He looked at her, then at the spare seat.

'My friend is at the till,' she said.

His eyes widened. 'Guess I'll go downstairs then.'

Lenina folded her arms and glared out the window.

The faceless masses streamed by in unending procession, most with their heads down against the wind. One woman, with a massive Alsatian on the end of a chain, fought to calm the creature outside a large department store. She tied the chain to a loop in the doors and slipped inside, leaving the dog to watch her through the glass.

A man with his face wrapped up to the eyes in a thick red scarf weaved through the crowds like a slalom skier with a pushchair out in front. The baby inside bawled and kicked, tiny hands waving from the depths of woolly blankets.

Two men in their middling twenties laughed and pushed each other as they crossed the road, sharing a cardboard box of fried chicken. One of them dodged to the side, steering clear of a shuffling form in grey approaching from the other direction.

The man in grey paused and turned to watch them, fingers twitching in his tattered gloves. He followed them for a step or two before the blast of a car horn pulled him up short. Shaking a fist, he hurried back on to the pavement and kept walking.

Lenina nerves fired with a rush of adrenalin. She stood, pressed her face to the window and watched the man continue on his way, scratching the back of his head with one grubby hand. A nest of ginger curls protruded from beneath his hat.

Lenina slumped back into her seat. She felt lightheaded and clutched the arms of the squishy green chair while trying to think. It couldn't be the same man, could it? She leaned forward again and watched his progress. When he turned, exposing his face for the first time, she knew.

Ramona returned with two mugs and two slabs of chocolate cake on a tray. 'I bought you one anyway. You need to counteract all that bloody running.'

Lenina gazed at her friend without really seeing. Her hands shook as she brought them to her mouth.

'What? You look like you've seen a ghost.'

Her stomach clenched. Lenina pushed herself off the chair, biting her lip.

'What's wrong?'

'I need to go,' she said.

'What? No, I'll eat the stupid cake. You don't have to leave.'

She shook her head and stumbled from the coffee shop, scrunching her jacket into an untidy bunch over her chest. Once again assailed by the bright autumn sunlight, she angled left, away from the main road to the indoor market. Beneath the sloping roofs, surrounded by the call of fruit and vegetable vendors she felt safer. Calmer. The headache began to recede. Head down she threaded through the stalls, dodging prams, yapping dogs and young student types struggling to secure their five-a-day.

'Strawberries, madam? Two punnets for a pound.'

Lenina shook her head, shying away from the sweet-smelling selection.

Her handbag buzzed. Even through the noise of the market she could hear the hip-hop jingle that was Ramona's ring tone.

The thought of answering, of dealing with her friend's incessant questions, made her stomach writhe. Tucking the bag beneath her arm she ploughed through to the other side. Here the goods changed from fruit and vegetables to mobile phone accessories, second-hand clothes and books with a fusty smell. She dodged past all of them and paused on the side of the road, one hand pressed to her forehead. Cold sweat slicked her palm.

The phone rang again.

Lenina snaked one hand into the bag to retrieve it, licking her lips as she worked on what to say. 'Hi.'

'What the hell? Is this about the wedding? The dress? There's nothing wrong with it.'

Lenina sighed. 'It's not the dress.'

'What else could it be?'

She thought of all the other things she'd told Ramona that day and felt a pang in her chest.

Am I really that shallow?

'I'm going home.'

'No, no, wait for me. We'll go together.'

She hung up without speaking, shoved the phone into her bag and marched through a narrow passage of shops. On the other side she saw the stranger again, gazing through the window of a vintage boutique. He leaned against the glass watching a cluster of men fiddling with bowties, bowler hats and walking canes.

She backed away, gaze pinned to his back. As she watched, the man stiffened, straightened and tilted his chin. He sniffed. She heard the sound as if he was standing right beside her. And the growl that followed.

Lenina turned and walked the other way, peering back over her shoulder. She reached the end of the row just as the stranger appeared at the start.

Cold fingers of fear crawled down her back.

Faster now. Back into the market. Past the books and clothes. Into the food section. Out the other side. Through a narrow passage between two banks, a favoured resting place of the city's many homeless people. Empty today, the small recess in which they often sat filled instead with a small pile of vomit. The ginger stranger loomed into view on the other side, blocking the exit. His smile was crooked and yellow.

Lenina froze, staring into his eyes. Her knees buckled.

'Why are you following me?' he whispered.

'I'm not, I–'

'I've seen you before. Tell me.' He stepped into the passage with her, using his bulk to edge her towards the gap in the right hand wall.

Lenina backed up until heels touched the brickwork and she brought her feet close together to avoid the puddle of vomit. 'Please, I'm not following you.'

His hand touched her throat. The tips of his fingers brushed the bandage where he'd set his teeth the night before. His nostrils flared and his breath hit her face; a hot, stinking billow of old meat and cigarettes. 'You wanna die?'

She looked into his eyes again. Fell into the smoky grey of his gaze and felt darkness creep in around her. 'Not again– please– I can't.'

The menace in the man's eyes winked out like a snuffed candle. He frowned and peered close, searching her face, as if seeing clearly for the first time. When his gaze fell on the scratch on her cheek his hands jerked back. 'You should be dead.'

Lenina sucked in a breath of air and tried not to move. 'What?'

The man's voice took on a tight, rasping quality. 'You can't be here. You're dead. I saw you.'

She waited.

The stranger backed off. Tendons on his neck stood out like ropes. He stared so intently that she imagined his gaze boring a hole through her skull.

It gave her time to look at his face, better light giving away more detail.

Thick grime caked his skin. Four pale scars marred his cheek in stark relief against his scrubby ginger beard and hair. Grey eyes, round and wide, showed white all the way around. His lower lip trembled.

He sniffed again, leaning forward as if to catch the air near her face. Whatever he smelled made him close his eyes and emit a low, keening moan. His face paled. 'She'll kill me— the Kiss— I didn't mean to— you should be dead.'

The tremble in his voice made Lenina stand straight. She stared at this man's face and the shaking of his hands and realised that he was scared.

No, terrified. Of her.

He shied away, pressing his back to the wall as though he meant to sink into it. 'You only got a drop.'

'A drop of what?' she whispered.

'Blood.'

Then she felt it. A niggling tug at the back of her mind. A tickle. A stroke. It was a feeling she had no name for, but she recognised it as clearly as the warmth of sunlight on her face. She knew it because the man in her dream had experienced the same thing on the field of battle and in private with his lovers. Shivering in that narrow passage, Lenina felt the grey-eyed stranger in her head and knew his thoughts. His fear.

'Jason,' she murmured. 'Your name is Jason.'

The man shrieked and covered his face. He seemed to be whispering something, the same words over and over, but his fingers muffled them.

'What did you do to me?' she demanded. 'You did this, didn't you? You understand it. How can I know your name? Is that a vampire thing?'

The word slipped free of her mouth before she could catch it, but the change in Jason was dramatic. He stood straight, gazing at her with such horror in his eyes he might have witnessed the end of the world.

'Vampire,' she repeated. 'But they're not real. That can't be right.'

Lips ringed with crimson. Bright white fangs. Bare throats littered with teeth marks. Lenina cringed beneath the onslaught of images and clutched at the wall. 'Is that what you did? Did you give me the nightmares?'

His fear and confusion reached a tsunami-like peak then crashed down on her thoughts, drowning her emotions until she felt nothing but him.

In her mind's eye, Lenina saw a child with olive-dark skin and flowing dark hair. She had brown eyes, but they darkened rapidly until the whites disappeared and became black. Fangs peeped from between her lips.

Lenina whimpered. 'Who is that? What are you doing? Stop it!'

The man – Jason – shoved past her, dashed out of the alley and back into the market. He managed only three steps before crashing into Ramona. His charge knocked her flat and he fell with her, the pair of them tumbling over the pavement like scattered bowling pins.

Ramona shrieked and called out, 'Rape!'

He scrambled upright and took off at a run.

Lenina stumbled back into the open.

'Nina,' her friend exclaimed. She stood and rushed forward to grab her shoulders. Her eyes were big and shiny, face pale beneath the liberal dusting of freckles. 'Are you okay? Who's that man? What happened?'

Several curious onlookers stopped to stare. Some even pulled out mobile phones to record it on video.

Closing her eyes, Lenina concentrated on the steady thud of Jason's fear still filling her mind. It ebbed but only a little, seemingly a product of the growing distance between them rather than a lessening of the emotion itself.

When she opened her eyes she saw Jason vanish around a corner, along with all the answers.

She took a deep breath through her nose. It came out through her mouth slow and steady.

'Nina, talk to me.'

But Lenina didn't talk. She ran.

Gaze fixed on Jason's back, she followed him through the market and out on to back streets.

Far ahead, he pounded along the pavement ducking and diving around others moving in the opposite direction, jacket flying behind him like a cloak. Such speed and agility made Lenina doubt her assumptions about his age. More startling was the fact that she was slowly gaining on him.

'Wait!' she bellowed. 'We have to talk.'

He shook his head, holding his fists over his ears as he ran. Without looking, he darted into the road.

Car horns filled the air followed by the squeal of brakes.

Like a gazelle he dodged through the first lane, narrowly avoiding a horrible, crushing death.

In the next lane, a car screeched to a halt directly in front of him but he never paused, simply bounding over the bonnet like an Olympic hurdler.

By the time Lenina reached the road the traffic had stilled, drivers leaning from their windows to stare and curse. She weaved through them, gaze fixed on Jason's back as he left the city centre and dashed past the cluster of buildings making De Montford University.

Across another set of lights. Past a pub. Over a bridge. He entered the grounds of a small park linked to the primary school on the near side of the road and used the path leading to the far end.

As Lenina entered the park, Jason was a small figure, shoving his way past dog walkers, couples with prams and kids on bikes.

She sped across the grass, hoping to cut him off as he rounded the bend. So intent on his retreating back, she didn't notice the woman with the pram.

The woman shrieked.

Lenina stopped dead, her momentum toppling her into a poor imitation of a baseball slide. The impact jarred her spine and rattled her skull. She came to a painful stop after four feet, knocking her arm against a fence.

'Are you okay?' The voice seemed to come from a thousand miles away.

Groaning, she flopped on to her back and stared at the darkening sky.

The woman's face appeared above her. 'Are you crazy? You could hurt someone running like that. Is someone chasing you?'

'No.'

'Are you hurt?'

She winced. 'No.' Though true, with the rush of adrenalin spent, Lenina felt cold and shaky. She eased into a sitting position, cradling her jarred elbow.

'Wait, go slow.'

'I'm fine.'

The woman crouched beside her, one hand still on the pram. 'I thought you were going to hit us.'

'So did I.'

'Do you need help?'

'No.' With slow movements, Lenina clambered to her feet and tested her balance. 'I'm so sorry. What about you?'

'We're fine. You've got amazing reflexes.' The woman gave a shaky smile.

'Thanks.' Limping past her, Lenina returned to the path and looked. There was no real need; she knew Jason was gone.

Sighing, she found a bench and sat, resting her forehead on her knees.

The shakes continued, full body trembling until her teeth chattered and her hands could no longer grip her knees. Cooling air swirled around, but her skin flushed hot, then cold, then hot again. Tears caught on her eyelashes and she scrunched both eyes shut.

Deep breaths. She had to calm down.

On the back of her closed eyelids she saw him again. Grey eyes. Yellowed teeth. Trembling lips.

The more she tried to avoid him, the more she saw, until she had an impression of Jason leaning against a wall in a narrow, litter-choked alley. He stared at his hands and she saw through his eyes. Watched his fingers shake until he curled them into fists.

His fear began to leak away, replaced instead by sure, steady resolve. Thin lips mouthed the words, *I have to get rid of her.*

Lenina jerked her eyes open and leapt off the bench.

She looked left and right, shivering as every curious look became a death-glare, each stranger morphed into a stalking spectre of bloody murder.

Though the images died, the imprint of Jason's thoughts remained.

He was coming back and he meant to kill her.

Chapter Twelve

Lenina set off at a brisk walk which soon became a jog. Then a run. Out of the park and back along the main roads. Her frantic flight took her back past the cluster of buildings making De Montfort University, bumping through the crowds of students with normal lives and normal troubles. Then past the hospital, an ugly cluster of glass and concrete jumbled up with older buildings of weathered stone.

By the time she reached the giant bulk of the rugby ground, she knew she could run no further and thrust out her hand to flag down a cab.

'Oadby please,' she told the aged taxi driver.

He glanced at her ruffled hair, flushed face and grubby clothes. 'You all right, mi'duck?'

'Fine,' she gasped. 'Please just drive.'

He did, stabbing two buttons on the meter that hiked the starting price to £3.

She didn't care. It didn't matter. Nothing mattered as much as getting away.

With each passing mile Jason's presence faded. By the time they reached the main route leaving the city, some of the panic eased off. Replacing it came a wave of nausea that brought out goosebumps on her arms.

From the depths of her bag her mobile rang with Ramona's tone. She yanked it out and pressed it to her ear.

'What the hell, Nina? I've been calling for ages. Where are you? Are you okay? Why did you chase that guy?'

Lenina put the phone in her lap and let her friend wear herself out with questions. She couldn't answer them sensibly anyway. After a moment or two she raised the mobile back to her ear.

'I'm going home, Romey.'

'I'll come meet you. I don't think you should be alone right now.'

'I won't be; Nick finishes early today.'

'Will you at least get a bus rather than jogging?'

'I'm in a cab. I'll be fine.' Her stomach tightened, doubling her over and drawing gasps from her lips. 'I need to go.'

The driver paused at a set of traffic lights and swivelled in his seat to peer through the plastic partition. 'There's a £50 fine if you throw up back there.'

'I'm okay.'

'You're hyperventilating.'

The phone rang again. Lenina clutched her knees until her fingernails bit through the denim and let the call ring out. When it did, she turned the phone off.

'Just go,' she told the driver.

As the lights changed, the driver turned forward again but he looked back regularly, often swerving as he tried to see what she was doing. After the third such slalom across the lanes, Lenina scrabbled for her purse.

'Let me out. You're going to kill us both.' She shoved a wadded ten-pound note into the tray at the base of the partition. 'Keep the change, just let me go.'

No complaints. The driver pulled into the car park of a large supermarket and unlocked the doors.

Lenina threw herself free of the vehicle, landing on her knees. Her stomach clenched with ferocious intensity and seconds later she vomited, retching and spitting until her stomach contracted on emptiness.

The cab driver gave a disgusted groan as he drove away.

A security guard approached with his hands outstretched, as if she were a potentially violent animal. He crouched nearby. 'You okay? Do you need help?'

Bitterly wondering where such help had been last night, Lenina shook her head. She wiped her mouth, side-stepped the lumpy puddle and began walking again.

Rain began soon after. A drizzle at first which quickly evolved into an angry downpour. Turning her face skyward, she let the rain wash her mouth clear and spat the tepid mouthfuls on the paving slabs.

Lenina thought of her warm, comfortable bed and moved faster, her feet automatically choosing the path home she had used hundreds, if not thousands of times before.

The house was only ten minutes away now.

At the north gate of Grick Park she stopped dead, staring across the rain-slicked grass.

Nick's voice filled her head, begging her not to cut across the dark and lonely park.

Surely it made no difference now. The worst was already done.

She opened the gate and slipped through.

Though not as late as the day before, the rain made the park similarly dark. This time, without the lull of her music or the comfortable rhythm of running, Lenina felt awkward and out of place.

Halfway through she turned off the path on to the grass, angling her route towards the middle where white lines marked the edges of three familiar football pitches.

With each step, the bite marks on her throat itched and burned.

It didn't take long to find the spot.

Tears ran down Lenina's cheeks and mingled with the driving rain.

As though her body were attuned to the site, an echo of last night's panic fizzed through her limbs. Growing warmth filled her belly. Her lungs tightened. Breathing became difficult.

Here, she thought, bending to touch the grass. This was where he bit her. Where she bit back and filled her mouth with his blood.

As if to think of him was to call him to her, Jason's presence filled her head. She felt him like she had earlier, close enough to be peering over her shoulder.

He sensed her. A prickle of unease trickled down the link between them. Then the connection died and her mind was her own once more.

Peeling off across the grass again, Lenina ran with her face in her hands as if by not seeing she could erase the images dancing behind her eyelids.

Long teeth. Sandy dunes. Flesh stained red.

Saar, the man from her dreams, bent over a twitching body in Roman armour and feasted from his throat.

She heard distant barking and banked left away from it, aiming for the dim grey of the industrial estate hemmed in by high rail fences. Buildings loomed out of the darkness like thick, stubby fingers, unlit but for the occasional sparkle of a wet security camera catching the rising moon's glare.

She clung to the fence, resting her forehead against the twisted metal.

Rain hammered her head and shoulders. The barking grew louder.

Saar, she thought. A soldier in Cleopatra's time. A man who drank blood, grew fangs and talked of 'children', even though some of those were clearly older than him.

Closer now, the furious yapping brought her attention to the ground.

A small terrier blinked in the rain then growled again. It backed off a step then bounded around her ankles, worrying her laces.

'Go away,' she snapped.

The dog barked harder.

'Get lost.'

More barks and a growl, followed by a nip at her toes. Sharp teeth punched through her trainers.

'Get away from me!' Rage burst like a pricked balloon. She kicked out with a wordless grunt, not caring, not seeing, not thinking at all. The side of her foot struck the dog in the ribs with a loud crack, catapulting it across the wet grass. The small creature hit the ground with a sickening thud more than twenty feet away, then slid through the oozing brown mud a further six feet. It didn't move after that.

Lenina's hands flew to her mouth.

Before she could check on the creature, she heard shrieks from behind.

'What have you done? God— oh no— Poppy!' A woman shouldered passed her and threw herself down beside the silent dog. 'You killed her.' Raw horror filled her voice.

Lenina chewed her thumbnail until it bled. 'I'm sorry— I didn't mean to.'

'What sort of crazy person kicks a dog?'

'She bit me.'

'She's only a baby!'

'I'm so sorry.' Lenina reached out, but the woman twisted free like a greased eel and shouted into the darkness.

'Police! Help me, police!'

The shrill voice seemed to fill the empty park, bouncing off raindrops until it built to a deafening crescendo of panic and anger.

Lenina pressed her hands over her ears, but then the woman was in front of her, clawing at her face. She hid beneath her hands. 'Stop it.'

'You killed my dog.'

'I'm warning you, lady, leave me alone.'

But the woman screeched and dived in again, folding Lenina's fingers back with strength born of madness. She struck out, with a closed fist this time, and Lenina caught her wrist a trembling inch from her cheek. Then the fist opened and sharp fingernails scored her cheek.

Lenina's vision tunnelled. Loud thudding filled her ears and it took long seconds to recognise it as a heartbeat. Not her own, but the rapid drumming of the other woman's heart, powered by a rush of adrenalin.

Fangs reappeared in her mouth. She felt them this time, heard the little click and grinding sound of them extending from her gum line. They shot downward in response to an absent thought, linking blood to the rhythmic tattoo of that racing heartbeat.

She opened her mouth, acclimatising herself to the new mouthful of weaponry. She growled. A quick step pressed her against the woman and she snaked one hand around the back of the damp head and pulled her close. It might have been preparation for a lover's embrace if not for the saliva flooding her mouth, or the appreciative rumble of her stomach. Or the fury in her mind.

Free hand beneath her assailant's chin, Lenina pushed up, tilting the woman's head back to expose her throat, long and white beneath a fluffy, pink scarf.

She ripped the scarf away. Lowered her head. Placed her fangs against that trembling flesh and bit down.

The woman screamed.

Lenina heard the sound and the increase in her heart rate which followed. Both sent a surge of pleasure crashing through her body and she groaned through her mouthful of flesh.

When the blood hit her tongue the flow was fast and powerful. Swallowing it brought a warmth to her body that chased out the chill of the rain. Thin lines of fire raced through her limbs.

The woman in her arms made a strange choking sound.

Lenina heard it and deepened her bite, sinking to the ground with the woman cradled against her chest. She sat in the grass and suckled like a newborn enjoying that all-important first drink at the breast.

Minutes later . . . hours later . . . Lenina raised her head.

The thudding of drums that she knew to be a heartbeat, slowed to a barely audible patter. When she pulled her teeth free of the woman's throat the sound stopped completely.

The body in her arms gave a sigh, then slipped free of her arms and rolled across the grass.

Lenina noticed the woman's eyes were still open, blank and unblinking, fixed in an expression of horror that would last forever.

A large part of Lenina longed to run away again. To put as much distance between herself and the truth as physically possible. A smaller part luxuriated in the afterglow of her actions and applauded her.

Thanked her.

For the first time in hours her stomach neither rumbled nor ached.

She felt full. Even glutted.

Three small trails of blood oozed down the side of the woman's neck. Before the rain could dilute them, Lenina lowered her head and licked them away.

The last explosion of sweetness on her tongue stole her breath. It clung to her gums, her teeth. Tiny drops of it lingered on her lips and her tongue stole out to lick them away even as tears gathered in her eyes.

The points of her fangs receded back into her gum line.

Lenina swallowed a sob and struggled to her feet. She stared across the grass. Gasped.

Everything looked brighter. Clearer. The entire world was picked out with diamond hard edges and deep, rich colours, even in the poor light, with a level of detail reserved for close-up shots in nature documentaries.

Every blade of grass was visible against its companion. Broken windows in the face of the dark and lonely industrial estate. The wisp of fine hair across the dead woman's upper lip.

Lenina smelled the churned-up earth. The fresh, faintly metallic scent of the rain. The musk of wet dog fur.

She glanced at the bruised and broken carcass and finally lost her grip on the sobs. Tears ran freely and she lowered her face to her bloodied hands, as if to save herself from the sight of those cooling bodies.

Not that it helped. She would see that dog and its owner forever, stamped on the fabric of her memory, never to be erased.

Chapter Thirteen

6 September 33 BC

Saar leaned forward, meeting the proffered kiss with a soft moan that rumbled through his chest like the purr of a giant cat. From above, her hair forming a dark curtain around their naked bodies, Kiya smiled at him.

He touched her cheek. 'You're so beautiful. Your eyes, your skin, your delicious mouth.' He nipped her lips, lapping away the drop of blood that followed.

She writhed against him, kissing her way down his face and chest. Her lips hovered over his hip before brushing down his thigh, stopping at the birthmark beneath his rear. She kissed it.

He twitched. 'Don't.'

'But I love this mark, like the deadly claw of a bear. Or the tooth of some giant snake. It's beautiful and tastes so good. Just like the rest of you. From the sweetest nectar of your lips to the juicy meat of your—' Kiya jerked upright, looking over her shoulder as footsteps approached their chamber.

Though he tried to catch her, she slipped through his grip like a fish and darted off the end of the bed to hide in the shadows at the back of the room. Grinning, he followed her. 'It's safe, dear love.'

'No one must know of us,' she hissed. 'The queen does not allow it.'

'Mosi will tell no one. Will you?'

He looked across the vast chamber, skipping over the beautiful dressings and gifts to view the wide arch at the far end. The silky coloured drapes which cloaked the entrance twitched aside, exposing the newcomer. Saar laughed at the bemused expression on the other man's face.

'You're naked.' Still dressed for scouting, Mosi wore his sword on one hip and held his spear beneath his arm. Sand crusted his feet and legs as far as his knees. 'I thought you needed me. I felt you call.' He tapped the side of his head with one finger.

As he did so, Saar felt Mosi in his mind, a warm presence that coiled around his senses and held tight in a loving, spiritual hug. He reached out to touch that presence, a flex of will that manifested physically as a slight smile.

'I did. The time has come for you to meet somebody else dear to me.'

Mosi looked at the ground. 'You're naked.'

Saar glanced down then back up again. He grinned, stepped forward and let the light from the strategically placed mirrors fall upon his body. 'This isn't the first time you've seen my body, Mosi. Don't be embarrassed. I'm not.'

'And what of me?' Kiya's voice rang with impatience.

'Take the linen from the bed if you wish.'

'If you will be naked before this man, I need not hide.' She employed the air of a petulant child, but Saar chose not to comment. Instead he extended his hand. 'Come then, dear love. Meet the second love in my life.'

'Second?' Her voice became sharp. Clipped. As she stepped out from behind the drapes, her eyes narrowed. 'At last.' Up, then down, she took in Mosi's attire and his face before turning back to Saar. 'So this is the one?' She set her hands on her hips and assessed him once more. 'I suppose I can understand his appeal. But he's skinny and weak compared to you.'

Saar grinned. 'Many men are. Don't be jealous, you both have my love, but in different ways.'

She snorted. 'I offer you the warm embrace of a woman's most delicate flower. What does he give you?'

'Love. Devotion. Unquestioning obedience.'

Another snort. 'Really? And is my offering of these things not enough?'

'You question everything I do.'

She glared.

'Of course it's enough.' Saar's grin wilted. 'Will you not try to understand? He's dear to me but no more or less than you.'

'Men who act as you do are considered dirty. They aren't real men in the eyes of others or those of the gods. Did Set not sully Horace in such a way?'

Saar flinched. 'Is that really what you think of me?'

Her answer loitered on her tongue. 'No. Love takes many forms. But I needn't like it. I've no desire to share you. With anyone.'

'Mosi is the first. You and he are my god-touched children.'

'Yes, him. A soldier. Before me.'

'It is *because* of him that I learned of the ability to share my gift. If not for Mosi, you wouldn't have the power you so enjoy.' Eyeing his naked lover, Saar sighed. 'I want you both to hear my plan. Success depends on the three of us working together.'

'Both of us?' Kiya looked again at Mosi. She folded her hands beneath her breasts, pushing them up and out. A fine flaunting of her womanly assets. 'Even him?'

'Even him.'

A long silence filled the chamber.

Saar heard the rumble of chariots outside, soldiers drilling in the large yard to the side of the palace. The occasional clash of weapons rode the light breeze which carried scents of sweat and warm metal.

He closed his eyes. Took a deep breath. When he opened them again he turned away from Kiya and extended a hand to Mosi.

The other man didn't move.

'Please, Mosi. Come to me.'

Still studying the floor, Mosi flicked a hand over his shoulder. The gesture lingered from the days of his long hair and his fingers caught nothing but air. He shrugged and fussed with the short strands at the back of his neck. 'I can hear these plans another time. I have no desire to cause Kiya discomfort.'

'She'll grow accustomed to you. Perhaps even love you as I do.'

As he spoke the words, Saar felt the heat of Kiya's gaze against his back. He chose to ignore it. Instead he reached out and grabbed Mosi's arm, pulling him close.

Still he resisted, dragging his feet across the stone floor. 'Please . . .'

'Be silent, Mosi. Look at me.'

At last the younger man looked up and Saar smiled. He stared at those beautiful eyes, the long, thick lashes, and full kissable lips. 'Do as I ask. Remove your weapons. Sit with us.' To add weight to the request he took the spear and laid it on the ground.

Cat-like, Kiya prowled around them, her crossed arms and jerking head a clear indication of her feelings. She took up one of the chairs near the wall and watched.

'Look at me,' Saar repeated, conscious of the tension returning to Mosi's back and shoulders. 'Look only at me.'

He took the sword and put it beside the spear, then unfastened the knot holding the first section of toughened leather straps in place across Mosi's chest. The second section protected his stomach and Saar pulled that away too, holding his gaze the whole time.

He heard Mosi's breathing quicken and resisted the urge to smile.

'Saar . . . ?'

'Let us all be on an even footing. Besides, I like to look at you.'

At last he removed the linen shendyt from Mosi's waist and bent down to unfasten the flat straw sandals.

Saar took a moment to enjoy the view before kissing him once on the lips.

'Now, sit.'

Obeying his own order, Saar snagged a chair and turned it to face Kiya.

Mosi copied him.

'Now that we are *on an even footing*, what do you want to discuss?' The appearance of fangs in Kiya's mouth matched the bite in her voice, but she kept enough of a hold on her temper to keep her eyes a warm, steady brown.

'Antony.'

Whatever Mosi might have expected it wasn't that. He stared, lips slightly parted, one hand twitching on the arm of the chair. By contrast, Kiya gritted her teeth and leaned forward in her seat.

'This has been too long in coming,' she said. 'What will you do to him?'

'I'm undecided. But it pleases me to know that I'm not the only person who senses his inability to lead.'

'He spends more time in the queen's bed than he does with you or your soldiers. I would know. Believe me, dear love, he is a fool. He has not half the wit or intelligence that you do.'

Saar grinned as a fierce rush of pleasure warmed his insides. 'You flatter me.'

'I speak truth.'

'King Antony is a cautious man, true, but he isn't foolish. What quarrel do you have with him?' Mosi spoke softly from his corner of the lopsided triangle made by their chairs.

'Antony is selfish, arrogant and short-sighted.' Saar spoke quickly, glancing at Mosi with a frown. 'You know this. His selfishness leads us to outright war with Rome and will ultimately put our great country in their hands. He must be stopped.'

'And how do you plan to do that?'

'An army.'

Both Mosi and Kiya looked confused.

'You and I are already part of the army.' Mosi glanced at his discarded weapons. 'You are the queen's personal protector. How will an army help us?'

'Not *an* army. *Our* army.' Saar leaned forward. The warm, slightly rough surface of the wood scratched his thigh, but it was a minor irritant. His hands shook and he clasped them together to help control the excitement building in his gut. 'We have a gift. A wonderful, powerful gift, passed to us by mighty Set himself. Our blood holds power. You've seen it.'

An eager nod from Kiya. 'I can last for days without sleep. Food holds no lure for me but my body has never been stronger. I'm faster. I hear the whispers of the slaves in other rooms throughout the palace and when I follow the queen, I can see the smiles on the faces of the people for hundreds of yards in every direction. I hear their thoughts in my head and change them to suit my whims.'

'And you, Mosi?'

He scratched the back of his neck again. 'Yes, in the years since you first touched me I've felt stronger and faster, too. None but you can best me with a sword or bow, though many have tried. Small objects move when and where I will them and my body finds sustenance in the physical touch of another. This is power unparalleled.'

Saar nodded. 'We're the finest examples of what a man or woman can be. If our army were filled with others like us, we would be unstoppable. Never again need we fear invasion.'

Kiya's voice trembled. Her eyes grew round and shiny. 'Is that possible? How many times can you share this gift? It comes from blood, would it not weaken you? And what of Set?'

'I don't know. Set values strength, so I would choose carefully. But what god would reject additional tribute? And think on it. How strong would Egypt become if every soldier were as we are? Perhaps we could grow beyond our current borders and reclaim lost lands.'

'Yes.' Kiya bounced on her chair. 'We'll recruit hundreds to your cause and make our homeland great again. We'll name them The Red Fang of Alexandria.'

Saar cocked an eyebrow.

She cast a playful glance at his bare thigh. 'The mark which coaxed your mother to enlist you in the army. The mark which so resembles the fang of a snake. Name your army after it.'

'Is that necessary?'

'Yes. All great men have memorable titles. Saar . . . leader of the Red Fang Army. It's perfect.'

Though he smiled, Saar couldn't help but notice the silence from one corner of the triangle. He glanced at Mosi's pensive frown, tapping foot and lowered gaze.

Carefully he reached down the invisible line that joined their minds together, groping for answers at the other end.

Sensing him, Mosi looked up and, with a grunt, shut off the connection. 'Don't,' he whispered. 'Let me think this through. I must be clear in my own mind.'

'Why?' Kiya sneered. 'Do you not trust *our* love to do what's right? He has an excellent plan that will ensure our survival now and for years to come. What more is there to think about? Why else would Set give him this gift if not to protect us?'

'But it wasn't a gift.' Mosi's voice hardened. His right hand made a fist while the left groped over his shoulder for hair he'd cut long ago. 'It was a foul trick, which Saar has since come to use for good.'

'How can power and strength be a trick? You're weak, Mosi. Seeking trouble where there is none, to avoid doing what must be done.'

Saar stood.

The abrupt motion cut short Mosi's response and caused Kiya to snap her mouth closed.

He waited, staring at each of them in turn until he felt their unease prickle down the links between them.

'This is a delicate plan,' he said at last. 'We can't rush. I've had months to consider this but you haven't.' He glanced at Mosi. 'I expect and welcome your questions.' Sensing Kiya's urge to speak, he raised a hand to silence her. 'Dear love, you trust me in all things and I'm grateful for that. But you're not a soldier. Yes, I need you in executing this plan, but I must hear what Mosi has to say on the matter. His thoughts are valid.'

She slumped in her seat, crossed her arms and said nothing.

'Well?'

Mosi sighed. 'It's a bold plan. Much can go wrong. What if the . . . gift . . . can't be shared any further, or the results differ? What if it weakens you? And what of Antony?'

'What of him?'

'Will you share the power with him and the queen? Surely Cleopatra should be first in line to receive such power. It would make her a formidable force if she could bend the will of men the way you do when she visits Rome.'

Saar snorted. 'She has power enough in that regard.'

'Maybe, but physical strength would protect her. And her children. Octavian has the support of the Senate and I fear you're right, war is coming.'

Leaving the cluster of chairs, Saar walked to the window and looked out over Brucheum.

In the warm golden glow of afternoon sunlight, he saw the bustle of people in the street far below. In this, the Greek portion of the city, men and women wore expensive clothes, shoes and jewellery in bright colours. The road, patterned with small white and blue tiles, led to the pavilion where three dancers pranced on a high pedestal to the cheers of those watching. Small children ran through the crowds, and their laughter reached even this high window in the palace.

The soft pad of footsteps made him glance over his shoulder.

He saw Mosi approach and stepped sideways to make space.

'I love them too, Saar. This is my home. And you— before you, I had no hope or life beyond that in Gyasi's whorehouse. You saved me from that and I love you for it.'

Saar smiled.

'I would follow you anywhere. Into any danger.'

'I know.' He shuddered, aware in that moment that the link between him and his lover had been reopened. Through it he felt the warmth of pride, respect and deep-seated need. He chuckled. 'Do you have somewhere else to be?'

'No.'

'Good.' He turned then, and gripped Mosi's face between his hands. The other man was smaller, almost feminine, but the hands that closed over his were strong. They shared a chaste kiss.

Then Saar felt slim, delicate hands brush across his back and knew Kiya had joined them.

'I don't have to like it,' she whispered, 'but that doesn't mean I won't join you.' With that, her soft lips picked a path down the middle of his back, following his spine to the tops of his buttocks. Again she lingered over the curved birthmark on his left thigh. She kissed it.

He groaned and heard Mosi echo the sound.

'We'll discuss the rest of my plans later,' he whispered, leaning forward for another, far less innocent kiss.

Neither Kiya nor Mosi raised any objections.

Chapter Fourteen

Lenina stood outside her house, blinking at the warm glow in the windows through diagonal sheets of rain. She hugged herself and chewed her bottom lip. Though it bled, filling her mouth with sweetness, an hour of aimless wandering served to deaden the taste.

Standing over the body, Lenina had struggled with what to do next. The rational and law-abiding side of her demanded that she pull out her mobile and call the police.

The rest of her, coupled with the fight or flight reflex successfully keeping humans alive for millions of years, had other ideas. That part instructed her to hide the body. Anywhere. Quickly.

She wrestled with it at first. Guilt and fear crippled her thoughts. Then, on the far side of the park she saw three strangers hurrying through the rain beneath a trio of umbrellas.

Risk of discovery made the decision for her.

Lenina grabbed the woman by the legs and dragged her across the grass.

Her damp, cold hands struggled with the dead weight, eventually forcing her to heave the woman on to her shoulder.

That, by contrast, was easy. Lenina paused to marvel at her new strength.

She hid the body beyond a cluster of bushes in a corner of the park, pushing it into a deep hollow that had once formed a pond. Shielded by evergreen shrubs, she hoped it wouldn't be found until she could decide what to do.

The dog she threw in as an afterthought.

Now, far from the park and back on the familiar paving slabs of her own driveway, Lenina stared at her house and wondered if she could enter.

Was it even her house any more? Did vampires and murderers deserve to live in beautiful, semi-detached properties in a quiet corner of the East Midlands? Did they have fiancés? Could they get married?

She didn't think so, but neither did she think she could stay outside any longer.

Locking herself in the bathroom, she peeled off her wet clothes and left them on the floor, climbing into the bath to stand under the shower. In a curious mirroring of the night before, she let the hot water sluice blood and tears off her face and hands.

Steam filled the room, white and thick, hiding everything until Lenina felt lost and adrift.

The bandage on her neck flapped loose, useless against all the water.

She peeled it away, puzzling over how the events of the day had numbed even physical pain. But when her hands brushed the skin at the base of her throat she stopped and scrambled out of the bath.

With shaking hands, she cleared condensation off the mirror, a long smear across the glass through which she could see.

The bite marks were gone.

Her skin still dripping, Lenina perched on the edge of the bath and stared at the floor. Despite the water all over her body, the insides of her mouth felt as dry as sand.

It took several minutes, but eventually she convinced herself to have another look.

The result was unchanged.

The skin of her neck and shoulder were as smooth as they had been at the beginning of the week. No teeth marks, no bruising. On her face, the faint scratches from the park woman's clawing fingernails were gone too. The only sign of any mark at all, was a thin red scratch from the point of Jason's dagger.

In a distant way she recalled Saar, the Egyptian soldier from her dreams, telling his men that he could heal any injury. That he was strong and so too were they.

Lenina sighed. Bit her lip.

No more hiding. No more stalling. She knew what she had to do.

***

Wrapped once more in her big, fluffy dressing gown, Lenina took her laptop into the kitchen and put the kettle on.

Minutes later with a mug of tea at her side and a search engine opened, she typed *vampire* into the search bar.

The search turned up all the nonsense she expected. Costumes, fan clubs, films, books and songs. Fictional characters, poetry, accounts of 'real life' vampires and diseases which had once been mistaken for vampirism. Myths, legends and fables from America, Eastern Europe and Japan. And pictures. So many pictures.

Red lips, sharp teeth, bloodied throats and dark handsome men with pronounced widow's peaks and sultry eyes. Then came the more contemporary images: pale teenage boys with moody stares, floppy hair and glittery skin.

The tea grew cold beside her as the list of useless websites grew longer.

She jabbed her thumb into her mouth, gnawing the nail until it split and peeled away between her teeth. The very act reminded her of the dreams. The dreams in which her voice deepened, her body grew large and strong and her name was Saar of Egypt. It seemed ridiculous, but the whole situation resembled something from the script of a movie anyway. She tugged the laptop closer and typed: *Sar*.

The search engine suggested several alternative spellings before she could convince it that she meant what she typed.

The results list comprised a miserable selection of unrelated businesses, acronyms and partial surnames. Sighing, she clicked the first suggested spellings, *Zaar*.

The search engine immediately flipped to *tsar* and began listing biographies of Russian rulers from Yuri I and Ivan II to Vasily I. Lenina glared at the screen and tapped her finger to her mouth, trying to sound through the name in her head. The accents of her dreams resembled nothing she knew. Long, lazy sounds with harsh consonants and the occasional dropped syllable.

Instead, she turned her thoughts to the people. The soldiers used bronze weapons and wore leather or straw sandals. Men and women wore coloured paints around their eyes as well as simple linen skirts on their bottom halves.

'Shendyt,' she murmured.

Egyptian soldier Sar. Once more the search engine corrected her: *Saar*.

She skimmed the results list for several pages until one entry made her pause.

. . . Saar's love affair with . . . and of course Cleopatra, as Pharaoh of Egypt was known to . . .

Her fingers hovered over the track pad. More than once the man in her dream had mentioned Cleopatra. Swallowing the lump of unease in her throat, Lenina clicked the link.

The page opened with ominous music and a tacky animation of a vampire stereotype leaning over a comic depiction of the last Pharaoh of Egypt. Cleopatra's large eyes and thick black hair were unmistakable, synonymous with the film made famous by Elizabeth Taylor.

Heartened, Lenina began to read. Her enthusiasm faded minutes later when she realised that the site, amateur at best, a joke at worst, contained little fact and more than its share of speculation and make-believe. Some details tallied with what she knew of the Ptolemaic period, but the rest came straight from one lonely source text. A book written by a man who claimed to be one of the world's first vampires.

Lenina tangled her fingers in her hair and tapped her foot against the floor. The author, using the pen name Xerxes XIV, wrote of his ties to the Ptolemaic vampires in a book named *The Start of It All, The Birth of The First of Us*. From the blurb, the book appeared to be a long-winded biography of one Egyptian soldier who served under Cleopatra before Octavian's forces made Egypt part of the Roman republic. Though crazy and probably a waste of time, Lenina grudgingly acknowledged that this was her only clue. The website contained a digital version of the source text, compiled from its original Coptic and made available to download for a small fee. There seemed little choice in the matter. Lenina purchased the book and two minutes later, opened the file.

Saar, heroic and loved by all, knew that we, men and women blessed by Set, are the true rulers of this world. He created thousands of god-touched warriors to help him further Set's plan to make his followers the most powerful creatures on the planet.

'Seriously?' She rubbed her eyes and skipped forward a few pages.

But Saar could only work with the raw material he was given. He could not make worthy god-touched followers from humans plagued by weakness. So he left his Egyptian roots and journeyed south, seeking others to bless with his gift. His search took him across the world to many different peoples, from Mongolians to Japanese samurai, Aboriginal wild men to European dignitaries. Saar spent years searching for his ideal human.

Lenina yawned and skipped back through the text, waiting for something to catch her attention. When it did, she froze, gazing at a name she knew incredibly well. It was followed by another.

Mosi was a great favourite of Saar's despite his humble and vulgar beginnings. He wasn't a special man, nor a particularly intelligent one, but his grasp of the Five Powers matched Saar's like no other. For that reason he quickly became Saar's right-hand man, second only to the love of his life, Kiya.

Rain drummed at the windows, filling the silence with gentle white nose. The occasional rumble of thunder came with it and a flash of lightning briefly brightened the kitchen. Normal things. Natural things. Phenomena she couldn't possibly hear or see alongside names plucked straight from her dreams.

Mosi. The man Saar once loved. The man he battled on the blood-soaked sands outside Alexandria. The man who betrayed Saar in the last battle against Octavian's men.

Kiya. Dark-haired, long-limbed and beautiful, she had a sharp tongue and a temper to match. The same woman Saar wept over as her body crumbled into sand.

Lenina pressed her hands flat to the table, anchoring herself in the kitchen with the touch of something solid and real.

A deep breath in. Another one out. Part of her recoiled from the names written in the book. That same side of her longed to crawl into bed and hide beneath the duvet, shutting out all the terrible truths of the last twenty-four hours. The other part of her crowed with vindication and relief.

The visions weren't nightmares. Nor the frightening imaginings of a mind on the verge of breakdown. Mosi and Kiya were real. Saar was real. His life played before her eyes each time she slept, moving backwards from his last battles to show his gradual rise to power. Lenina knew then that Xerxes was wrong. Saar hadn't just loved Kiya, but Mosi too. The other man's betrayal hit him hard *because* of that fact. She kept reading.

Relations between Kiya and Mosi were strained at best, volatile at worst, but no others cared for Saar more than they. No others were afforded such preferential treatment.

These two were the first of Saar's original fourteen children; Hasina, Aswad, Ife, Faki, Jamila, Jafari, Kakra, Atsu, Moswen, Musa, Nubia and Adofo.

Seven men and seven women, chosen by Saar for their skills, intelligence or connections. They helped create the other god-touched warriors he then recruited to his personal army, Red Fang.

A shiver of cold coursed down Lenina's back. God-touched. Red Fang. Seeing the phrases strengthened her recollection. Hadn't Saar called his soldiers god-touched? Hadn't Kiya insisted Red Fang was a suitable name for the army they intended to build together?

Scraping her chair closer to the table, Lenina scrolled to the beginning of book to read it properly. She read about Saar's plans to secure leadership of Egypt with an army of men loyal to him. His failure caused by Mosi's betrayal. His search around the world for suitable substitutes which would enable him to rekindle his fight to rule in place of humans, whom he thought to be weak, soulless and foolish. The book culminated in a lavish account of the Battle of Waterloo, in which Saar, having sided with Napoleon, lost spectacularly to Duke Wellington's allied forces in 1815.

Though no trace of Saar's body was ever found, every God-Touched less than four years old perished that day. Many believe this was a direct result of Saar's death as he was the primary link to Set. Without him to bind us together, the weakest of our number couldn't hope to survive.

But we maintain hope.

Sacred texts held by Red Fang tell of secret ways to restore Saar to a living god-touched body. 'The Prophecy,' as it is widely known, speaks of a Vessel suited to this purpose.

The Vessel will be known by a symbol unique to Saar, but the exact details are the subject of much speculation. The popular belief is that the Vessel will bear a mark much like the one representing Red Fang, a curved slash resembling a long tooth, often called the Neeva. However the Prophecy and the specific details it contains remain the business of Majestics and not any God-Touched younger than First Generation.

In their search for the Vessel, Majestics gave all Elders a specific role: seeker, watcher or soldier. Seekers search for the Vessel, watchers ingratiate themselves into human society, while soldiers are our first line of defence against all those who seek to do us harm.

Lenina wiped her grainy eyes and licked her dry lips. She pushed back from the laptop, shaking her head.

The room seemed to spin, fragmented images whirling through her mind in a colourful kaleidoscope of memories. In the silence of her large modern kitchen, it all seemed so foreign and out of place. Yet parts of it were familiar and not only from her dreams. Something about the tale Xerxes told and the emotions he toyed with captured her heartstrings and plucked them like a harp's. Despite that, Xerxes had written only a fraction of the real story. She knew that with a certainty that frightened her. His simplified and indulgent account skimmed the surface of the man called Saar, no doubt a result of the rose-coloured glasses he wore when looking at his hero.

The front door opened with a soft click. Soft thuds and a strong smell of wet leather told Lenina who it was long before Nick put his head around the door frame.

'Hey.' He dropped his motorcycle helmet on the table and unzipped the top half of his oversuit. 'You didn't call. How was the doctor?'

She had to think. That morning and the simple worry of calling the doctor seemed a million years ago. She gazed at her fingers. 'No appointments until Monday.'

Peeling off the top half of the suit, Nick fanned his t-shirt against his chest. 'I suppose Ray had a fit about that.'

Lenina turned away. She couldn't bear to look at Nick's cheery face, such a mismatch with the rest of her day.

'What's wrong, babe?'

Where could she possibly start?

'Is it the goodie bags again? I told you, just put in cufflinks and earrings or whatever it was you wanted.'

'It's not that.'

'Then what? The dress?'

Lenina drummed her fingertips against the table. Anger roughened her voice. 'Not everything is about this stupid wedding.'

'Wow, okay. But it's all you've talked about for months. Nothing else exists right now except flowers, horse-drawn carriages and white doves.'

She wondered if Saar ever worried about such mundane things as weddings. Tears gathered in her eyes and ran free, splashing against the laptop. 'I've done such horrible things. I'm a monster.'

Nick actually smiled. 'Every woman gets a bit stressed when planning something like this. You're no monster.'

'No, you don't understand—'

He grabbed her hand and held it. His fingers brushed hers and she realised he was stroking her engagement ring. 'I haven't made any vows yet,' he whispered, 'but I'm with you for better or worse. Nothing you can do or say will take away what we have. Tell me what's got you hissing like a *koperkapel*.'

She arched an eyebrow at him.

'A snake from back home.'

Lenina looked away from her fingers. She met Nick's eyes and saw the sincerity there, the love. The thin film of sweat on his cheeks and forehead made his skin shine while the heat gave him a warm glow.

He squeezed her hand. 'Tell me.'

'I'm a vampire.'

He blinked at her.

'The man in the park. When he bit me he turned me into a vampire. I think. Or perhaps it's when I drank his blood. I don't know. But I *do* know that I'm a vampire now. Or God-Touched . . . they never say vampire. Is that the wrong word? I don't know.' By the time she finished speaking, Lenina had to gasp to breathe.

Nick squeezed her hands. 'Come on, babe. This is a joke, né? You don't even believe in that stuff.'

'I didn't, but then I found this website and it had all this information that matched my dreams and—'

'Dreams?'

She took a deep breath. No matter how she tried to explain it, Lenina knew it wouldn't make sense.

'It doesn't matter. None of it's important except the first bit. I'm a vampire.'

Nick pulled back and crossed his arms. 'Right. So you drink blood now, né?'

Lenina saw the woman on the park again. The glassy eyes. Bloodied throat. With the image came a name, floating up like an air bubble from the oceanic depths of her mind. *Pauline Lock*. Though she had no idea how, Lenina knew the name belonged to the dead woman.

She bit her lip. 'Yes. I've already done it.'

'You drank blood?'

A nod. 'Today. In the park. I killed a woman. I kicked her dog.'

Nick stood, hunching his shoulders against his ears. His voice trembled, a soft stream of Afrikaans expletives before dipping back into English. 'That's a really shitty joke, Lenina.' He turned on his heel. 'I'm going upstairs.'

Chapter Fifteen

Nick's use of her full name felt like a punch to the face.

Further tears blurred Lenina's vision as he walked away, damp boots squeaking on the tiled floor. She might have laughed if not for the ache in her heart. Instead she gasped and clutched her chest, remembering the slow crawl of fear as Mosi turned his back on her, leaving her alone to hear his terrible final words play over and over in her head.

No— not Mosi.

Lenina clutched the table, sinking her fingernails into the wood until small splinters came away in her hands. *Nick* left her. Not Mosi.

But it felt the same, as if her heart was filled with hot lead, firing agonising darts of heat through her limbs until every moment was pain. Like the loss of an integral part of herself. Knowing that Saar and Mosi had never reconciled their differences only made it worse. How could two people so much in love hurt each other that badly?

She stood, ready to throw herself at Nick's feet and beg forgiveness. She would lie if forced to, deny the truth of her discoveries and play the happy bride once again. If only he would hold her. Look at her with love and desire the way he once did.

As she planned what to say, she gazed at the window, watching rivulets of rain form wriggling tracks down the glass. Sighing, she likened the sight to a similar one in the window of a homoeopath's office in Lusaka. The woman inside had gestured her in, pointing to large trays of minerals including quartz, haematite, halite and bloodstone, while praising their healing properties. Gerald hadn't known what to do and opted to linger outside, watching the locals rush through the drizzle.

The smile fell from Lenina's face as the memory faded away. She had no idea who Gerald was.

Lenina had never set foot outside Europe, let alone travelled as far afield as Zambia, of which Lusaka was the capital. She shivered as a sensation like the slide of cold jelly slithered down her back. Shaking hands clutched the tabletop once more. Gerald *Lock* . . . Pauline Lock's husband. Lenina saw him in her mind's eye, a tall, barrel-like man with a bristling black beard and arms like a gorilla. She heard the deep, earthy rumble of his voice, softened by emotion as he asked her to marry him.

'No,' she whispered. 'Not me.'

Jerking her head to the side, Lenina clawed free of the foreign memory. But more followed. Gerald waving from far out to sea, bobbing on the waves with a blue and white surfboard. Stroking her round stomach, kissing the stretch marks around her belly button. Then Lenina saw a screaming, red-faced child. Felt the delicate weight of those tiny limbs as the doctors laid it against her sweaty chest. A similar scene, though this time, as the doctor wrapped the baby and handed it over, a young boy with hair the colour of field mice stood on tiptoe beside the bed.

'My little sister,' he said.

Shrieking, Lenina ground her fists against her eyes, knocking her head against the table over and over. It dazed her, but didn't stop the images; a constant, full-colour film reel of Pauline Lock's most vivid memories.

At last she saw her own face, barely recognisable with features twisted by anger. She saw the long fangs in her mouth, glinting in the watery moonlight beneath the empty black pits of her eyes. The last thing she recognised was the night sky and the pinprick silver of stars, lined on one side by damp grass.

When she returned to her own mind, Lenina lay on the floor, knees pulled up to her chest. Her cheeks were damp. She shoved her fingers into her mouth and pressed down to muffle the rising scream.

It didn't work.

Shrill shrieks fled her lips, the agonised call of a beast trapped and dying, alone and afraid. Her limbs ached. Weariness pinned her to the floor. Lenina curled into a tighter ball when she heard Nick dash back into the kitchen. She imagined Pauline Lock's body still lying in the park, close to the broken remains of her feisty dog. For the first time, the full weight of the truth sank in. She shuddered.

How many times would she have to repeat that experience? How often? Would she take on *every* set of memories?

Saar certainly seemed to have done so.

Nick grabbed her and heaved her upright, pressing her body against his. She clung to him, gasping for breath, sucking in the familiar scent of leather, sweat and newsprint. The smells of home.

'What's wrong?' he demanded as he stroked her hair.

'You left me. You walked away.'

'Only to go upstairs. I'm sorry. I needed to think.'

'You didn't even look back.' Lenina shook her head. A crawling ache began to consume her skull, from the back of her neck to her forehead. A full, bursting sensation, as though her head held too many thoughts. She bit her lip hard enough to make it bleed. It didn't help.

'You abandoned me when I needed you, just like before. You don't love me.'

'I think you're overreacting a little bit, babe.'

'No!' She jerked free of his arms.

A low buzzing filled her ears. Soft at first, then louder, as though thousands of tiny bees had nested within her skull.

Again she shook her head but that only made it worse.

Escaping into the living room failed to improve things. Though she saw the familiar room and the furniture it contained, over it Lenina saw smooth mud-brick walls, wooden chairs and tables inlaid with gilt beneath diaphanous hangings of linen dangling from high vaulted ceilings.

She gnawed her thumbnail. 'You left me because you were too stubborn to see the truth. Kiya was right, you were too soft hearted to see what needed to be done and that I had to be the one to do it.' Now she was talking, the words seemed to have no end and she let them flow, flinging them like spears, designed to hurt and maim.

Nick followed with his hands held out before him, speaking softly as he might to a skittish horse. 'Who's Kiya? Speak sense, babe. You're scaring me.' He held out his hands but Lenina twisted away.

'You knew what would happen but you left anyway. Then you led those Roman heathens into our city and let them raze it to the ground. They killed our queen.'

'What are you talking about? Calm down. Come sit down, I'll get you some tea, né? We can talk about this properly.'

'No, you left!' Lenina heard the words, but they didn't feel like her own any more. They came from her mouth but the agony behind them took its roots elsewhere. Somewhere deep in the past.

Nick wiped his face with both hands. 'Damn it, I knew we should have gone to the hospital. You need counselling. This is some kind of psychotic break.'

'I'm not crazy,' she shrieked, shaking a fist in Nick's direction.

A loud crack stopped them both.

Slowly, fearing what she might see, Lenina turned towards the source of the sound.

Above the fireplace, a large mirror in a heavy oak frame boasted huge, jagged cracks. Her startled reflection peered back at her, reflected dozens of times in the trembling fragments.

'What happened?' Nick's voice filled the hush.

'I don't know. I didn't touch it. I didn't mean to.'

'No, your neck. The bite marks are gone.'

Lenina touched the smooth skin at the side of her throat. 'Vampires heal. He calls himself God-Touched, but it's the same thing.'

Maybe the soft whisper of her voice made all the difference. Perhaps the look in her eyes. Maybe Nick saw the healed flesh about her throat and realised that rational explanations were thin on the ground. Whatever it was, when he next looked up, Lenina saw the bright gleam of fear shining in his eyes.

'You're not kidding are you?'

She shook her head.

Nick's back hit the bookcase. His look of surprise suggested he hadn't meant to move. 'And you killed a woman?'

'On the way home.'

He laughed, but not like he was happy. 'On the way home? Like picking up a pint of milk?'

'I don't know how else to say it. I didn't ask for this. I didn't want it. I don't know how it works. Jason just attacked me.'

Nick twitched, his fingers flexing on the spines of books he couldn't see.

'The man on the park. The homeless man— he isn't homeless. His name is Jason. I saw his thoughts— I could read them like those books. I just knew. He wants to kill me.'

'Babe, slow down—'

'You need to help me.' She moved towards him.

Before she could advance more than a step he gasped and shimmied away, rocking the bookcase with his frantic motions. 'Stop. Don't come any closer.'

The words were a knife in her heart.

'Nick?'

'Stay where you are.' He moved again, sideways now, towards the fireplace and the broken mirror. His gaze never left her face.

Tears stung Lenina's eyes. This latest betrayal tore her soul free and slapped it in a blender. The look in his eyes ground her up like mince. 'Don't do this. I need you.'

'You murdered someone!'

'I didn't mean to. I wasn't thinking straight. It wasn't me.'

'I need to get out of here.'

Nick stepped forward, but in that moment Lenina's body shook with a jolt of hungry, angry energy. Bright and vibrant colours crawled across her vision, bringing out exquisite detail in everything from the carpet to the shimmering highlights in Nick's hair. The grain on the wood in the bookcase. The sharp edges in the mirror. She could hear the rustle of his oversuit against the jeans he wore beneath and the hiss of his breath as it fled his lips. His heartbeat, thud-thudding within his chest.

With a bound like a cat she dived across the small space between them and shoved both hands into his chest. He reeled back, his spine cracking against the fireplace, head crashing into the mirror. Deadly shards of broken glass showered down around him, their tinkling loud in the sudden still.

Rebounding from the impact, Nick fell to his knees, gasping as his hands struck the carpet and met the bite of broken glass. The sweet scent of his blood spiked the air along with something else. Spicy. Meaty. Like the exotic offerings of a distant land.

Lenina opened her mouth. Her fangs were there again, sliding forward from the recesses in her gums. She flicked her tongue over them, enjoying the smooth hardness and the wicked tips.

Bleeding, panting, Nick struggled to his feet. When his gaze met hers face all colour drained from his face and neck.

'You smell like food,' she told him.

Thrusting her head forward, Lenina buried her nose in the fabric of his shirt and inhaled. Remnants of leather. Sweat. Cotton in need of a wash. With a grunt of impatience, she grabbed the fabric and ripped it, exposing his bare chest and the soft curls of pale hair between his pectorals. Another sniff. There it was . . .

'You smell like fear.'

Lenina linked emotions to the strange new smells and understood them with a deep part of her mind. The part related to cavemen and survival in the barren wilds surrounded by vicious beasts.

That part of her mind took the smell and translated it into a message that made her mouth water.

Nick tensed. The simple reflex gave away his intent as well as if he had shouted it. As he turned to flee, Lenina grabbed him by the shoulders and spun him around. A sweep of her foot hooked his legs from beneath him. He went over with a cry; she followed him down and sat on his hips.

He slapped at her stomach and chest. 'Let go!'

It took no effort at all to grasp his wrists and pin them down near his ears. She pushed upwards, stretching his struggling body against the floor. Soon she lay flush against him and felt the pound of his heart against her chest. He strained, muscles bunching in his arms and shoulders. When nothing happened, his struggles intensified.

Each frantic, pointless effort made Lenina's mouth water. Her skin tingled. Every motion of his body against hers seemed charged with energy and her hyper-sensitive skin turned it into something more.

She shivered and leaned closer to enjoy more of the delicious smell.

Beneath her, Nick began to shake. His chest heaved up and down. Sweat beaded on his upper lip. 'Let go. Please— my wrists.'

She heard another voice make a similar plea. This one female. Shrill. Frantic. She spoke with the ugly, fast-paced tongue used by the rich Greeks, nothing like the soft, lilting sounds of old Egypt.

As Saar's thoughts once more intruded on her own, Lenina shook her head. But she couldn't clear them. She felt him swelling within her, pushing on her senses, shoving aside everything she knew and understood to be part of herself.

Bones cracked in Nick's wrists. She felt joints pop out of place and closed her eyes as his agonised screams filled the room. The sound pierced her brain like a knife. Make it stop.

Lenina gripped Nick's face in both hands and wrenched his head to one side to expose his throat. There, beating the flesh like a moth against a light bulb, his pulse. Beautiful. Teasing. Inviting.

Nick screamed again.

She barely heard it.

Lowering her head, Lenina put her fangs to the side of his throat and used the sharp points to slice his flesh.

The flow of blood was immediate, a hot gush against the back of her throat. She swallowed and opened her mouth wide, desperate to catch every drop.

Shrieking, Nick drummed his heels against the floor. He scrabbled at her neck. Fighting with both hands. His fingernails clawed her skin as he fought to prise open some space between her mouth and his flesh.

Lenina felt nothing but pleasure. Tasted nothing but sweetness. She moaned.

Fire raced in a liquid line down her throat, scorching a course to her stomach where it settled, grew, then spiralled into thin threads of pleasure that fed her entire body.

The smell of fear spiked again and took on a fresh edge that brought to mind the word *terror* before all rational thought died and vanished.

Chapter Sixteen

Lenina returned to her waking mind lying flat on her back. A sticky residue, thick and sweet lingered around her mouth and jaw. Groaning, she sat up. Nick lay beside her. His glassy eyes pointed at the ceiling, features locked in an expression of terror and pain. Blood choked the wounds on his throat.

When she stood, the world swayed and she found a liquid quality to her legs that she usually associated with post-coital weakness. Gazing at Nick, she felt the first tremors of fear ripple through her body. Her bottom lip wobbled. She crammed her hands against her mouth. Fangs sliced the backs of her hands and left tiny ribbons of blood.

'Nick?'

He didn't move.

'Nick?' She bent and pressed her hand to his chest.

No rise, no fall. No soft gust of warm breath from his parted lips. Of course not. His fixed expression and pale flesh told a comprehensive story.

He was dead.

She said the words aloud, as if to test how they felt. 'He's dead.' It tasted bitter on her tongue.

Movement outside the window caught her eye. She ducked down, a flash of speed, and crouched behind the sofa. A slither of a face peered through the gap in the curtains then shrank out of sight. Lenina crouched lower, pulling her limbs close together to make her body as small as possible. Every sound, sight and smell took on new strength, as if this latest infusion of blood had fired up her senses tenfold.

She heard the rustle of cloth outside the front door, then the familiar trill of the doorbell slicing the room's silence. Soft knocking followed.

'Hallo? I heard shouting. Is everyone okay?'

Lenina recognised the voice of her elderly neighbour, Mrs Ferdinand, and clamped down on a groan. Instead, she growled, hunkered down and waited.

'Lenina? Nick? Is it your television again? Hello?'

Her fingertips began to prickle. She imagined grabbing the old woman, tearing at the grey, threadbare dressing gown she wore to expose her wrinkled throat. She licked her lips.

'Is someone on the floor? Should I call the police?'

It would only take a moment . . . she was small. Frail. Compared to Nick, Mrs Ferdinand would be easy to subdue.

Just as Lenina made up her mind, she heard the retreating shuffle of slippered feet on the drive. She exhaled.

Dragging herself back towards Nick, Lenina gazed at his splayed feet and bloodied throat.

'Dead.' Though less bitter this time, hearing the word took her breath away. Like a punch to the gut.

Before she could dwell too much, colourful images filled her head, joined by smells, sounds and exquisite tastes. Nick's life spilled through her mind, from his earliest memories in South Africa, to his last moments on the living room floor. She saw a tall, slim man with a curly moustache and military short hair. Without ever meeting him, she knew this was Nick's father. In her mind's eye, he morphed from smiling, fit and healthy, to bent, weak and grim as leukaemia stole his life. Nick watched the transformation with the confused innocence of a child and she joined him, feeling the ache in his heart on the day of the funeral.

Nick's journey through school had alternated between shyly asking girls on dates and skulking in corners at parties. By the time he'd reached England and college, his thin, wiry frame had given way to broad shoulders and growing muscle as he took up running and basketball.

Then Lenina saw herself. Visiting Nick's memory of their first meeting brought tears to her eyes. For the first time she understood his fear, followed quickly by elation as she responded to his joke in the registration queue on the first day of university. She saw his nerves, preparing for their date and the thread of terror through the whole meal they shared. His stomach turned flip-flops as he nibbled pepperoni pizza and the smell of hot cheese and grease repeatedly sent him to the bathroom. The game of mini-golf which followed saw him little better; hay fever gave him streaming eyes and a runny nose for all eighteen holes.

The fear gradually changed, first into respect, then love. She watched it happen over the years, culminating in his proposal, down on one knee in the middle of the High Street singing a line from a Whitney Houston track.

Lenina fell to her knees. She didn't want to see the rest. Pouring over wedding brochures. Picking venues. Gleefully arguing over honeymoon destinations.

Then fear came back as he ran across the grass in Grick Park. Anger as he punched the scruffy ginger-haired man in his filthy grey hat. Frustration as she refused the hospital in favour of the GP.

She saw him sitting at a desk, teeming with folders and loose sheets of paper. He picked up the phone beside his computer and dialled for the local doctor, seeking advice on counselling and stress-related mental illnesses. Then he came home, nerves bringing a cool sweat to his forehead as he pulled off his motorcycle helmet.

With a great heave, Lenina wrenched free of the memories. She didn't want to see her angry face or feel Nick's pain as she drained his life away. The images kept battering her mind, knocking like a ram at the door of her senses. She leaned against them and scrunched her eyes shut, digging her fingernails into her forearms.

It worked. Barely.

Back in the room and in her own head again, the last traces of Nick's memories faded from her eyes: her own face, a snarling rictus of fury, covered in gleaming, red blood.

In that moment Lenina knew her life was over.

The one man who loved her, almost from the moment he'd first seen her, lay dead on the floor. His blood filled her stomach, spreading warmth through her limbs while his body grew cold.

'I killed him.'

She pressed her hands to her mouth. The sob escaped anyway, a single burst of sound that filled the room and seemed to bounce back at her.

Footsteps outside the door stole her attention. Her head snapped up, gazing through the gap in the curtains. Had Mrs Ferdinand really called the police? Were they here?

Lenina rushed to the glass and squinted out. The moon hung low on the horizon, beginning its ascent through the blue-black sky behind the houses and trees. Nick's bike stood on the drive beside her car and a vaguely man-shaped mass lurked near one of the flower pots.

The moment she noticed it, the back of her brain fired to life. A powerful rush of thoughts flowed through her mind and spilled over like a river in spate. Not like the memories of Nick or Pauline Lock, but more personal. Controlled. Selective. Immediate.

She knew without looking that Jason stood on the driveway. He stared at the house with poorly suppressed excitement, laced by a single thread of nerves. Lenina ran for the door, fingers fumbling with the chain and deadbolt. Before she could use either, the door burst off its hinges and slammed into her face.

She fell. A rush of cold air and rain whistled through to meet her. By the time she shoved aside the heavy hunk of wood and scrambled to her feet, Jason stood before her, damp hat hanging sideways off his tangled hair. The cool grey of his eyes assessed her, gaze sliding up, then down again with slow consideration.

'I'm too late.' He inhaled, deep and long. 'You gave your first tribute.' His voice trembled.

'How did you find me?'

Jason tapped the side of his head. 'I'll always know where you are, love. I just gotta concentrate.'

'You can't be here.' She backed up. 'Leave me alone.'

He gave a wry smile and stepped through the doorway. 'Can't, love. I gotta do this.'

Lenina closed her eyes, as his thoughts intruded on hers. Worries of failure and torture spun through her mind. Long wooden stakes. Starvation. Burning.

The different methods of ritualistic torture made her pity him until she remembered that his success depended on her death.

She put her hands to her head, rifling through the tangle of panic until she found a gap in the back of her mind. It hung open, and through it marched Jason's fear, like the charge of eager football fans breaching the pitch.

For the first time, Lenina knew what to do: she stuffed up the gap with a mental wrench of will, like slamming a door in Jason's face. It blocked his mind from hers and immediately shut off the flow. Panic faded instantly. Though sweat continued to bead on her forehead and slide down the side of her face, this level of fear seemed manageable without the added weight of his on top.

The vampire flinched. 'You can't do that.'

She straightened her shoulders. 'Get out of my house.'

He hesitated.

'Don't you need an invitation or something? You can't come in here.'

'Invitation? Who told you something stupid like that?'

'Get out!'

Without the benefit of an open link between them Lenina could no longer tell what he planned to do. But when she saw him shift his weight and reach into the grubby folds of his jacket his objective became plain. He pulled out a long dagger with a gold handle and filthy blade the length of his forearm. The sight of it made Lenina's lips curl back from her teeth. She glared at the weapon and felt a surge of hate so strong that her knees buckled. Before she could consider what it meant, Jason lunged.

Lenina threw her weight sideways and slammed into the wall beneath the coat hooks. Jason's clumsy charge shot past her, taking him to the foot of the stairs where he spun around and repeated the motion.

His arm arched high, then down; a blinding flash of motion with the dagger at its tip.

Lenina saw the descent of the blade in slow motion, the rust-encrusted point aimed for her chest. It seemed she had plenty of time to twist aside and save herself from certain death, but she knew no human would stand a chance against such speed. She ducked down the wall, side-stepping across the narrow hallway to straighten on the other side. Her own speed blurred the walls and dangling coats into a streak of browns and blacks. Jason's arm swiped over her head.

Fast. Inhumanly fast.

He was faster.

Before she reached the opposite wall, Jason adjusted his aim, cutting back with his wrist cocked to deliver a devastating backslash.

The tip of the dagger caught Lenina's left cheek, a hair's breadth from her eye. A last-second jerk of the head saved her vision, but the sharp weapon sheared through flesh and scraped bone. Blood gushed down her face, staining the air with its scent and colour.

The world returned to normal speed. Lenina clutched her cheek.

The wound burned, as if the blade had delivered a deadly dose of poison.

Jason whirled to face her, once again blocking the way out with his grubby, foul-smelling bulk. 'I'd ask how you did that but it doesn't matter. You need to die.'

'Wait!' She raised her hands palm up. 'You don't have to kill me. You don't have to do anything.'

His lower lip trembled. 'You're a mistake. I gotta fix it.'

Lenina struggled to respond in a way that would secure her life.

'Everyone makes mistakes. Even vampires.'

He moaned softly, pressing his fists to the sides of his head. 'She'll kill me.'

'She won't. Whoever it is, she doesn't have to know. It's just you and me.' The whole time she spoke Lenina kept the dagger in her peripheral vision. The point turned towards the ground. She kept talking. 'This is our secret. Just walk out that door. No one else needs to know.'

'You don't know what she's capable of. She'll kill me but it'll take weeks to die. Months. She learned torture with Saar in—' Jason stopped talking, glancing over his shoulder with a wild look in his eyes. The source of his distraction remained a mystery, but when he returned his gaze to hers, Lenina knew the damage was done.

She ran into the living room, aiming for the kitchen. On the way she saw Nick, still lying on the carpet, his wound darkening in the oxygen-rich air.

Jason followed. His heavy footfalls thudded across the carpet. The hot gust of breath hit her neck before she got near the door. Spinning round, Lenina meet his charge with an upthrust hand, her fingers pressed together to make a fleshy blade. His momentum drove the side of her hand into his throat, a crushing force against his windpipe.

He dropped the dagger. Doubled over. Clutched his neck with both hands.

Without thinking, Lenina followed the jab with a powerful thrust of her knee into Jason's stomach. She heard air rush out of him and swung her fist around to club the back of his head.

Jason fell on to his face, his fingers twitching. 'How?' he wheezed.

Lenina had no answer but she knew that the fight had escalated well beyond her own sheltered, middle-class skill set.

Dabbing her fingers to the left side of her face, she traced the line of the wound. The burning sensation faded, but in its place came an intense bristling, like a tide of itching powder from her face down through the rest of her skin. The shrill wail of approaching police sirens soon broke the still of the room and she knew then what had coaxed Jason to move.

He stood, retrieved the dagger and tucked it back into his coat. She watched him, hands loose by her sides, ready to match any move he made.

The pink tip of his tongue flicked out to catch a spot of blood on the side of his mouth. 'I'll be back,' he whispered. 'I can't let you live.' Without waiting for an answer, he ran past her, a blur of speed that took him back through the hallway and out the pulverised front door.

Seconds later the rumble of several car engines arrived on the drive.

Loud shouts broke out followed by a crunching sound. A man screamed. Something heavy hit the floor. Then a set of pounding footsteps took off into the night.

Lenina reached the door in time to see a uniformed police officer on the floor clutching his bleeding nose. Jason, a small smudge in the distance, crossed the road, rounded the corner and vanished from sight.

A second officer rounded the stationary police car and crouched beside his companion. After satisfying himself about his condition, he looked towards her. 'Are you okay, Miss?'

She knew what she had to do. Sinking to the floor, Lenina put her face in her hands and conjured a fit of hysterical sobs. 'He attacked me,' she cried. 'He killed Nick.'

Chapter Seventeen

8 May 36 BC

Despite the hood shielding his face, Saar stole glances left and right before entering the building. Inside, he saw a woman, round through the stomach, with blue and green smudges around her eyes and a long string of green beads around her neck. She hauled her heavy body off a pile of silks and cushions and bowed to him.

'Good evening, how may we entertain you today?'

Saar lowered the hood. 'Good evening, Gyasi.'

'Back so soon?' She smiled. Rather than enhancing her beauty, the gesture nulled it, highlighting the wrinkles around her eyes and the teeth missing from her upper jaw.

'What happened?'

She sighed. 'One of the men became violent.'

He arched an eyebrow.

'We dealt with him.' The stubborn set of her jaw dared him to question how.

Saar advanced, grasped her chin and angled her face to the light. A bruise hid beneath the blue and green paint.

'He hurt you.'

'We hurt him more.'

A stab of concern tightened his stomach. 'How fares the child?'

Gyasi cradled her stomach. 'I have some pains, but no more than usual.'

'Let me bring you to the palace,' he began.

'The queen would never allow it.'

'But I can—'

'No. You can't save everyone.' She tossed her hair and fisted her hips. 'Now . . . are you joining us today?' The arch of her eyebrow let Saar know what she really meant.

In answer he pulled off his cloak and slung it over one arm.

Gyasi grinned. 'Good. I have a surprise for you.' Passing through an arch on the right, she led him through the building.

As he walked, Saar glanced into various rooms. On high tables and pedestals, beautiful girls pranced and swirled their trailing gowns. Acrobats, often seen outside at festival time, played with leather balls, long ropes and chimes. In other rooms, men and women beat drums and plucked sweet-sounding strings.

Many faces he didn't recognise, but those he did belonged to high-ranking officials in law enforcement, finance and construction. Most ducked away or tried to hide their faces, but Saar felt no scorn. He knew what it was to need more and require less than savoury means to get it.

Since returning from the Pharos, his appetite for many things, including flesh, had blossomed to the point that Kiya complained of fatigue and soreness. He needed more. Of everything.

Gyasi chose a room at the rear of the building where few of her customers ventured. It was plain but for a low bed and a window in the far wall.

'Wait here.' She darted out once more.

Saar sat on the bed, stripping away his dagger and sword. He heard Gyasi return long before he saw her.

The white hangings in the doorway twitched, then pulled aside, revealing his host who wore a smug smile. 'This is Kontar,' she murmured.

Saar's breath caught in his throat.

Looking up through thick black lashes, Kontar flashed a bright smile. 'The great Captain Saar. At last.'

Gyasi continued. 'When I mentioned your last visit, Kontar insisted on joining you, should you return. I hope that suits you?'

Struck dumb Saar simply nodded.

'Good. Then I'll leave you.'

The room seemed even smaller with Gyasi gone.

Kontar was tall and slim. Long black hair, held back with a plain strip of leather, fanned down his back until it brushed the top of his narrow waist.

'I've never seen a man with hair so long,' whispered Saar. He stood. 'May I touch it?'

Kontar stepped so close that a deep breath would cause their chests to touch. He flicked his head and a thick section of that beautiful hair swung forward and brushed Saar's arm. He closed his eyes and let his skin translate the silken whisper of those strands into a teasing caress. The hair swept over his other arm. His face. His neck. The backs of his legs.

When Saar reopened his eyes, Kontar crouched in front of him, using his hair to stroke his calves and shins.

He licked his lips. 'I've never seen you here before.'

'Gyasi allows her customers to see only those they may enjoy spending time with. When she understood you might appreciate my company, she took the risk.'

'A fine risk.' Gripping Kontar's shoulders, Saar pulled him up to face height. No kiss – that was a pleasure for later – but he did rub his face along the side of Kontar's neck to bury his nose in the hair at the back. The smell brought to mind fruit and hot spices.

'You asked to serve me today. Why?'

For the first time, the younger man looked unsure. He stepped away and leaned against the wall. His fingers fiddled with the knot of rope holding his robe closed. 'I want to be a soldier.'

Saar became very still. His mouth dropped open. 'Then you must enlist.'

Kontar glared at the floor. 'I've tried. Every year since coming of age. But I'm too weak to join. You told me so, yourself.'

'Forgive me, I've no memory of you.'

'No forgiveness needed; I've grown since then. I ask only that you reconsider.'

'Why?'

When Kontar met his gaze, Saar recognised the fire in his eyes. He saw it reflected back at him from the surface of the water set by to wash his face each morning.

'Octavian's influence grows every day and soon he'll turn his attentions here. If Antony does marry our queen, the insult can't go unanswered.'

Saar lifted his eyebrows. 'You're well informed.'

'I see many soldiers.' Kontar flicked his hair over one shoulder.

'Really? When? How many?'

Kontar studied his face. 'The knowledge distresses you. Is it that your soldiers come here, or that they come to see me?'

'Neither.' Even to his own ears, Saar knew he'd answered hastily.

A smirk from Kontar. 'Your body betrays you. I see your discomfort.'

He snatched his weapons from beneath the bed. 'I must leave.'

'No— forgive me, Captain. I meant no offence. Don't forget why you came. You've yet to touch me.'

'The fact that I want you so much makes me uneasy. No common man knows the political woes of this country as you just described them and certainly no male whore.'

A frown furrowed Kontar's brow. 'I know only what your men let slide from their slack, drunken mouths.'

Saar strode towards the door.

Kontar leapt ahead, blocking the way with his arms spread. 'Wait! Don't leave me, Captain. My family is dead and I grow too old to continue working here. Make me a soldier.'

'Step aside.'

'Not before you reconsider.'

'Move.'

'Please Saar!' He lunged forward.

Maybe Kontar meant to touch him. Or embrace him. He never knew. Saar reacted as years of training instructed he should, but with a speed he barely recognised. The sword in his hand slashed up, then down, bisecting angles across Kontar's slender body. The other man gasped. Clutched his chest. Blood blossomed through the linen robe.

Before the sound fully registered, Saar struck again, two more slices with his stolen blade, fine lines across his stomach and ribs. Kontar hit the floor. The heavy thud brought Saar back to himself and his mind caught up with the actions of his body. Writhing, moaning, Kontar clutched his wounds.

Kazemde's promises of strength and speed returned to Saar in the same moment he smelled the blood. It wormed into his nostrils and bored into his senses, making his mouth water. His stomach writhed at the glorious, wet sight and an urge to taste the crimson fluid crawled into his mind.

He dropped the sword. And the dagger.

Saar threw himself down, slicing his palms and knees on the fallen weapons in his haste to reach the dying man. As his own blood mingled with Kontar's he pulled the younger man into his lap. Sacrifice . . . tribute . . . is this what it meant?

'Forgive me! This power— it's too new. I can't control it.' He longed to call for aid, but how would he explain?

Kontar reached out, but his fingers skidded on slicks of blood. 'You move so fast. The favour of the gods lives in you. I knew you were great, that's why I wanted to join you.' His eyes fluttered closed.

Saar shook him, biting his lip to hold back cries of desperation. 'Look at me.'

'I'm cold. I can't— I'll never be a soldier now.'

Saar ran his bloodied fingers over Kontar's mouth. No, Kontar would never be a soldier and Saar would never kiss those lips.

Kontar sighed, his body limp and lifeless. His eyes rolled back in his head.

Saar gnawed his thumbnail. A heavy weight filled his stomach. This was no battle, no righteous death.

'Re, forgive me,' he whispered.

Kontar's eyes snapped open, showing a white, blank glow. He gasped and clutched at the air. His body shot from still and silent, to violent thrashing in the space of a heartbeat. He rolled free of Saar's grasp and on to the floor. Bubbles of white foam poured from his mouth, tinged pink by the blood on his lips. He screamed and scratched his face until deep, bloodied furrows joined his other wounds.

Saar cursed. Leapt to his feet. Backing up, he pressed against the wall beneath the window. One hand clutched his dagger. He couldn't remember picking it up. The metal burned his palm. Lines of blood slid down the blade.

Kontar's heels beat a rapid tattoo on the floor. He thrashed like a fish scooped from the Nile, first shrieking, now moaning, all the time clutching his face. Black ooze gushed his ears and nose.

Saar gagged. He remembered that smell. His body tingled, as though plunged in cold water.

Dropping the dagger, Saar crouched beside the thrashing form and ripped away the ruined linen robe. Four wounds; deep, red and dripping. The clean edges gaped like mouths, obscene smiles on Kontar's chest and stomach. Smiles that closed as he watched. In the space of seconds Saar witnessed several weeks' worth of healing. He gaped, tracing the vanishing wounds with trembling fingers.

Kontar sat up. Shoving Saar's fingers aside he felt his own chest. 'You cut me— what happened?' As he spoke the white glow faded from his eyes until his usual brown colour took over once more. Before Saar could answer or consider what it meant, the younger man shrieked and covered his ears. 'Those sounds,' he sobbed. 'The light burns. Why does the air smell of death?'

It took both of Saar's hands and all of his considerable strength to hold the frantic man in place. Eventually, Kontar slumped against him and wept. Saar held him and stroked that long, beautiful hair. He strained his hearing, but beyond the faint traces of music and laughter from other rooms he heard no one else.

Kontar gnawed his bottom lip. 'Am I dead?'

'No. You have my word.'

Beyond that fact Saar didn't know what to add. Instead he kept silent and let his gaze fall on the bronze dagger. Red stains marked its tip and caught the decorative swirls on the blade.

'From blood all power comes,' he whispered.

When he looked again he saw more blood, including his own, smeared across Kontar's lips.

Saar laughed. A small bubble of sound that burst from his lips before he could stop it. 'All power . . .' More laughter, frantic now and he gripped Kontar ever tighter, staring into his wide, frightened eyes.

'Forgive me,' he begged. 'I've blessed you. Cursed you. I don't know which.'

'Let me go.' Kontar's voice was very small.

Saar straightened and retrieved the dagger, studying it.

There: his own dried blood mingled with that of Kontar which was fresh and dripping. Mixed with that, just visible to his heightened sight he saw dry black particles of blood far older than his own.

Kontar growled low in his throat. His gazed followed Saar's hand, which he cradled in his own. Then, without speaking, he pushed Saar's bloodied fingers into his mouth.

'No!' Saar yanked his hand back but the blood was already gone and Kontar's stare raked his body, searching for more. Just in time, Saar jerked the dagger out of reach and stood back, watching the younger man lower his head to the floor and lap at the spilled blood.

'Don't— you mustn't.'

Though he tried to stop him, Kontar kept licking until his tongue rasped stone. Next he shoved the crimson portions of his ruined robe into his mouth and sucked on those. When finished, Kontar sat back on his heels. His chest rose and fell with each shuddering breath. 'I need more.'

Saar felt limp. Weary. 'What have I done?'

The room faded away. Before Saar could question it, he stood on a dusty stretch of road watching dozens of men march out of sight. They carried swords, spears and bows, and moved with the pace and careful precision of men on a long march. Among them strode a young man with a small, jagged scar across his nose. Pride swelled Saar's chest as he watched his brother march away to war.

A lonely street at night. A man with sweaty skin and a crooked smile pulled his hair. The man thrust him against a wall, pulled his shendyt to one side. A terrible stab of pain followed, then rhythmic thrusting, grunting and soft words moaned against his ear.

The army training grounds. Dozens of boys of various heights and strengths, lined up for inspection by the existing soldiers of Cleopatra's army. A tall, heavily built man with short, curling hair and commanding eyes, looked him up and down and shook his head before walking away. Saar recognised his own younger face, before shame and despair welled up inside him.

When he next opened his eyes, he stood back in Gyasi's room. Kontar gazed at him, clutching his head with both hands. Saar swayed and touched the wall to regain his balance.

Kontar lowered his shoulders and shrank in on himself. His shoulders trembled. 'How did you do that? I could feel you inside my head.'

'I saw . . .' Saar gripped his hair and yanked it. 'I saw you. I *was* you. You have five brothers. A sister who died soon after birth. I saw your life, like pictures on a scroll.' He wiped the dampness on his cheeks, refused to acknowledge it as tears. 'I saw you in the street. A man attacked you – even before you came here – he tore off your clothes and took you.' The words stuck in his throat. 'In the street. You were so alone. Scared—'

'Stop!' Kontar pressed his hands over his ears as though to block out the words. 'You can't— you mustn't know what I've done.'

'I can't help it. I didn't ask for this and I—' He broke off. 'No . . . I wanted to know the minds of men. I wanted control. Power. This is exactly what I asked for.'

'You're a shadow in my mind. I feel everything . . .' Slowly Kontar emerged from behind his hair. 'You're afraid. Why?'

Though he longed to deny it, Saar's own knowledge of Kontar's mind wouldn't let him. 'Because I've done a terrible thing. I've made you as I am. Tied you to Set forever.'

'My whole life I've wanted to be like you.'

'Not like this.'

Kontar stood. He flexed his hands and made fists, looking about the room with an expression of wonder in his eyes. 'I feel like I could conquer the world single-handed should the desire strike me. I could run for miles. Lift the pyramids. I could tug stars from the sky and use them as a path to touch the sun. If this is what it means to be like you then I want nothing more.'

'But Set will own you forever. He demands blood tribute for this power.'

A slight widening of his eyes. And then, 'I give up worse things every single day I work in this place. Take me with you. Show me what to do.'

'I can't.'

'Don't leave me here,' Kontar's voice cracked. 'Please. I'll do whatever you need.'

Saar hesitated. 'Perhaps you could join the army?'

'Yes! Yes, I'll join. I'll cut my hair. Change my name if you must, but let me join you. Please.'

Chewing his thumbnail, Saar ran his free hand through Kontar's long mane of dark hair. 'Everything will be different if you join me.'

'I know.'

He sighed. 'When my mother saw the mark on my thigh she took it as a sign that she should enlist me. My oldest uncle told her she could do Alexandria no greater service. I loved him very much.'

'It would be an honour to take his name.'

Saar turned and strode to the doorway. 'Then, come, Mosi. We must leave immediately.'

Chapter Eighteen

Lenina scratched the back of her hand. Brutally clipped fingernails scored fine white lines on her skin, flaking away crusts of blood lingering between her trembling fingers.

She stared at the cardboard cup of tea on the table, noting that the little curls of steam had ceased to rise. The sugary scent of the black fluid stung her nostrils.

'Miss Miller, is there anybody you would like me to call?' Detective Inspector Brad Thorne leaned against the wall, watching her. His expression, much like the first time they met, resembled the look of a man chewing something he disliked the taste of. This time, however, a hint of sympathy lingered in his eyes. At his side, Tristen looked everywhere but at her face, his fingers fussing with a button near the collar of his black and red overshirt. Dark waves of chestnut brown hair frothed around his face and neck. Bloodied handprints dotted his sleeves. In a distant way Lenina recalled that she had put them there. He had found her in the back of the police van outside her house.

Surrounded by whirling blue lights, curious onlookers and dozens of law enforcement professionals, she sat on the low step and huddled in a black, scratchy blanket provided by a kindly police officer wearing too much make-up.

When Lenina saw Tristen, her handbag slipped from her fingers and she jumped up to meet him.

In that moment she wanted nothing more than his arms around her.

His green eyes on hers. His peppermint breath across her cheek. It made no sense. She hated it. Yet his very presence soothed her. He held tight enough to make her gasp and didn't let go even when Inspector Thorne arrived behind him.

'Are you okay?' Tristen's voice quivered. He pulled her close and stroked her hair. He seemed not to notice when his hands came away bloody. 'Your face – what did he do to you?' He held her all the way to the hospital then watched while a team of doctors cleaned and stitched her face.

Hours later, in a cold white room at the back of the hospital, Lenina longed to feel his arms around her again. But he refused to meet her gaze.

'Miss Miller?' Thorne stepped away from the wall and placed his hand on the table. 'Can you hear me?'

'Hey,' snapped Tristen. His eyes narrowed to thin slits. 'Give her a minute.'

Though grateful for his intervention, Lenina knew she had to answer. 'I'm listening, Detective.'

'Would you like me to call anyone? There must be someone you want to talk to. Friend? Family?'

'No.'

'Somewhere to stay? You can't go back to your house tonight. Do you have somewhere to go?'

'No. Yes.'

'Which is it, Miss Miller?'

Tristen slapped the flat of his hand against wall. 'Brad, take it easy.'

'No, *you* do your job.' Thorne gritted his teeth, took a deep breath, then let it out slowly. 'We need to get her somewhere safe.'

She ran a finger around the rim of her coffee cup. 'I have a friend nearby. I'll stay with her.'

His voice softened. 'Would you like me to call her?'

'No.'

From the corner of her eye she saw him gazing down at the top of her head. Then Tristen shuffled his chair closer and wedged himself between them. His gaze brushed hers, melancholic and desperate. It slid away again just as fast, a guilty action quickly suppressed.

Thorne's fingers twitched on the table then slipped away. 'I'm sorry for your loss, Miss Miller.'

The door opened a crack. Through it came a young sandy-haired nurse. 'Are you officers nearly done? I have some paperwork for you.'

The bigger man huffed a heavy breath. He glanced at Tristen, then waved away the nurse. 'I'm coming. Miss Miller?'

She looked up.

'Detective Blake will look after you now.' His voice became heavy. 'I know it's easier said than done, but try to get some rest.' He stepped out. Stuffy silence filled the space left by his body. The smell of cigarettes and takeaway burgers lingered in his wake.

'Lenina—' Tristen began.

She raised a hand towards him. 'Don't. Please.'

More silence.

Eventually he reached across the table. He touched her fingers and the contact was electric. A shiver rippled through her body. Her mouth became dry. Very slowly, Lenina pulled her hand away.

Tristen bit his lip and moved his hands to his lap. 'Talk to me.' His voice was low. Hushed. Desperate.

'And say what?'

'Anything. Whatever you need to say. I want to help you, but—'

'You can't help me.' She wiped her face, catching the edge of the soft dressing covering the horrific slash on her left cheek. The stitches ached and pulled on her skin, delivering a stab of pain each time she spoke. Requesting more painkillers was pointless; she'd already had. The doctors insisted that she wait at least three hours before her next dose. Joys of a vampire metabolism.

'Let me try. I can't imagine what you're going through but please, let me try.' His hand snaked out again, palm up. Small wrinkles formed at the corners of his eyes. 'Please?'

Lenina reached across the table and placed her hand in his. He closed his fingers around hers and squeezed, as if he could force his own strength into her. A tiny smile touched his lips. 'I'll do whatever you need, Lenina. Anything.'

Like when they first met, the words seemed loaded with additional meaning. Though she tried to shake it away, the weight of his gaze and the touch of his hand made her palms moisten. Her lips parted.

A door slammed open somewhere outside the room. Loud shouts and curses accompanied the tramp of many footsteps and the squeal of gurney wheels. Another door crashed shut. The spell between them splintered and died.

Lenina looked away and worked to steady her breathing, abruptly aware that she'd been holding her breath. She freed her fingers.

Tristen leaned back in his chair and returned to fiddling with the buttons on his shirt. 'We'll process the clippings from your hair and fingernails as soon as possible. We should have some information by the start of next week. Brad already called Gwendolin, you won't need to do that.'

Mention of Nick's mother threatened to shatter the carefully erected wall Lenina had built around her emotions. She swallowed. 'Thanks.'

'You won't get your clothes back, but you can keep those trousers. And that shirt.'

Lenina glanced at the rolled up sleeves of the borrowed sweatshirt. Stripped even of her underwear, the foreign clothing rasped against her skin with unforgiving coarseness.

'Thanks.'

Through the silence Lenina heard the bustle of the rest of the hospital. The clack of keyboard keys and the occasional raised voice. The air smelled of stale coffee, antibacterial gel and sickness.

'Let's go. I'll take you to your friend's house.' He held out his hand. When she took it, a faint tingle across her palm echoed the first time they touched. His fingers tightened on hers.

In the car, a plain grey vehicle, with a police radio in place of a CD player, she curled around her seat belt and gazed out the window, watching the world outside slide through her reflection. It blurred, much as Jason had when he'd plunged down with that dagger. The thought of his persistence made her cringe and test the integrity of the mental door holding his thoughts away from hers. Would it also protect her location? It hadn't before.

The car idled at a set of traffic lights and Lenina found her mind drifting, picking apart the encounter in her house with the care and attention she usually reserved for museum samples. Part of her baulked at the cold analysis of her actions, the rest was grateful for it.

Nick was dead. Probably lying on a cold metal table to be prodded and poked by medical professionals with no idea of who he was or what he meant to anybody. He would mean nothing to them but a number and a name, probably written on a small piece of card, attached to a pale big toe with a thin piece of string.

His face swam before her, the kind smile, crooked nose, dimpled chin. And his eyes: so very, very blue. The image changed. The smile became a scream. The chin a bloodied stretch of skin. Blue, washed out and empty.

She tasted his blood. So sweet. So smooth. Gliding down her throat like the liquid silk and touching every part of her with its warmth. Better than food. Better than sex. Better than Pauline.

The truth struck her so hard she thumped back against the seat, staring out the window while her fingers trembled.

Two deaths. One night.

I really am a monster.

Where then were the tears? The frenzied confessions of guilt? There was no guilt, just the gentle pulse of pleasure as she remembered the blood. The taste. The smell. The power.

Who would be next?

She unclipped her seat belt and yanked at her door handle.

Tristen gave a cry of alarm. 'What are you doing?'

'I can't stay with you. It's too dangerous. I might— he could—'

The car slowed but didn't stop. 'Sit back, Lenina. Put your belt on.'

'No. I have to leave. Let me out.'

Stoney silence.

'Open the door!' Breaking the lock would be easy, as would leaping from the car even as it moved. She could roll across the tarmac and leap up unharmed, running before he had any chance of catching her.

Her skin tingled with the need to flee.

'I know you're scared, but this isn't the way. You need to let us help. Let *me* help.'

'You can't.'

'I'll protect you.'

'What about everyone else?' The words burst free before she understood them, but as soon as they were loose, Lenina knew the truth. Jason found her once; he could, and would, do so again.

She turned her attention to the imagined door between herself and the ginger haired monster. Still in place. Still sturdy. For now. She added several chains, a padlock and a deadbolt to the projection in her head. The sense of solitude in her own mind deepened.

Better, but not foolproof.

Lenina faced Tristen. 'I can't go to Ramona's house. What if he knows about her? She won't be safe.'

From him or from me.

'What do you want to do?'

'A hotel? B&B?'

Shadows striped Tristen's face and shoulders in a rhythmic pattern as he drove. His hands gripped the steering wheel at a textbook two-and-ten but his attention strayed from the road.

'I can't let you do that. You need to be with someone.'

'So I can put them in danger too?' Her insides writhed as she considered it. In that moment, she had no idea who was the bigger threat. 'I'm not myself. And that man attacked me in my house. I won't risk leading him to my friends.'

Tristen pursed his lips. 'Fine.' He stamped the foot brake, bringing the car to a squealing stop on the side of the road. Ignoring the toots and waving fists from other cars, he performed a daring U-turn and sped off in the opposite direction.

Catching her sidelong look he fixed his gaze on the road and squared his shoulders. 'We're going to my house.'

Panic fluttered through her belly, followed by a stab of pleasure. Then confusion. 'Is that allowed?'

He wouldn't meet her gaze, looking instead at the road with an expression of deep concentration. 'You'll be safe and among company. If this guy has been following you he won't know anything about me. You can have my bed; I'll sleep downstairs. However we do this, I'm not leaving you alone tonight.' At last he met her gaze, pausing at a set of traffic lights to stare into her eyes.

Even in the darkness the green of his irises was visible, bright and vibrant like a pair of emeralds. His hair billowed around his face, dancing in the gusts from the air conditioning.

When the lights changed he returned his attention to the road. 'Are you sure you don't want to call someone?'

'I will. Soon.'

Lenina returned to watching the streets roll by.

After hours of hustle and noise, question after question, and constant looks of pity on every face she saw, sitting in silence suited her. The pity bothered her most. While there was no way for the officers to know the truth of Nick's death, knowing she didn't deserve their kind looks and gentle words made her stomach writhe. That, more than any other thought, stopped Lenina reaching out to her friends and family. Instead she sat in Tristen's car, enjoyed the steady rhythm of his breathing and the faint traces of peppermint on his breath each time he spoke.

After ten minutes he nosed the car on to a drive lined with pruned hedges. Lenina gazed at the red brick, polished windows and small garden filled with flowers. Two small gnomes with silly hats and fishing rods stood to one edge of a tiny pond made of shiny plastic.

'This is where you live? Seems . . . not like you. Too homely.'

'I'm homely.' Tristen appeared hurt.

She patted his hand. 'You're young, good looking and single with a good job. I expected a bachelor pad.'

'You think I'm good looking?'

Lenina nibbled her thumb nail. 'Did I say that?'

He shrugged, though not without a tiny smile. 'Maybe I misheard. But . . . I was married once.'

'Really?'

'Her name was Ava. Pretty woman. Smart. Funny. She looked like you too. Something in your eyes.'

'What happened to her?'

'She died.' The flat way he said it told Lenina that part of the conversation was over.

The off-white carpet, tasteful decor and spotless furniture forced Lenina to rethink her opinion of single men even further.

Tristen ushered her along the front passageway into a large, open room. Within, a three-piece sofa suite separated the living space from the dining area. The smell of new leather filled the room. She left her handbag on the dining table and aimed for one of the armchairs.

'Would you like a drink?' He loitered near an open arch on the left, leading through to the kitchen.

The thought of putting anything else in her mouth made her stomach growl. 'No, thanks. I just want to lie down.'

'I'll clean the bedroom first, then you can go upstairs.'

She watched him leave, cupping her face in her hands. How had she come to be here? How did everything deteriorate so quickly? The band of her engagement ring scraped her eyebrow, a quick stab of pain. Lenina's breathing caught in her throat as she twirled the band around her finger, watching the light caress the diamonds on its crest.

Nick hadn't deserved to die. Had Jason been the one to kill him, the loss might be easier to bear, but Lenina couldn't blame him. His bite had started it all, but the choices were hers. Replaying the events in her mind made no difference to the fact.

Something inside her *wanted* to hurt Nick. Something longed to hear him scream and beg and refused to release her until she fed those desires. A dark creature lurked deep inside over which she had little or no control.

That thought frightened her, far more than the memory of what she did to the man she supposedly loved.

But I did love him. Didn't I? We were getting married.

She heard Tristen moving directly overhead, opening and closing cupboards. His features swam before her mind's eye, kind and gentle. The teasing tilt to his smile. The low lure in his voice.

The truth hurt so much she whimpered and grasped her chest.

How could she have loved Nick when there mere sight of Tristen made her want to pull off his clothes? When his touch sent warm thrills of pleasure shooting through every limb?

Leaping to her feet, Lenina snatched up her handbag. She ran for the hallway. No choice remained but to leave. To run away. Put as much distance as she could between herself and any other innocent. And Tristen.

A flash of red caught her eye and she spun towards it, hands curled into fists. A mirror threw her own startled reflection back at her, dry trails of blood still forming streaks across her cheeks and forehead. The stitches beneath the dressing resisted her attempts to frown.

Slowly she pulled the sticky, white dressing away to reveal the wound beneath. She gasped.

The wound started as a deep gouge below her left eye. It curved across her cheek bone before tapering into nothing, a finger's breadth from the corner of her lip. Along its length, the ugly black stubs of surgical thread twitched like insectile legs. It bisected the previous scratch made by Jason's dagger, though that first wound couldn't compare to the second round of damage. All the make-up in the world wouldn't hide that from a photographer's lens.

A moment later Lenina realised that she needn't worry about photos. Without Nick there could be no wedding.

'It's not as bad as it looks.' Tristen's voice came from the top of the stairs. He descended holding a toothbrush and a large white towel. Though his tone remained light, the intensity in his eyes deepened as he stared at her left cheek. 'You weren't supposed to take the dressing off until tomorrow.'

Though unsure, Lenina thought she saw a flash of anger in his eyes. Before she could dwell on it, he sighed and held out the towel and toothbrush.

'I wanted to see. What if it scars?'

'It won't.' His voice quivered and that strange look returned to his eye. This time Lenina was quick enough to recognise regret. 'And it doesn't matter, you're still beautiful.' He touched her chin. 'I'm sorry this happened to you, Lenina.'

The way he said her name made her knees quake. He leaned closer and Lenina saw a flush rise in his cheeks and neck. His breath tickled against her nose and lips, and his heartbeat began a lively triple step.

Each exhalation brought her a little wave of mint and faint traces of something else. Something sweet. Smooth. Warm. Lenina knew it was the smell of desire. As if her brain had flicked a switch to assign emotions to familiar scents, she knew the name of this one instantly. Tristen placed his hands on her hips. His fingers worked beneath the hem of her oversized sweatshirt until they touched bare skin.

'Wait,' she whispered.

He did. But his hands didn't move.

When she met his gaze, she saw raw need burning in the brilliant green depths, speaking a language she knew and understood with the basest parts of her anatomy.

'Don't cry,' he murmured. 'I'm here. I'll look after you.'

It would be so easy to let him. To fall into Tristen's arms and let this strong, kind, sweet-smelling distraction whisk her away to a place where the crazy events of the last two days had no power.

'It's my fault,' she burst out, gnawing her trembling bottom lip. 'I did this.'

'Don't say that.' His hands tightened on her hips. Pulled her closer. 'It's nobody's fault.'

Curls of dark hair brushed her nose. The soft strands carried that familiar scent of peppermint and caressed her cheek like velvet.

'I'm a horrible person,' she wailed.

Tristen stopped her words with a tender kiss. When he pulled away again, his chest heaved as if he'd run the minute-mile. 'It's not your fault.'

The next kiss was gentle but insistent. He cupped her uninjured cheek and tilted her face towards his. Lenina opened her mouth, and he took the invitation to deepen the embrace.

His free hand dived beneath the hem of her sweatshirt and groped the swell of her breast. He groaned deep in the back of the throat. 'Is this okay?'

No. Lenina wanted to scream. To push him away and run as fast as she could. But she also wanted to touch him. Hold him. Kiss him. Taste him.

The warring desires left her gasping. Trembling.

'Touch me,' she said.

Tristen lifted the sweatshirt over her head and ran his fingers over her skin. 'So beautiful,' he murmured. Leaning close, he brushed his nose through the hair at the back of her neck, separating the braids with his fingers. 'You smell so . . .'

More kisses, along the side of her neck, her ear, the hollow of her throat, growing steadily more frantic with every touch of his lips.

The light touch of his fingers sent electric thrills shooting along every nerve. His taste on her lips was the sweetest she had ever known and in that moment Lenina wanted it more than anything else.

His overshirt made no noise at it hit the floor. Neither did his t-shirt.

Lenina let her hands travel over his bare chest, picking out the subtle shapes of muscle beneath his skin. When he crushed her close to his chest, she kissed the side of his throat, and allowed her teeth to scrape his skin. She ran her fingers through his hair.

He moaned. A whispered, 'Yes,' bubbled from his lips.

The rest of his clothes vanished as quickly.

Lenina had a vague impression of green, silky boxers flying through the air before Tristen knelt before her, tucking his fingers into the waistband of her borrowed trousers. He eased them over her hips as though unearthing an invaluable treasure, his gaze never once leaving hers.

Hooking one arm beneath her knees, Tristen swept her into his arms and carried her up the stairs.

The neatly made bed squealed as he settled her on it, stretching his naked body over hers with another slow kiss.

Chapter Nineteen

Lenina huddled beneath the duvet, her limbs still singing with pleasure. She watched Tristen roll off the bed and stretch.

Rimmed in silver moonlight, his body resembled the sculpted perfection of an ancient Greek statue. She imagined running her hands over him again, picking out each muscle with the tips of her fingers. Feeling his body join with hers in the ultimate display of intimacy.

He smiled at her.

She looked away. 'We shouldn't have done that.'

His smile wilted at the corners. 'I know this is hard for you, but—'

'You do *not* know how hard this is.' Shame gave her voice a raw edge.

'Fine. You're right. But we just shared something amazing. Don't push me away now.'

'Nick's body is in the morgue. It hasn't been a day. I cheated on him.'

'You didn't, you—'

'We were getting married.'

'That's right. *Were.*' Tristen sat next to her and tugged the duvet down to her chin. 'You've been through a trauma. You're scared. Don't feel guilty about reaching out for comfort. Any normal person would.'

Staring into his eyes, Lenina wished she could believe him. But the sickly, crawling sensation twisting her stomach into knots refused to let her off so easily.

'I'm not normal.'

'You got that right.' He touched her shoulder. 'You're an intelligent, strong, beautiful woman.'

'I'm a monster.'

Any answer Tristen planned to make died as his phone rang. He crossed to the dresser and snatched it up. 'What?'

'You need to come down to the station, Tristen.'

Lenina heard the voice perfectly, even from so far away. She felt an inexplicable jolt of fear and watched Tristen's face as he spoke warily into the handset.

'Brad? Why are you calling my home line?'

'You didn't answer your mobile. You need to come back in.'

'I'm supposed to be on leave.'

'We have another murder.'

Tristen gave Lenina an apologetic glance and briefly covered the mouthpiece. 'Sorry, I have to take this.'

She nodded, pulling the duvet even closer around her and turning her back to him. Despite his lowered voice, she heard every word.

'What happened?'

Thorne chuckled, a dry sound, followed by his familiar smoker's cough. 'A woman in Grick Park. Bitten *on the throat*. Dead dog right next to her. Her name is Pauline Lock.'

Lenina froze. A chill raced through her limbs and her mouth filled with a familiar sour taste.

'Grick Park?'

'Same place Lenina Miller got bitten. Where is she, Tristen?'

Tristen cleared his throat. 'With her friend.'

'Bullshit. Her friend's here, busting our nuts because that batty old neighbour rang her up to gossip. Chief Hobb is trying to get rid of her. Where's the girl?'

Lenina closed her eyes. It might have been funny if not so tragic. In her mind's eye she saw Ramona marching into the police station, her expression as fiery as the red curls surrounding her face.

'Lenina was concerned for the safety of her friend. Given the circumstances, I think she's right.' Tristen's raised his voice, each word clipped and harsh.

'Where is she?'

'I . . .'

'You took her home with you.' The flat disbelief in Thorne's made it a statement, not a question.

'It's not a crime, Brad.'

'She's a *witness*.' He sighed. 'I'm coming to get her. If she's worried we can put her somewhere safe, but she can't stay with you. Stop thinking with your dick. We have a murder to investigate.'

'Brad—'

'Shut up and listen to me. Don't touch her. Don't talk to her. Don't even offer her tea. You can't be seen making moves on the woman whose fiancé just got murdered.'

'I'm not making moves.'

Silence from the other end said more than words ever could.

'Be ready in half an hour.' Thorne hung up.

Tristen placed the phone back on the cradle then turned to face her. While he struggled to find the words, Lenina arranged her features into what she hoped was an innocent expression.

'That was Brad. I need to work. He's coming to take you to a safe house. I don't want— you mustn't think that I—'

She sniffed. Shook her head. 'That's probably for the best.'

'I'll get your things so you can get dressed.' He left the room with a visible slump to his shoulders. When he returned with her clothes and handbag, she refused to meet his gaze.

'I'll wait for you downstairs.'

Nodding, she waited for him to close the door behind him before shrugging the duvet off her shoulders. Two minutes later she sat on the end of the bed with no memory of getting dressed. She stared at the opposite wall, tracing the patterns in the wallpaper as her mind whirled like a Ferris Wheel.

Finally she pulled her mobile from her handbag. Five missed calls waited for her. Four text messages. All from her father. As she read through them, her nerves twisted like a corkscrew.

Hey chuck, not heard from you. Can you call me?

Did you get my last message? Give me a call, chuck.

Where are you? Call me.

Lenina, answer your phone!!!

The panic riding in that last message brought on a wave of dizziness. Then, as if to think his name was a summons, the phone rang in her hands. *Dad Mob* flashed on the display.

Hand shaking, she pressed 'connect' and lifted the mobile to her ear. 'Daddy?'

'Thank God, chuck.' Ray exhaled hard. Behind the sound of his voice was the rumble of rushing traffic and white noise provided by a radio station with the volume turned low.

'What's wrong?'

'You didn't call. You wouldn't answer your phone. Nick's phone is dead. No one's answering the land line.'

She hesitated.

'Ramona called me, but nothing she says makes sense. What's going on? Are you okay?'

'I'm fine, Daddy.'

'Did something happen to Nick? He always answers his phone.'

'Nick is—' the tightness in her throat cut off further speech.

'Chuck? Talk to me.'

'He's dead.' She made herself say it slow, firm and clear.

In the silence that followed Lenina heard the low murmur from the radio. She imagined her father behind the wheel of his ancient BMW, gazing out the window while drumming his fingers on the wheel.

The image was so clear that she could almost feel the beaded seat cover beneath her, smell the lime-shaped air freshener her mother always hung from the rear-view mirror.

'Daddy?'

'What happened?' His voice cracked. 'Tell me.'

Her stomach writhed at the thought of sharing her lies. 'He . . .'

'Chuck, I know this is hard, but you have to tell me what's happened.'

She dropped the phone. Though Ray continued to call out to her, she couldn't move. Instead, she pressed her hands to her face and sucked deep breaths through her nose, swallowing repeatedly to tamp down the taste of bile on her tongue.

'. . . to you now.' She heard the tail end of Ray's words while wiping a dribble of snot against her borrowed sleeve. 'I'm already on the motorway.'

Lenina snatched up the phone and crammed it against her ear. 'Don't come here.'

'I'm not leaving you alone over a hundred miles away.'

'I'm with the police now. Detective Blake is here.'

'Blake? The young one with the ponytail?'

'Yes.'

'Is the other detective with you?' Ray's voice dropped low. She recognised the change of tone from her early childhood when blaming her younger brother for broken furniture and stolen biscuits no longer worked.

'No.' Her voice became small.

'Stay away from that detective. Go to Ramona's house. I'll be there in two hours.'

'Daddy, please—'

'Do it, Lenina.' The use of her full name stole her breath. 'Text me when you get there.'

The phone buzzed then died. Lenina crammed the phone into her bag and ran from the room. As she reached the top of the stairs a heavy hand knocked twice at the front door. She froze.

Tristen stepped into view, hastily tying his hair back before pulling the door open. Huddled on the step, shoulders hunched against the rain, Detective Thorne nodded a grim greeting. He pushed his way through. Beneath his suit jacket, greasy stains formed a trail beside his tie. A missing button on his off-white shirt left a large gap, through which a patch of pale, flabby stomach was visible.

He shuffled his feet on the carpet and shoved his hands into his pockets. 'Where is she?'

Tristen glanced towards the stairs, his eyes widening when he saw her poised on the top step. When Thorne followed suit, his gaze touched her injured left cheek then slid away. 'Miss Miller, I know you're frightened but you can't stay here. Gather your things and I'll take you to one of our safe houses.'

She saw Tristen lower his face to his hands, rubbing his jaw with the tips of his fingers.

'My dad is on the way.'

'Good. Once we get there you can tell him you're safe but he won't be able to visit you straight away.'

Lenina felt a small measure of comfort in that thought. When Jason found her again, at least her family would be safe.

'I'm ready.'

'Great, let's go. Excuse us, Tristen.'

The younger man frowned. 'What about the murder?'

Thorne shifted from foot to foot and fiddled with the knot of his tie. 'I'll handle it for now.'

'Why? What's wrong?'

'I didn't want to do this here,' he murmured, gaze flicking briefly up the stairs. His voice lowered. 'Chief Hobb knows what you did. You're suspended until he has a chance to speak with you.'

Tristen's hands formed trembling fists at his sides. He glared at his partner before dragging his coat off a hook near the bottom step. 'You're not leaving here without me.'

'Don't make this any worse.'

'You're not taking her.'

Shaking his head, Thorne nudged him aside. 'Goodnight, Tristen.

Let's go, Miss Miller.'

Lenina followed. As she passed, Tristen snagged her hand and held it tight. She squeezed back and tried to continue, but he didn't let go. Instead he stepped forward, swung her behind him. Standing between her and the way out he stopped with his arms folded.

'What's wrong with you?' Thorne snapped. All traces of sympathy and patience fled his voice. 'Don't be an idiot.'

'Leave now, Brad. Walk away.'

'You know I can't do that.'

'Just go. I won't offer again.'

Grunting, Thorne clamped his hand down on Tristen's shoulder to drag him aside, but the younger man ducked and twisted away. He gripped his own fist and drove forward with his elbow, slamming the hard angle of bone into Thorne's face. A strident crack preceded the thud of Thorne's knees hitting the carpet. Then his shriek cut off everything else.

Lenina had time to see blood gush from his nostrils before Tristen attacked again, leading with his knee. It struck Thorne in the chin, snapping his head back. His teeth clicked together. More blood flew from his mouth. The big man slumped on to the carpet. Tristen stepped clear of his writhing body the same way he might avoid a muddy puddle. He dragged Lenina back into the living area and pushed her into an armchair. She moved with him, too stunned to object, though her gaze slid past him when Thorne stumbled in after them clutching his bloody nose.

'Leave,' said Tristen. He didn't look back. 'Please. I'll deal with you later but you have to go.'

'*Deal with me*?' The words slurred. Thorne's voice was thick with clots of blood. 'Meaning?'

'Meaning walk out of here while your legs still work.'

Growling, Thorne launched forward. He caught Tristen by waist and pulled him to the ground. The pair rolled across the carpet, locked together in a tangle of flailing arms and legs.

'Stop!' Lenina circled them, trying to find a way in. She looked at Tristen, then Thorne, twisting her fingers. Her hands jerked towards one man then the other.

Neither of them needed help. In a display of grace and strength that belied his age, Thorne shoved his feet into Tristen's stomach. The younger man flew back, skidding across the carpet and rolling into the back of the sofa. Thorne lurched to his feet. Lifting his fisted hands before his face, he balanced his weight on the balls of his feet.

Lenina stepped forward.

'Stay back, Miss Miller.' A bubble of pink-tinged spittle frothed from Thorne's mouth as he spoke. He spat a tooth on to the carpet.

She backed off, pressing her back to the wall near the arch to the kitchen.

Tristen bounded to his feet. He did it with a flip like a break dancer and huffed a wisp of hair out of his face. He had a line of blood on his chin. 'Not bad. Finished?'

'Screw you,' Thorne hissed.

'Wrong answer.' Then he moved, an incredible blur of speed that Lenina barely managed to follow.

Tristen's leg flashed up, heel cocked, knee locked. The side of his foot caught Thorne in the chest, then again in the chin, knocking his head back with stunning force. Once more Thorne hit the floor, straight down like a felled tree. This time he didn't move.

Lenina swallowed and tasted bile. 'You're crazy,' she whispered. 'Detective Thorne?'

A low moan.

She rushed to him, kneeling on the floor by his face. Warm blood slicked her fingers when she touched his cheek. For once the urge to taste it was absent; she felt nothing but revulsion and fear.

'Are you okay? Can you stand?'

'Broken ribs,' Tristen murmured. 'Probably punctured lungs too; he's not going anywhere.' He crouched beside Thorne's groaning form with his hands dangling between his knees. 'I warned you, Brad. We could have avoided all of this. Believe it or not, I need you. We work well together.'

Lenina stared at Tristen as though she had never seen him before. Perhaps she hadn't. Though his green eyes were the same, and his breath still smelled of peppermint, his expression matched nothing she'd seen on his face so far. It was fury mingled with frustration and weariness.

He rubbed his hands over his jaw then leaned close to the other man's chest. 'You're dying. I can hear your lungs filling up. I shouldn't have kicked you so hard, I wasn't exaggerating when I said I needed you.'

Thorne coughed. Blood ran down his chin.

'I can't always measure it with humans. You're all so frail.'

Lenina stiffened. Through the wet bubbling of Thorne's laboured breathing she heard Tristen's words again and felt a shudder, like the cold dabble of clammy fingers down her spine. While Tristen stared at his dying partner, Lenina stood and inched towards the door. She stepped into the hallway just as he called out to her.

'Don't run, Lenina.'

She bolted. Skidding to a stop at the front door, Lenina grabbed the handle and jerked it open. Rain slanted in to meet her, cold and heavy. Through the gap she saw Tristen's car and another marked car, complete with blue and white lights on the top. She caught sight of the empty street and the grey-black sky before the door jerked free of her grip and slammed shut.

Several loud clicks signalled the locks sliding magically into place. She tried the handle. The door didn't move. The sound of footsteps made her turn.

'I said, "Don't run."' Tristen blocked the hallway behind her.

She pressed her back to the door. 'What are you?'

'You know. Why else would you run?' He smiled and, as she watched, the emerald green of his eyes faded away beneath a blinding flash of white. She shrieked and rushed at him. Wide eyes and grasping hands told her he hadn't expected that. Ducking beneath his grip, she darted towards the sitting area, spinning round as she passed through the door. A fractional pause, then she slammed it shut on his advancing face. She heard the shout and the satisfying thunk as it hit him in the nose and she used the precious seconds saved to hurdle Thorne's body and dash through the arch into the kitchen. She yanked open a drawer near the sink. Inside lay a selection of tea towels, place mats and sponges. Whimpering, she tried the next drawer. This one held cutlery, including a butcher's knife the blade of which gleamed in the half-light.

Before she could close her fingers around it, a hand cupped the back of her head and shoved her face down. The granite worktop rushed up to meet her. Pain exploded through her face, spiralling outward from her nose and forehead. The kitchen swam across her vision.

Lenina slithered to the floor, cradling her face in both hands. She heard rather than saw Tristen moving around her.

'You made this so much harder than it needed to be.' His voice remained low and steady.

Nauseated, she clutched her stomach and tried to steady the sensation of flip-flopping that came from the taste of her own blood. After two attempts she managed to open her eyes. An additional three seconds allowed her to focus. 'Stay away from me.'

When he crouched next to her, forearms resting on his knees, she wondered if Thorne had felt the same level of confusion and anger she did in that moment.

Tristen's eyes were green again, and his gaze wandered over her body, lingering on her left cheek. She tried to stand.

'I wouldn't do that yet if I were you.'

She ignored him. Gritted her teeth. Leaned against the cupboards and shoved herself into a kneeling position. A firm grip on the worktop helped her reach her feet. Blood dripped from her nose, running into the borrowed sweatshirt. With shaking hands she wiped it away and realised the damage was already healing. She sniffed, winced and tried again.

Tristen nodded. 'You'll be fine in a minute.'

Lenina opened her mouth, but before she could speak, he stiffened and whirled to face the archway.

An instant later she heard it too: footsteps marching up the drive.

Chapter Twenty

Time seemed to slow.

Tristen gritted his teeth. Balled his hands into fists.

Though her stomach and head shrieked a complaint at every move, Lenina shoved off from the cupboards and ran. Shouldering past him, back over Thorne's body and to the front door. 'Help me, please!' Desperation added volume as she went.

Locks clicked and the door swung open before she could reach it, admitting a scatter of rain and a shabby figure in grey. He peered through a scraggle of knotted ginger hair and stepped forward. Lenina glared at Jason and skidded to a stop. Her fingers itched as she balanced on the edge of attacking or fleeing.

'I blocked you,' she cried, checking the mental image of the door in her mind. Sure enough, the locks, chains and deadbolt remained in place. She felt no trace of him in her head, just the frantic shrieking of her own fear. 'How did you find me?'

'I wasn't following *you*.'

Tristen stepped into the hallway, kicking aside Thorne's legs to clear a path. One hand rested on his hip. 'Where have you been?'

Silence in the hallway. Lenina frowned. Looked toward the door.

Shuffling his hands, gazed fixed on the ground, Jason hunched his shoulders and lowered his head. When he spoke next, his voice quivered. 'Sorry.'

'I lost an asset. I had to buy time playing lovey-dovey. What took you?'

More hand shuffling. 'I stopped to give tribute. I had to make sure I was strong enough.'

'Are you?'

In answer, Jason lifted his head. His thin lips pulled into a sly smile.

Lenina screamed. Pain exploded across her skull and the carefully constructed mental door burst open. Imagined splinters pierced her brain like needles. Through the gap came a scalding wave of emotion from Jason, washing over her to drown out everything else. She felt his pleasure, his pride, his excitement. Beneath those more immediate emotions came more subtle ones and her body quivered as traces of love flowed through. Respect. Deep, visceral longing.

Lenina stared at Jason and understood. 'You know him.' Cradling her head in both hands, she gathered together the shattered pieces of her mental defences and tried to repair them. 'You bit him, like you bit me.'

Tristen snorted. 'Don't be so crass. I *Kissed* him.'

'*You* did?' She shook her head again, her gaze flicking across his face as if to find a clue in his expression.

'I invited him to share a gift with me.' Tristen eyed her injured cheek. 'When he accepted I sealed the agreement with a Blood Kiss.'

'He drank your blood?'

'If you insist.' He smiled and that brilliant white light returned to his eyes. 'Get in here, Jason.'

The longing she felt winked out, quickly replaced by fear. Lenina felt the change and shoved the last few pieces of the door back into place. The weight of Jason's thoughts leaned against it, but she gritted her teeth and pinned it shut.

He grimaced at her. 'You don't know what you're doing, love. You need more than that to keep me out.'

His words gave Lenina a new idea. Squeezing her eyes shut, she swapped the image of a broken door to a sheer, impenetrable wall, built with concrete slabs three feet thick. No door, no cracks, no way through.

Jason's smile faded. 'How?' He stared at her and, though his eyes narrowed with concentration, Lenina felt nothing. She slumped against the wall, panting.

Slow claps came from Tristen's direction. 'When you're quite finished, we all need to have a—' he broke off. Thrust out one hand. 'Wait!'

The order came just in time.

Breathless and dizzy from her mental acrobatics, Lenina didn't see Jason move until he stopped, the tip of his rusting dagger quivering an inch away from her chest.

His wild expression matched the rasping breathing making his chest rise and fall. She smelled old meat and fresh blood on his breath. The sight of the weapon brought on another wild surge of hate and fury. It bubbled up within her, threatening to overcome reason until an answering stab of pain from her left cheek drowned it out. She shuffled sideways and when equidistant from the two men, she shared her gaze between them. 'Why are you doing this to me?'

'Yes, it's always about you, isn't it?'

Jason's grip tightened on the dagger. 'She's not allowed to live. I gotta kill her.'

'Then you should have done it properly instead of cutting up her face.'

'I tried—'

'Shut up.' The light in Tristen's eyes flared, then dropped back to its creepy white glow. 'And give me that before you do more damage.' He raised one hand in a scooping gesture. The dagger jerked from Jason's grip, flying through the air to land on Tristen's outstretched palm.

Lenina clutched the wall. Dizziness came and went in waves. 'How did you do that?'

He smiled, but didn't answer.

She sank to the floor. That seemed preferable to falling. She bit her lip. 'If you made— *Kissed* him, then you knew what I was. You knew what really happened in the park.'

'And what really happened to Nick,' he added.

She stopped breathing. Just for a second. When she started again, the breaths were short and fast. Too fast. Dizziness welled up again. The hallway blurred before her eyes.

'I can still do it.' Jason's voice held a note of desperation. 'Before Kallisto finds out. No one will know but me and you—'

'Shut up.' Tristen didn't raise his voice, but Jason broke off as though slapped. 'It's too late now. I can't go back to the police after tonight. I need something to satisfy Kallisto and the other Majestics.'

'But then she'll know *I* did it. Please don't. She'll kill me.'

'Not my problem.'

Though unsure, Lenina thought she saw the hint of a smile on Tristen's lips. Bemused, she glanced at Jason, watching him shuffle his fingers.

He stared at her as though seeking answers, his stare performing that same slide over her features. They stopped on the stitches across her left cheek. Colour drained from his face. Sweat beaded on his forehead. His lips trembled. 'That's the *Neeva*,' he whispered.

Tristen's lips flattened. 'What?'

'On her cheek. Look at the cut— the way it curves. The *Neeva*.'

'Don't be stupid.'

Jason crawled across the floor. Though she tried to scramble back, the walls blocked her passage, forcing Lenina into stillness as his hands grasped her chin. Firm but gentle, he turned her face to the light. His fingers were warm, a peculiar energy prickling between his skin and hers.

'It is. I'd know this sign anywhere.'

'Not possible,' Tristen snapped. 'It's a myth.'

Jason ignored him, shuffling back and dropping to his knees. He leaned forward, holding Lenina's gaze until his forehead touched the floor in a clumsy, prostrate bow. He turned his hands palms up to expose the wrists.

'I didn't know, love,' the cocky nickname died on his lips. 'I wouldn't have touched you if I knew. You gotta believe me.'

Lenina narrowed her eyes. Though she scrabbled through her memories, nothing could account for this abrupt display of reverent respect and fear.

'Get up and bring her.' Tristen moved towards the living area. 'We don't have time for this.'

'Master, I serve you,' Jason spoke right over him. 'I didn't know it was you. Please.'

Inching her toes away from his fingers, Lenina looked at Tristen. 'What's Neeva?'

'It's an adapted form of the Hebrew word "niv".' His voice was tight, his lips pursed. 'It means fang.'

Then she heard it. Like an echo or a whisper directly between her ears. She heard Kiya's voice from one of her visions, picking the name of Saar's army in honour of the birthmark on his right thigh.

All great men have memorable titles. Saar . . . leader of the Red Fang Army.

With that memory came another, this one more recent.

Passages from the crazy autobiography on the Internet. Xerxes' account of the vampire known as Saar and his promise to return following his death at Waterloo.

'The Vessel.'

Tristen's eyes widened. 'How do you know about that?'

'I read about it.' She backed away again, trying to keep both men in her line of sight. Jason didn't move, but Tristen followed, backing her along the hallway until her spine met the front door. Like before, the locks clicked into place.

She licked her lips. 'The Prophecy is true?'

'No.' He almost shouted it, his hands bunched into fists at his sides. After a deep breath he continued. 'Some believe it. I don't.'

Lenina glanced at Jason. She had no need to ask what he believed.

'It doesn't mean anything. Most God-Touched can't even agree on what it involves. Who the Vessel is supposed to be. When he shows up. It's like the Second Coming of Christ— not happening.'

Turning to the mirror, Lenina looked again at her reflection.

The stitched up wound looked red and angry. A smooth curve across her left cheek, reminiscent of a large fang.

Even the colour matched.

Jason made a sound like a kicked dog. He crawled across the floor and touched her foot. 'You'll protect me,' he said, lifting his head at last. Gone was the terror of moments ago. In its place was hope, so raw he appeared childlike. 'I made a mistake, but you're the Vessel, yeah? Kallisto and the others have been looking for so long . . . she'll forgive me if you tell her to. She'll thank me for finding you.'

Snarling, Tristen stretched past Lenina and grabbed Jason by the scruff. He heaved the other man off the ground and shoved him against the wall, pressing the point of the wavy dagger to the base of his throat. He held the position for long seconds, breathing hard through clenched teeth. When he looked up again the white light faded from his eyes.

'She's not telling Kallisto anything. There's nothing to tell. She's not the Vessel, she's not Saar and she isn't saving anybody. She's just a girl *you* Kissed when you should have known better. Kallisto's going to eat you for breakfast.'

'But . . .' Jason's slate grey gaze flicked to Lenina. 'Tell him. Tell him you're the Vessel.'

From the expression on Tristen's face, she didn't think it would help.

Instead she said, 'I don't want to die.'

Jason mewled, deep at the back of his throat. 'But it *is* you. Your face— how can you not see it?'

'You cut me with your dagger, that's all. There's nothing special about it.'

'Saar's dagger!' he insisted. 'And it would have healed if it were a normal wound. Vampire powers manifest after your first tribute and you've done that now. You drank. So why hasn't it healed?'

Lenina watched the point of the dagger shift away from Jason's throat. She saw him sigh and sink down the wall, but her own chest tightened when the blade swung towards her face. She froze as Tristen laid the weapon against her injured cheek.

'He's right,' he whispered. 'I saw you outside the house . . . any other wound would have healed before we got to the hospital. Before we even arrived at the scene. Why not this one?'

Words clogged Lenina's throat.

Tristen pressed closer, leaning his body into hers, his heat a stark contrast to the cool metal against her face. 'What are you?'

The point pricked her skin. A tiny drop of blood ran down the blade.

With it, Lenina felt another scalding rush of hate and anger, this time accompanied by a memory. She saw the same dagger through Saar's eyes, admiring its gems and wavy blade. He handed the weapon to Mosi with a smile, a kiss and the words, 'A gift, my love. From the gods to me, from me, to you.'

Shaking her head cleared the image in time to see Tristen staring at her, his mouth hanging open. 'What did you say?'

Until then Lenina hadn't realised she'd spoken aloud.

'Say it again,' he snapped. 'Say *exactly* what you just said.'

'A gift,' she whimpered. 'He said it was a gift from the gods. "From the gods to me. From me, to you".'

A gust of peppermint-scented air billowed over her face. 'This dagger did belong to Saar. He gave it to Mosi and he passed it down the line to me. I gave it to Jason. It always passes with those words. Those exact words.'

Lenina fought to keep her voice steady. 'I saw him give it to Mosi. They were standing in Cleopatra's palace in a room filled with pillars like an entry hall.'

The moment she said the words, she saw what had followed not long after.

Saar lay on the sand, crippled by the pain of his dying soldiers and the agony of watching Kiya die. Bleeding, helpless, he watched Mosi crawl closer, holding a rusted dagger with a wavy blade. It plunged down. Hit his chest. Pierced his heart.

'Oh, God.' Lenina's voice trembled.

'Saar took the dagger the same time he took the gods' gift,' Tristen tightened his grip on her face. 'No one knows the exact details, but some say it once belonged to Set. Legend says it has the blood of Horus and Set in the metal, from when they fought over Osiris' death.'

Jason gave a small moan. 'That's proof. It *must* be her. No one else *sees* Saar or gets his memories when they join us. She knows the ritual words. Where else would it come from?'

The point of the dagger left her cheek and trailed down the front of her borrowed sweatshirt.

She held her breath, watching the rusty metal leave tiny flakes on her chest. It stopped between her breasts.

'You can't be the Vessel.' Tristen stared into her eyes. 'You're just a spoilt brat with bad luck. Jason wasn't even interested in you. He loiters outside bridal boutiques waiting for the *grooms* to show up.'

Scrambling off the floor, Jason rushed over and put a trembling hand on Tristen's arm. 'Think. Even if you distract Kallisto with my cock-up, you're dead if she knows you killed the Vessel. We both are.'

'She's *not* the Vessel!'

'Then test her. The dagger will know. Give it blood and we'll know for sure.'

Lenina held Tristen's gaze. She watched the battle behind his eyes and felt the tension through his arms and shoulders as he shifted his weight on the dagger.

'Fine.' His expression never changed, but an instant later Tristen's hand plunged forward, driving the sharp point of the dagger through Lenina's sweatshirt.

The breath she held rushed from her body, propelled by the terrible impact. Pain tightened her lungs and she struggled to draw a fresh gulp of air. Then the dagger slid out, blade red and dripping. Blood followed in a slow ooze, rapidly soaking the sweatshirt.

Lenina cupped her hands around the entry wound, as if she might be able to catch the precious fluid.

Eyes wide, hands shaking, Jason lunged forward and caught her as her knees gave way. He lowered her to the ground, apologising over and over.

Tristen watched, the dagger hanging loose in his grip. Crimson drops rained from the tip. 'If you *are* the Vessel, this shouldn't be a problem for you to heal.' His voice softened, his gaze darting left and right as though unsure of the outcome he wanted. 'A stab to the heart would kill a normal God-Touched as young as you. But this dagger won't kill the Vessel.'

Lenina had just the time to catch the scent of cinnamon on the air before darkness swept in and swallowed everything.

ALEXANDRIA 5 MAY 36 BC

Chapter Twenty-One

Saar placed the fish into the cloth sack slung over his shoulder and added a loaf of bread. Fresh from the clay oven, it warmed his hip as he strode through the market. The smell of it, sharp and slightly yeasty, put up a valiant fight but was quickly overcome by the scent of the street.

The heat of the day enhanced many of the less savoury smells, meaning that the occasional waft of rotting food still caught his senses. Rubbing his nose with his free hand, he kept walking, now seeking beer. He bought four jugs from a vender beneath a red and blue striped stall, bartering hard before finalising the price.

A woman greeted him at the corner of two bisecting streets. 'Captain Saar, are you well? Been visiting the palace?' She spoke using the language of the Greeks. 'Battling for our safety again?'

'We're safe for the moment,' he responded in kind, the foreign words awkward on his tongue. He masked his discomfort with a smile for the veiled compliment. 'I'm visiting my mother. I have food for her.' A quick gesture to the bags and jugs.

'You're such a good man,' she simpered. 'Little wonder the gods smile on you.'

Saar lowered his gaze. 'You're very kind.'

'I look at you and the hundreds of other men who go to war. They're injured or killed and yet here you are. Untouched by it all.'

'And you take that to be the blessing of the gods rather than skill?'

'Who is it but the gods who bless us with skill?' She grinned and walked on.

Leaving the market area, Saar stepped off the road marked out with white and blue tiles. Behind him, the tall spires of the twin obelisks were visible, sharp points jabbing towards the clear blue sky. Ahead, the point where the two largest roads crossed buzzed with activity: people walking into stores, chatting on the street, listening to the musicians playing under the shade of a tall tree.

He passed the mausoleum dedicated to Alexander, the city's namesake, and angled north. His route took him clear of Brucheum entirely and into Rhakotis. Saar walked towards the port and the fresher scent of sea air.

Children darted past him, laughing. Two girls and a boy, all wearing nothing but their skin. A smile touched his lips as he recognised one of the chase games he had enjoyed in his younger days before joining the army.

One of the girls shrieked, speaking familiar and comfortable Egyptian. The other girl and the boy laughed again and sprinted away, forcing Saar to step aside to avoid the frantic charge.

Two streets on and within sight of the port and a large ship carrying goods from Rome, Saar became aware that he was being followed.

He heard the shuffle of footsteps trying to match his own. A glance over his shoulder revealed nothing, but the creeping sensation of eyes on his back continued to itch between his shoulder blades.

Saar stopped. 'Who are you?' He turned in a slow circle to search the street. 'Why do you follow me?'

A man dressed in shabby black stepped out from behind a well. 'You have keen senses, Captain Saar.'

He frowned. Even after so many years he was unused to being so well-known. 'Thank you. Did you wish to speak with me?'

'Yes, spare a coin or two to feed an old man?'

'Of course.' Saar didn't hesitate in pulling a handful of coins from his pouch. He passed them over without checking their value.

'May the gods forever smile on you.' Gripping the coins in one gnarled, hairy fist the stranger shuffled on.

Saar watched him round a corner and vanish from sight. Only when he was gone did he realise that the conversation had taken place in Greek. Strange that such a shabby, obviously poor man would understand the language of the richer inhabitants of the city. Saar himself only knew the language because Cleopatra insisted on teaching him, treating his education as a pet project to fill her spare time.

His old home matched the others he could see making a circle surrounding a narrow well: flat roofs, white walls and a scattering of windows. He saw a pair of blankets drying in two of the windows and an overhang of flowers from the roof. In the doorway stood his mother, grey hair wrapped in a small piece of cloth to protect it from the dust she swept into the street.

She smiled as he approached, put the sweeping rushes to one side and shuffled forward to kiss him on the cheek. 'I hoped I would see you today.'

'I brought supper.' The smell of bread grew stronger as he held up the bag.

'You didn't have to do that. Silly boy. Come inside, shelter from the sun.' Though old and frail, her grip was like bronze, and she tugged him into the cool interior of the two-roomed house.

On a low table he saw the first traces of supper, a heel of bread and the tail ends of two tiny fish. Two clay mugs stood beside them, filled with beer. He picked up the first and tipped it to his lips, grimacing when he found it watered down.

'Mother,' he began.

'No, Saar. Just sit with me. Not another word. And put that bag away. I won't be needing it.'

'I bought it for you.'

Panya snorted. 'Yes. As though you yourself don't need to be fed and watered.'

'I have more than enough at the palace. Please let me do this for you.'

She pushed away the proffered sack and sat on a stool made from a sawn tree trunk. 'No. Tell me about your day.'

Saar rolled his eyes. He nudged the sack beneath the table with his foot, then leaned forward, propping himself on his elbows. 'I'm to meet with the queen today.'

Delight shone in Panya's eyes. 'I'm so proud of you. I've never heard of another soldier given the confidence and attention she gives you. What do you think it means?'

'I don't know.' Tearing his gaze away, he looked down at his fingers instead, tracing the callouses across his palms and fingers.

'Perhaps she'll take you into her household or match you with one of her serving women. Imagine . . . my boy a member of the Pharaoh's household.'

'She asked only for my thoughts on the defence of the city.'

'Let me hope, Saar. I live for hope.' Panya pulled the cloth off her head and fanned out the grey strands of her thin hair. Standing, she crossed to a flat stone on the floor covered with a faint dusting of white powder. Pulling grain from the bowl beside it she spread it on the stone and picked up another heavier one to begin grinding.

Saar watched her, enjoying the sight of her delicate hands working so confidently.

'I hear talk of another statue. Do you know what it is?'

Saar's pleasure dimmed. 'Yes. It's of Cleopatra.'

Panya raised her eyebrows. 'Another?'

'Yes.'

'Perhaps you can convince our queen that yet another statue is not a sensible way to spend hard-mined gold?'

'I'm but a soldier, why should she listen to me?' He grinned. 'Besides, I lack your wisdom.'

'Wisdom is age, Saar, nothing more. You'll learn that in time. Youth is for action and doing. Age is for thinking and advising. You'll see.'

'I'm a soldier. I'll never see your age.'

'Don't be silly. The gods have great plans for you. Did they not mark you to be the mover of great things?'

Saar touched his right leg, high up on the thigh, close to the surface of the stool. 'A dream. A hope. Nothing more.'

'Why else would they position you in a role at which you excel? And why else would they coax Cleopatra to favour you? Make no mistake, the world will speak your name for years to come.'

Saar grinned and stood. He crossed to the kneeling woman and wrapped his arms around her. He felt the bird-like frailty of her arms and ribs and made his hug as gentle as he could manage. 'You're kind, Mother. Your faith keeps me strong.'

'And your strength gives me faith.'

'I must leave.'

'Of course. Take care on the streets.'

With one last hug, Saar left his mother to her grinding, slipping out of the house and back the way he came. He was pleased to realise that he had successfully left the bread, beer and fish beneath the table.

Despite the late hour, the sun rode high.

Saar felt the comforting warmth on his bare arms and thanked Re for lighting the sky with his golden warmth. He thanked Osiris for the food he was able to give to his struggling mother and Horus for his ongoing protection. After a moment of thought he spent a few moments asking

Sheshat for patience and wisdom during his visit to the palace.

On the edges of Rhakotis, just before entering Brucheum, he became aware, once more, that he was being watched. He stopped walking. One hand strayed to his belt knife.

A familiar figure stepped out from behind a tree, shaking back a dirt-encrusted sleeve to reveal a grimy hand with long, broken fingernails. 'Stay your hand, Saar. I mean you no harm.'

Saar took his hand away from his knife and placed it instead on the back of his neck where the small hairs prickled and stood on end.

Such a dirty and unkempt man stood out, even in Rhakotis where the people were poorer and the clothes less colourful.

'Why do you follow me? I've already given you coin.' He resisted the urge to wrinkle his nose.

'A mere test. One you passed easily.'

'Forgive me, wise one, but I cannot linger. I must—'

'Meet with the queen. Oh yes, I know. But not before you meet with the raven-haired beauty who awaits you in the grain stores.' The hairs on Saar's arms leapt up to match those on his neck. The man laughed. 'Stay your fear, I won't reveal you. I wanted only your attention.' His voice resembled the rattle of stones down a rocky slope.

'You have it. What do you want?'

The man lowered his hood with a hand as dirty as the other. Freed from the shadows, the face looking out brought to mind a walnut, wrinkled and pinched. The skin was as dark as Saar's own, though probably from the sun rather than a product of his natural colouring. Hair, scraggly and thin, surrounded his face in wisps like spiderwebs. His teeth were yellow, slightly pointed and fewer than they should have been. Most startling were his eyes: they were red, as though daubed with blood.

Saar took a step back.

The man laughed. 'I've startled you.'

'Your eyes . . .'

'I'm old, Saar. And ill. The sickness ruins my body and will eventually consume my sight. Do you pity me?'

He swallowed. 'Yes.'

'I don't need your pity.'

Ashamed, Saar let his shoulders relax and reclaimed his frightened step. 'Then please, speak. Tell me your name.'

The man bared his sharp teeth. 'Kazemde.'

Saar widened his eyes. 'And what message do you have for me?'

Grinning wider, the man shuffled forward to avoid the passage of a team of slaves carrying a litter. A waft of sweet scents billowed through the air through the silken curtains.

'You know the old words? Very good. I *am* a messenger. An ambassador, with a plan to help you save your city.'

'What do you mean?'

'Everybody knows. We outside the palace aren't fools, though we aren't royalty. Our position is delicate and requires gentle handling. Already Rome fears us, what with Arsinae's execution and the birth of Cleopatra's young children.'

Saar looked at his feet. 'While not the most diplomatic way to deal with her sister, the queen was correct in doing so. Rome believed that she worked in league with Cassius. We'd be at war now if not for her decisive action.'

'Perhaps. But what of her relationship with Antony?'

The mention of that name brought Saar's head up with a snap. 'He sought our support in arms, nothing more. He won't return.'

'You're certain?'

'He has no love for Egypt.'

The old man tapped his lips with one skinny finger.

Saar gathered his thoughts. It took some effort. 'What does this have to do with your message? You're well versed in politics; are you an ambassador of the Senate?'

Kazemde gave another of those dry, rocky laughs that turned into a hacking cough somewhere in the middle. 'Do I look like a servant of the Senate?'

'No.'

'My message concerns power. The power of the gods.'

'I don't understand.'

Kazemde raised himself to his full height and though that wasn't very far, the effect was startling. 'Meet me tonight, when the moon rides high in the sky.' Gone was the rattle of stones from his voice. Instead, he spoke with strong, authoritative tones. 'Beneath the sands outside Alexandria is a cluster of caves. Go to the island of Pharos and enter the tower. Find the stone with a carved mark in the likeness of a bared sword and from there you may enter the caves.'

Saar hid a scoff behind his hand. 'There are no caves beneath the tower, only the bed of the sea.'

'The secret I keep is such that it must be well hidden, of course you know nothing of them.'

He backed off, shaking his head. 'Forgive me, but I must go.'

'I offer you a gift, Saar. Power to change the world. You need only believe and trust me.'

Without looking back, Saar walked on, passing into the Greek quarter to meet his queen.

'When you come, bring no weapons. No jewellery. Bring no doubt. Bring only yourself and the clothes on your back.'

'As you wish, old man.' He moved faster, aware that he would be late for his meeting with Kiya.

Kazemde gave one last shout. 'Tell Antony that I wish him many congratulations on his coming wedding to the Nea Isis.'

Gaping, Saar whirled around, but the man was already gone, vanished from the streets as though he had never been. Wiping his mouth, Saar searched high and low before running on, his mind now filled with thoughts of Antony.

Chapter Twenty-Two

Saar glanced over his shoulder, skimming the narrow passage in both directions. But for a pair of spear-slender cats slinking through the shadows he saw no one.

Satisfied, he kept moving, wedging his body through the gap between two large rows of grain bins. At the far end he saw a loaf of bread on a blanket beside a cold smoked fish and a handful of dried dates.

He sighed. 'This is a wonderful surprise, Kiya, but I cannot stay to enjoy it. Please forgive me.'

The woman in question stepped out from behind one of the bins, her silky robes fluttering behind her. Her large, dark eyes narrowed as she approached, an effect compounded by the dark smudges of kohl around them. 'You're late.'

'I was delayed.' He thought back to Kazemde and his curious claims about the tower at Pharos. 'I cannot eat with you.'

'Why?' She moved closer, running her delicate hands up and down his arms, a touch that made him shiver. 'Do you not love me?'

'Of course I do.' He kissed her lips. 'But I have other matters to attend. Higher things.'

She stiffened in his arms. 'Higher than me?'

'Don't misunderstand me, I—'

'I don't. You said it yourself. "Higher things."' Kiya jerked away. 'I may be a servant, but I'm no fool. I know what happens in the palace, perhaps better than you.'

He tried to touch her face. 'I would never—'

'You do.' She backed away. 'Much like the other men who seek my attention, you think me beautiful, dainty and foolish. I'm not a flower to be admired, nor a child to be coddled, I'm a woman. Remember that.'

Saar gazed at his toes. 'I meant no offence. I'd never insult you willingly or knowingly. I meant only that my worries are of things higher than myself. Problems that none but the gods can solve. I want to know the minds of men but I'm no god. I'm mortal just as you are and these problems may not be beyond you, but they are certainly beyond my humble knowledge.'

She smiled. The gesture was beautiful. Re's light seemed to fill her whole face and dimples appeared on her cheeks, visible as darker shadows against the rich brown of her sun-kissed skin. 'I never thought I would hear you say it.'

'Say what?'

'That something— anything— was beyond you, dear love. You who fixes everything.'

'I don't fix everything.'

The smile widened. 'You try. You feel all the troubles of the world so keenly. They touch you like no other man I've ever met.'

'You exaggerate.'

'Do I? Why else do you fight so passionately and walk the streets among the common men?'

Staring at the sacks of grain, Saar clenched his hands into fists. 'I'm captain. It's my duty to ensure that the people are buoyed up by the knowledge of our strength. They must see confidence in their leaders to feel the same themselves.'

'While that is true, must you also pander to the silly whims of Cleopatra?'

'She's my queen.'

'And mine, but she will not touch me. Never. My body is for you. Why can you not say the same?'

At last, Saar turned away from the grain. He put his arms around Kiya's slender shoulders to pull her against him. She sighed and linked her arms around his neck.

'I love you. Nobody but you. Cleopatra is young but powerful. I can't afford to displease her. Please understand that.'

Kiya pushed on to her tiptoes and kissed him. 'Eat with me.'

Juicy dates and warm bread lured him towards the blanket, but Saar shook his head. 'I'm sorry. I came only to touch your face and kiss your lips. I'm wanted in the palace.'

Her expression darkened. 'Cleopatra. Again.'

'Yes, but—'

'No, Saar, go. Stand in her rooms and let her touch you and treat you as one of her many other toys. I'll stay here.'

When he tried to see her face, she jerked away, sitting on the end of the blanket and reaching for the bread. She tore the soft flesh of the loaf between her fingers and shoved it into her mouth.

'I'm sorry, Kiya.'

She turned away, still shredding the loaf into inedible fragments.

After lingering for a moment longer, Saar shook his head and walked back the way he came.

Bright sunlit hallways and cool floors covered with rushes and rugs: Saar barely saw them as he marched through the palace, too preoccupied to offer a nod or a smile to those who passed. By the time he reached the doors he sought, his stomach had twisted into tight knots. Clearing his throat, he knocked once on the huge wooden doors and entered.

The chamber within was also bright and warm. Statuettes of cats and symbols of the sun god filled every available space. In amongst the treasures were coins, pots, flowers and the occasional tapestry woven from fine silks. In the middle of the room, reclined in a large stone bath lay Cleopatra, her thick black hair braided and piled high on her head. She swivelled when he entered, spilling milk over the sides to wash across the floor and dampen the rushes. The girls attending her immediately closed ranks to block her from view.

'My Lady Queen,' he said, stopping a respectable distance away. 'I had no idea you were still bathing. I'll return when you've finished.'

'No.' The voice came before he could turn away.

The cluster of women, dressed in diaphanous robes of white and cream, stepped to one side. Between them, Cleopatra looked over the side of the bath, her arms crossed beneath her chin. Thick rings of black kohl highlighted her eyes, and across her lips some red substance gave her the look of a perpetual pout. Though her face needed no such assistance to look appealing.

Saar gazed at her and understood Kiya's anger. He had to admit Cleopatra was an attractive woman, but her appeal faded once past the face and body. She was young and selfish, petty and fickle.

A cascade of grimy milk slid from her body as Cleopatra stood. Two more women approached with clay jugs and rinsed her skin with clear water. Then the queen put out one leg and one hand, a silent order for assistance. Once safely on the ground, she extended her arms and the women draped a gown of fresh white linen over her damp skin. She smoothed it into place, belted the waist with a golden cord and stepped towards him.

'So modest.' Her voice teased him like a physical caress. 'Will you not look at me?'

'It's not proper,' he murmured, watching his feet. 'I have no place to—'

'To see my body? I'm queen; I may show my body to whomever I please. Look at me.' She clicked her tongue. 'Look at me.'

When he raised his eyes, she held the golden cord in both hands. Water dripped from the shorter strands of hair at the back of her neck and ran down her shoulders. One drop slid through a gap in the linen, marking the path between her breasts.

Saar licked his lips. Swallowed. Looked away again.

Cleopatra giggled. 'Men. So hard, commanding and fierce, but put them before a woman and they lose their heads. Please, Saar. Look at me.'

He dragged his gaze back to hers. Forced it to stay there and watch as she untied the cord and opened the sides of the robe. She pushed it back from her shoulders and stood before him naked and beautiful.

'Do you love me?'

He flinched. 'You're my queen.'

'I know. Answer the question.'

'With all my heart, my flesh and my sword.'

She grinned. 'Really?'

'Of course, My Lady Queen.'

'Then touch me.'

Saar looked directly into her eyes. They were green, a colour brought forward and made brighter by the incredible contrast made by the kohl. The pale smoothness of her skin, so different to his own, was flushed.

'Touch me.'

Fingers trembling, Saar touched her bare shoulder.

She frowned. 'Touch me properly.'

'I— I'm sorry,' he fought the urge to look back to the floor.

'Here.' Cleopatra snatched his hand and held it against her left breast. She splayed her fingers over his, trapping him in place. 'I enjoy the rough touch of your skin. A soldier's hands.'

Beads of sweat gathered on his forehead. 'I think—'

'My lady, Cleopatra. What are you doing now?' The voice came from near the doors and, beneath his hand, the queen stiffened.

She glared at him then shoved his hand away, stooping to scoop her robe back into her arms with one smooth motion. Feeding her arms into it, she then stalked past him to reach the newcomer.

'Antony!' She paused with her hands outstretched.

Saar saw the pleasure in her eyes as surely as he felt his own heart sink.

'I thought you would never return, it has been many years.' Her voice became breathless.

'Just four.' The man crossed the room and swept the queen into his arms.

Saar glared at him, hating every inch of his smug round face and short curly hair. Even his clothing, a mix of cloth, leather and metal, made him want to punch something.

Cleopatra giggled. 'I've missed you. I've been lonely without you.'

'I'm sure you found willing servants to warm your bed.'

The look Antony shot over her shoulder might have frozen a weaker man, but Saar merely ducked his head and tried to look as innocent as possible.

When sure that he had his voice and emotions under control, he spoke. 'My Lord Antony, I thought you were in Rome?'

'I was.' The other man stroked the trim bush of hair about his chin and jaw. 'And I returned. Does that please you?'

Rather than lying, Saar cleared his throat and returned his focus to Cleopatra. 'You wished to speak with me, My Lady Queen?'

'Yes,' she tried to step forward but Antony's arm around her shoulders snagged her back. 'I have questions about the latest defence plan.'

Antony's nostrils flared. 'What defence plan?'

'Saar outlined a plan to improve our general defences.'

'I gave no order for that.'

The familiar prickle began to tease down Saar's spine. Four years apart clearly hadn't dampened that fire. 'In your absence I was charged with the city's defences. I take my responsibilities very seriously and I serve the queen.'

Dark eyes, above a hard hooked nose, narrowed to tiny slits. 'And I, as king, take my duties very seriously. We are strong and well prepared. Our naval fleet is unparalleled and our infantry has no match. No one within a thousand miles has any desire or means to attack us.'

The word 'king' made Saar flinch. So did 'us'. But he could see no way to question either without overstepping the line he already walked with reckless abandon. He angled himself towards Cleopatra. 'My Lady

Queen,' he whispered, 'these plans are essential. Without extra men on the borders and within the palace themselves, any attack could lead to innumerable casualties. Please consider what I have to say.'

Cleopatra, dwarfed beneath Antony's massive arm, gave him a winsome smile. 'You worry too much. If Antony says there is no need of any further defence then I'm sorry to have wasted your time.'

He gritted his teeth. 'Will you at least hear me? Perhaps some part of my plans will interest you.'

'She said "no", Saar.' Antony actually smiled. 'Now get out.'

He stared at Cleopatra, silently pleading, but she had already turned away, waving an absent hand towards the exit.

His shoulders slumped. 'My Lady, Queen.' Bowing once, Saar stepped around the pair and aimed for the door.

'Captain Saar?' The voice swung him round.

With Cleopatra still trapped beneath his left arm, Antony lifted his free hand and pointed at his face. 'If you touch my wife again I'll have your hands removed.'

'Wife?'

Cleopatra squealed. 'You returned to marry me?'

'Of course. I would never have left but for the small matter of the Parthians. Now that they're dealt with, I'll stay with you.'

'No!' The word burst free before he could catch it. Saar slapped his hands over his mouth but the damage was done.

Very slowly Antony turned away from the queen. His eyes narrowed and deep furrows formed in his forehead. 'Yes. In the way of *your* people. With ancient rites I'll marry Cleopatra and make Alexandria my home. Are you happy for us?'

Saar bit his lip. It was the only way to keep the scream from bursting free. 'Of course, My Lord. Congratulations.'

'King,' he snapped, arching one thick eyebrow. 'I'll be king, you'd do well to grow accustomed to that fact.'

'Yes, My Lord, King.' With a last, despairing look at Cleopatra, Saar spun on his heel and dashed from the room.

Chapter Twenty-Three

Over his crunching footsteps, Saar heard the yip-yapping call of a desert fox. Though the lights of the city were small and distant, the sky was clear enough that Saar had no need of the torch he held. It remained unlit at his side, the moon's white glow more than enough to light his way along the Hepastadion. The long line of piled earth stretched from the mainland to Pharos Island where the lighthouse watched the ocean.

Waves from the Nile washed over his path, showering his feet with cool droplets. Half way along he turned and trotted back towards the mainland. He shook his head, hands shaking as he cursed himself for a fool. After three steps he stopped. Looked back at the island.

It took every piece of strength he possessed to once more angle his feet towards the Pharos. As he did, his insides squirmed, a peculiar mix of fear and excitement.

He walked on.

At the tall stone wall surrounding the tower, he took a deep breath and approached the gate. Though late, two guards stood before it, there to defend the tower, but also to maintain the fire at the top of the third level. Saar looked up, marvelling at the incredible height. He could think of no other building as tall as this one and a fierce rush of pride swelled his chest.

'Stop!' The voice came from ahead of him. 'Who approaches the tower?'

He raised his hand. 'Saar, son of Yafeu, of Cleopatra's guard.'

The men at the gate straightened their shoulders. 'Forgive me, Captain. We didn't recognise you.'

'There's nothing to forgive. Let me pass, and return to your duties.'

The young pair, fresh and unscarred by battle, exchanged nervous looks.

'What?'

'None but Pharos attendants may enter the tower at night.'

Saar chewed his thumbnail. 'Strange. I've never heard this order, though I longed to give it.'

The second of the pair looked down at his feet. 'Lord Antony sent word at dusk, the light is an important guide to our ships and must be protected at all times.'

'I agree, but surely I'm not included in that order.'

'Anyone, Captain. Including soldiers unless they present Antony's token or seal. Other delicate or vulnerable points through Brucheum have received the same orders.'

Saar gritted his teeth, pondering if he felt able to lie. Finally he said, 'Antony's orders are sound and I'm happy to follow them. However I have urgent business within that cannot wait.' He thought again of Kazemde, with his withered hands, mottled skin and frightening insight into palace politics. 'Let me pass.'

With another of those shared glances the men shook their heads. 'Sorry, Captain.'

Stepping back from the gate Saar studied the walls. The pale stone was smooth and the gaps between them lined with molten lead to withstand the pounding action of the sea. There would be no climbing that way.

'Men,' he said, 'you do a fine job in protecting the Pharos, but my mission must go forth. Step aside.'

'If the mission is so important, why not return to the city? Obtain a seal and we will let you through.'

The idea of having anything further to do with Antony put Saar's teeth on edge. Desperation over the Roman's sudden return had fuelled this mad mission in the first place.

'No time. It must be now.'

The soldiers stood firm.

Saar sighed, levelled his torch and held it like a club. 'Please move.'

The younger of the men looked alarmed. His hand tightened on the shaft of his spear. 'Captain?'

He bit his lip. Thoughts of Kiya strayed through his mind. Of his mother. Of the latest limestone monstrosity built to honour Cleopatra, the self-styled 'new Isis.' He saw Antony and the gleeful expression in the eyes of the queen as she agreed to marry him.

Within hours, Antony had already made his presence known by issuing orders to the military over Saar's head. What else would he change if given the opportunity? If there was even the smallest chance that Kazemde had the answer, Saar couldn't afford to let it go.

'Re, forgive me,' he murmured. He stepped forward, thrusting up with the torch as he went. It cut a sharp arc through the air, and struck the first soldier in the face. Blood burst from his split lip and nose, almost black in the moonlight.

The man screamed and dropped his spear, falling against the gates to clutch his face. The second, though clearly alarmed, recovered quickly and advanced to parry. Saar struck at his spear shaft, snapping it. Then he kicked the man in the stomach, a powerful blow that sent him reeling.

Both men writhed on the ground. The second guard would recover in time, but the first looked pale and frightened.

Saar bent down to him, tugging off his overtunic as he did so. He wadded it up and put it beneath the moaning man's head. 'Your bones may be broken,' he said after a glance. 'Don't move until help arrives. Try not to speak.'

'Captain, why?' The winded man gave a wheezing gasp.

'To save us all. Please believe that.' Pausing long enough to swap his torch for the remaining functional spear, he stepped over the two men and through the gate.

It was quiet within, civilian residents having long retired for the night. Soldiers walking the perimeter kept watch for any intruder quick, sly or crazy enough to scale the walls. Hugging the inside wall, Saar searched the stones beneath his feet, seeking a mark in the shape of a bared sword.

Despite the brightness of the moon on the Hepastadion, the area inside the Pharos lay beneath the shadow of the tower, with patches of deep black amongst the paler ones. He heard approaching footsteps and hurried on, keen to keep a blind corner between himself and pursuit.

Only when he heard raised voices did he realise that the patrolling men would have to be blind not to see the injured pair at the gate.

Saar cursed and moved faster, bent double and straining his sight. The stones beneath his feet bore no marks, bared sword or otherwise, having been trampled flat and smooth by the passage of hundreds of feet.

The voices behind him became shouts and the sound of running feet cut the air. Saar gripped his stolen spear and turned to face them. Men he had trained with. Fought with. Laughed with.

His shoulders slumped. He couldn't harm them. Not for doing their sworn duty. It didn't matter that his mission was the same as theirs.

Dropping the spear he ran on, watching the stones as he went. On the second corner he ran into another soldier. Literally. Bouncing off his wide, thick chest, Saar stumbled back several steps.

'Wasret.' He steadied himself and took another step back.

'Captain! Why are you here?'

He hesitated.

'I heard shouts. Help me defend the tower.'

Saar backed further away, his gaze darting to and fro.

Wasret gaped. 'You?' He drew his sword and, though his shoulders shook, his grip was firm. 'What have you done?'

'Nothing. This is for the good of us all.'

Wasret's sword never wavered. 'What could possibly be so important that you flout the king's orders?'

Rage bubbled through Saar's attempts to reason. 'He is *not* king.'

'He will be, second only to the queen in the line of command.'

'Antony isn't fit for any command. Cleopatra has no need of him.'

'You've finally lost your senses. Age has dulled your mind, no soldier should live as long as you have.'

'I don't have time for this, let me by. This is for the good of the city.'

'You know I can't do that.'

Though Wasret was bigger, stronger and younger, Saar had the skill and experience on his side. He knocked aside the advancing sword with the flat of his hand and took a large step forward. Grabbing Wasret about the shoulders, he drove his forehead into the larger man's nose. Wasret grunted but didn't fall, angling his sword for a back slice. The blade bit flesh and Saar caged a cry of pain behind clenched teeth.

'Here!' Wasret bellowed. 'He's here!'

'You don't know what you're doing.' Saar winced as he spoke.

'I know Antony will have you killed for this.'

With a jolt Saar realised Wasret was right. His hatred for the Roman interloper paled in comparison to the smouldering fury he received in return. If caught, there would be no safety.

A smile widened Wasret's lips. 'Yes . . . you understand. Antony will kill you. Cleopatra will do as she pleases and this strange quest will come to nothing.'

'Then I mustn't fail.'

Diving between Wasret's widespread legs, Saar flipped on to his back and kicked at the backs of the taller man's knees.

The screams filled his ears, stabbing his brain like knives. Nausea boiled through his gut and threatened to paralyse him, but the image of Antony's leering face spurred him forward. Saar scrambled away from Wasret's shrieks and ran on.

The sound of shouts and tramping feet grew louder. Rounding the third corner of the outer square, Saar saw more men approaching and clenched his fists. He cut right. An arrow whistled through the air near his cheek. Double doors loomed before him, leading into the lower section of the tower itself. Sand scuffed beneath him as he dived through. Inside, Saar spun about and slammed the doors shut, pulling the shaft which lowered the locking bar.

The core of the tower was formed of limestone, sparsely decorated. A set of steps led to the next level, just visible in the shadows cast by torches hanging from the walls. He heard pounding on the doors and knew that men stationed in the octagonal second level would soon arrive to help. Grabbing one of the torches, he carried it around the walls, watching the floor as he went.

Three circuits later, with no sign of a curved sword anywhere, Saar wiped sweat off his face. He tried to stop his fingers shaking, but the true implications of his actions made it difficult. If caught, he would never see his mother again. Nor Kiya.

Saar bit his lip as he considered the possibility that Antony himself had sent Kazemde to find him. It would be just like the man to choose such an underhanded method of removing obstacles.

The air seemed hot. Sticky. Close. He rolled his shoulders, conscious of the ache in his back from Wasret's lucky sword strike. More sand shifted beneath his feet. His skin tingled as fear crawled over him, making the hairs on his neck stand on end.

'No . . . it has to be here.'

On his hands and knees, Saar crawled across the floor, nose scraping the dust. One hand held the torch aloft, giving his gait a painful rolling quality as he neared the bottom of the steps. Heavy pounding rocked the main doors. The wood whined beneath the impact. His hand brushed a jagged peak in the stone, slicing his palm and staining the cold surface with red. A faint scratch appeared on the stone, picked out by a smear of blood. Small. About the length of his finger.

Dry air caught in his lungs. Saar dropped the torch and scraped the stone with both hands, smearing his blood all over it until he could see the rest of the scratch marks. A curve like a scimitar and a shorter straight mark. Like a handle. Or a hilt.

Saar laughed. His breath flooded out in a great rush. 'It's real!' Grabbing the torch again, he jabbed around the edges of the stone slab, alternately working his fingers into the tiny gap.

Nothing.

'No!' He beat the stone with his fists. Stamped on it. Struck the sword mark with the butt of the torch.

'Please, no!'

The shadows of men descending the stairs began to flicker across the room. Their shouts grew louder.

'I'm Saar! Kazemde sent me.' He beat it again with both fists and leaned on one corner. 'Please help me.'

The slab began to rumble.

He had the vague impression of soldiers arriving at the bottom of the stairs before the slab tipped up and dropped Saar into darkness.

He screamed as he fell; relief, fear and desperation mingled into one. He fell until he imagined he might land in the belly of the earth, never again to see sun or stars.

Then his feet hit water and he plunged into a pool of salty, icy cold. Using hands and feet he struck out for the surface, but it never seemed to come. The current tugged him on, spinning him, twirling him, twisting him round. He floundered in darkness so deep, he no longer knew which way was up. Pain filled his chest, rushing through his lungs like the stale air he longed to release. He let it go, then fought back a rush of panic knowing he needed to replace it.

Gold stars swam across his vision. His skin grew numb all over except for the wound on his back that burned in the chilly salt water. Terrible thudding filled his ears, the desperate racing of his own heart.

His fingers struck sand. Fighting waves of nausea, Saar flipped round. Both feet kicked off the solid surface and he pushed himself through the darkness. Salty water squeezed through his lips. The ocean flooded into his mouth and Saar screamed with the last scraps of breath left to him.

Cold air touched his face.

Gasping, Saar floundered in the water, his hands clutching at nothing. Echoes of splashing water and his own ragged breathing bounced back at him.

Something hard knocked his head. Under once more. This time Saar led with his hands, feeling above his head until his fingers flexed in the open air again.

The bobbing water lifted him up and down and with each movement his palms brushed stone. With one arm extended to feel the roof, the other groping for the sides, Saar caught his breath and let the water carry him on.

His gasps continued to echo around him, like the sinister whispers of an invisible watcher hanging over his shoulder.

Chapter Twenty-Four

Saar's numb fingers slipped away from the wall. The impact with the water splashed his face and brought him back to full consciousness though opening his eyes made no difference to what he could see.

The water carried him on, with no way of knowing how far. Gentle sloshing filled his ears with a rhythmic quality he equated to marching drills outside the palace. The comparison soothed him, but not enough to ignore the shivers in his limbs. Though head and shoulders above the surface, everything else felt numb and thick in the water.

He licked his cracked lips and turned slowly, facing back up the tunnel. Still nothing.

When the ceiling dipped suddenly and cracked the back of his head, Saar found comfort in the fact that it hadn't hit his face. Regardless, as the lapping water closed over his head again, he felt a chill that had nothing to do with the damp around him. What if he continued underground forever? What if the ceiling dipped and prevented him from snatching another breath of air? Would he be cast out to sea?

Breaking the surface, he blinked the droplets from his eyes and concentrated on staying afloat, this time with one hand feeling ahead.

His fingers waved through the darkness.

Saar gasped and waved his hand again. Hope made him shout aloud and the sound bounced back at him, over and over until it filled his head. He didn't care . . . he could see his fingers.

Encouraged by the thought of light and an exit, he pushed off from the wall and began to swim, aiding the current in taking him forward. With each stroke he saw his hands plunge in and out of the water. Around him the walls began to glitter, tiny mineral deposits lined the rough surface. The ceiling lifted away gradually, until the sound of his breathing echoed around him. Saar had just the time to recognise the difference before the water fell away and he plunged into another pool.

Shafts of silver light stretched across his face and high above long spikes of jagged rock pierced down from the rocky ceiling. Between them he saw flashes of night sky, dotted with stars. To the left, the walls of the tunnel stretched back and widened, a large opening with a flat, sandy floor. Beyond that, a flickering orange glow made Saar cry out again. Twisting in the water he swam towards the torch light.

A lifetime later he dragged himself on to the sand, squeezing the damp grains beneath his fingers. It hurt his skin, but Saar didn't care, clinging to the earth like he once grasped his mother.

Gradually his breathing slowed. Muscles relaxed. His teeth chattered and though Saar could see his fingers digging into the sand he could no longer feel them. Reaching his feet took several attempts but when he did, he inched towards the golden light. Another tunnel. But for the single torch at its entrance, no light fell here. Though dry, flat and straight, Saar could see nothing once it angled away.

Another tremble from his legs convinced him that an attempt to climb through one of the holes in the ceiling would be foolhardy. So he took the torch from the wall, put his free hand on the wall and walked on. Brisk walking soon chased away the goosebumps and dried his clothing. Eventually his shivers lessened, then stopped completely. A bead of sweat slipped down his back.

So soon after the fear of drowning, Saar pondered the depth of his new course. The distance from his home. The stillness weighed on him like three layers of armour until his steps became slow and shuffling.

The tunnel began to curve. Beneath his fingers, the walls changed from rough-hewn rock, littered with jagged edges, to smooth stone with faint ridges. Seconds later, he realised that his fingers traced not the natural contours of rock, but the man-made etches of carved glyphs. They arced up then down, a constant stream he could just see vanishing beyond the nimbus of light thrown by the torch. Beyond that light he might well have stood on the edge of the Underworld and never known it.

'I knew you would come.'

Saar yelped when he heard the voice. He dropped the torch. The flame died, plunging him into darkness.

Shame rose quickly to mingle with fear and he placed both hands over his chest. They were clammy, the fingers trembling as he flattened them to his skin. He heard panting, and several seconds passed until he understood it was his. Until that moment, he hadn't fully understood the silence of the tunnel. 'Who's there?'

'Come closer.'

From the direction of the voice came a new glow, just visible as Saar's eyes adjusted to the loss of his torch. He hurried towards it, telling himself that the haste in his steps was to do with impatience, not fear.

As he left the mouth of the tunnel, he saw a circle of waist-high torches with purple flames grouped around a vast stone altar. He gazed at the stone slab, mentally measuring it as at least his own height in width. Twice that in length. On the altar lay a dagger. The blade was long, perhaps a foot in length with an edge that formed a sinuous wave on both sides. The flats of the blade were marked with curious shapes and spirals, perhaps a dialect, but not one Saar knew. Smooth gold formed the handle, studded with gems of white and blue with a pommel at the end in the shape of a skull. From its jaws a long tongue protruded, a thin coil of silver.

Tearing his gaze from the weapon, Saar took in the rest of the chamber. Smooth walls, built in a domed shape with a small hole at the top through which more stars were visible.

Proof of the outside world eased some of the tightness in his chest. After so long below ground in such deep, thick silence, it was easy to doubt the existence of a world beyond that immediately around him. When cool air breezed through the hole in the ceiling, Saar inhaled deeply and reminded himself of home.

In the middle of it all, behind the altar, stood a figure he recognised well.

'Kazemde.'

The old man smiled. He approached from the far side of the altar, both hands hidden within his voluminous sleeves. With the hood thrown back he looked as he had in the market place, though darker. Colder. More . . .

Saar shivered.

'Power. That's what you feel.'

'You know my thoughts?'

'I read your body. Reading minds is for higher creatures.'

He stepped closer. 'You tried to kill me. You sent me to fall to my death.'

Kazemde spread his hands. 'And yet here you are.'

'I almost drowned.'

'But you didn't. You survived. As always. The gods favour you.'

'Luck favours me.'

'Few men have the "luck" you have. All these years, so many battles. But you need more than luck to save your city.'

Talk of Alexandria reminded Saar of why he had made this terrible journey in the first place. He chewed his thumbnail.

'Antony has returned. He plans to marry the queen.'

'Of course and in so doing he will become king at her side.' Kazemde appeared unconcerned.

'He's already married to Octavia. Do you think her brother will let such a slight go unpunished? But Cleopatra is besotted, she'll do anything Antony asks, even if it means war.'

'A delicate situation.'

Saar pounded his fists against the altar. 'Then help me.'

Kazemde bared his teeth. 'What do you know of Horus?'

'You insult me. Horus is the god of the sky. The sun. The moon. God of war. He watches me above all others. Why?'

'What of his relationship with Set?'

Saar's eyes narrowed. 'Even the smallest child knows the tale. Set killed his father, Osiris, and scattered the bloodied remains. What does that have to do with what you offer?'

'Everything.' Kazemde bent and retrieved a large stone bowl from behind the altar. The sides were etched with pictures, symbols Saar recognised as those for both Horus and Set. In the dim light, he struggled to see what liquid it held but for the fact it was black and thick.

'Horus attacked Set and sliced from him those dangling sacs with which he might one day bear a child of his own. In retaliation, Set pierced and stole the left eye of the falcon-headed warrior and so their battle ended. From the last battlefield Set collected the spilled blood and kept it as a reminder of how jealousy can spiral out of control. How war between two can infect the lives of many.' Kazemde set the bowl on the altar and stepped back. 'This is his gift to you.'

Saar snorted. 'That bowl contains the blood of Horus?'

'Blood of the gods, cherished over the years to be gifted to one worthy of its power. Look around you, read the messages on the walls. This was once a temple.'

He shook his head. Unease lifted the hairs on the back of his neck as he gazed into those steady red eyes. 'You mean to make a fool of me.'

'Why would I stand before you and waste my time? Yours? Though I have many years' claim in this world, I've none to waste in bringing gifts such as these before weaklings and non-believers. Hundreds of men have died for this power. Others have killed to possess it. Only those strong enough to use it may do so. Many have tried, all failed.'

'Many? Like who?'

'Sensuret. Ramesses.'

'Lies. These Pharaohs lived before your time.'

'Really? How old am I?'

Saar stiffened and looked more critically at the figure before him. 'Forty summers. No more than that.'

A laugh. Kazemde coughed, wheezed and beat his chest. 'You flatter me.'

'How many then?'

'Two thousand.'

The room seemed to pitch and dip. Fingers splayed, Saar clutched at the altar and held on, waiting for his knees to regain their strength. 'Impossible.'

'Believe what you wish, but I have seen many things. I know many things. And this,' he nudged the bowl, 'is your only hope.'

'No.' Yet even as he spoke, Saar remembered the startling accuracy in Kazemde's words about Antony and his union to the queen. He licked his lips. 'You're a spy.'

Kazemde smiled. 'Would a spy know of the blemished skin beneath your seat shaped like the curve of a lion's fang? The mark which convinced your mother to enlist you as a solider before you finished nuzzling at her breast?'

Saar gripped his right thigh, high up beneath his buttocks. 'Nobody knows of that mark.'

'Just your slave-whore, Kiya?' Kazemde smirked. 'And Cleopatra, I suppose.'

Growling, Saar lurched across the altar to grab the laughing figure. Eel-like, the old man wriggled out of range, with speed that belied his frail frame.

'Now I know why you insisted "no weapons", you knew I would kill you.' He clutched his head with both hands. 'Antony will kill me for what I've done today. I'll never see my loved ones again. And for what? Lies, tricks and insults.' Spinning on his heel, Saar walked to the mouth of the tunnel and back into the darkness.

'And if you return to the city with no aid? Antony won't let you defend the city, so how do you expect to save it?'

He froze. 'That was a private conversation.' His steps dragging, Saar returned to the altar. He leaned over it, flinching back when his fingers touched sticky patches of blood. 'What have you done?'

Unconcerned, Kazemde shrugged. 'Nothing is free. You of all men should understand that. The power of blood is bought *with* blood. Take it if you dare.'

'Why me?'

'The fact that you ask makes you a perfect candidate for such power. You're strong. Kind. The good of the city is your only desire and that makes you pure. That purity gives you the power to use this gift. Imagine what you could do with the blessing of the gods.'

Saar touched the bowl. So smooth beneath his fingers. Cool. The black liquid within clung to the sides like ichor and left dark smears in its wake.

Over the faint crackle of torch flames he imagined the sound of whispers. A soft voice calling his name.

He shuddered. 'How does it work?'

'Drink it.'

The whispers intensified.

Saar picked up the bowl and brought it close to his face. Rank waves rose from the liquid's dull surface, bringing to mind rotten food and dead things baking in the sun.

He gagged. 'Why does it smell so foul?'

'I've waited many years for a man suited to this gift. Even great things cannot last forever.'

The whispers grew louder until they were no longer whispers but clear voices. Saar whirled as they called his name. Shivered as they demanded he drink.

'Who's there?'

'The way to this temple is shut. It is but you and I here.'

Again he turned. His gaze darted to and fro across the chamber. Shadows took on sinister shapes in the corner of his eye, but each time they shifted before he could face them. 'I hear others. They tell me to drink.'

Kazemde's eyes widened. 'Why do you resist?'

'I fought my men to reach this place.' His fingers trembled on the sides of the bowl. The dark liquid within sloshed up the sides. 'I hurt one and crippled another. If not for the water their blood would stain my hands and face.'

'Then you've already paid with blood. The gift is yours. Take it. Drink.

Become all that you can be.'

'What will it do to me?'

'You'll see like an owl, hear like a cat, smell like a wolf. Tastes will become stronger for you. Your body will be more attuned to the changes in the air. You'll be sensitive. Faster. Stronger.'

Saar straightened. 'Stronger?'

'Like no other man on earth. Touched by the blood of gods, their strength will mingle with yours.'

Still he hesitated, staring into the dark depths of the stone bowl.

'Drink the blood of the gods and you'll be as close to them as one can be and yet remain human. You'll be all powerful. Long-living.'

'I just want to save my homeland.'

Kazemde nodded. 'Powerful men make the decisions. You know that better than anyone. With this gift you'll be able to fight Antony with the gods at your back.'

Cool stone touched Saar's lips. He hadn't noticed his hands rising until the gritty rim met his mouth. The smell grew worse, tangled with the scent of old blood on the battlefield. A smell he knew well.

His hands shook. 'Will I still be me?'

Kazemde's lips parted. His eyes widened. 'No one else has ever asked that question.'

'Will I?'

'You'll be as much yourself as you ever have been. With power comes freedom; nothing will stop you being your true self. Drink. Or else return to the city and face certain death.'

Saar closed his eyes. Parting his lips, he tipped the bowl against his mouth and poured the foul-smelling fluid into his body.

Chapter Twenty-Five

It tasted bitter. Cold. Rotten. Sickly. Saar thought of many words to describe the taste of that foul black liquid, but couldn't settle on a single one. The thick substance clung to his lips and tongue, forcing him to swallow over and over to be rid of it. When he did empty his mouth, the taste lingered.

Saar returned the bowl to the altar. After wiping his mouth, he put his hands on his hips and waited.

'I feel nothing,' he said after a pause. 'No strength, no wonderful power.'

Kazemde backed up enough to put the altar between them. The red in his eyes spread across the whites like ink.

'You lack patience. Power will come, just wait. Believe.'

'I believe,' he snarled. 'I believe your fine words and grand promises have brought me to my death. I must return to the city. I must—' a gasp choked off his words. Violent shudders rippled through his body.

Saar fell to his knees, gripping his stomach. The muscles pulled inward, a frantic contraction he could see beneath the skin, like pulling sheets of cloth through a loop. His throat burned. The black liquid scorched a path to his gut where it coiled like a fiery beast seeking refuge.

'What have you done to me?'

A smile touched those thin, bloodless lips. 'I? I forced nothing on you.'

'The pain . . .' Back bowing, head dropping low, Saar opened his mouth and vomited; a black torrent of thick liquid that smoked when it touched the ground. With just the presence of mind to keep away, he saw Kazemde slip around the altar and crouch beside him.

'Poison.' Breathing hurt. The air, once so warm and soothing on his skin now seared his throat like burning oil.

'Blood is a potent gift. Not many have the strength to accept it, no matter the desire. Ramesses couldn't.'

'Ramesses was a coward. Why would he want the blood of Horus?'

Kazemde cackled, showing off his yellow teeth. 'Horus? I didn't say Horus.'

Saar stared into those crimson eyes. Though he fought it, his lips trembled. 'You did.' Sweat beaded on his brow and trickled down the side of his face. More ran down his back. 'The blood of—'

'I told you Set collected blood from the field of battle where he and Horus fought. Not once did I say Horus' blood.' Another cackle of laughter, matched by an ugly grin.

Saar screamed, clutched his face between both hands and shrieked until his throat was raw. Invisible bands of bronze compressed his chest to hinder his breath. The terrible liquid spread through his skin like needles of flame, following the path of his veins until it touched every muscle. Something warm and thick flowed from his ears, his mouth, his nose. Though the smell of it clogged his nostrils, Saar knew it was blood. His heart beat faster.

'Set's blood? That slayer of kin? No— I don't want— not him. I serve Horus.'

Kazemde wagged a finger. 'Set claims all creatures powerful enough to do his bidding. He'll be pleased to own one as strong-willed and well-placed as you. You'll be richly rewarded.'

'No!' He lunged across the floor, but the older man moved with another uncanny burst of speed. Leaping up, he landed on the altar and crouched there, neck thrust out like a vulture.

'Should you survive, you'll be the strongest man alive. Wars will be won through your power and skill. Thousands will know your name. You'll be loved. Feared. Just survive. Like you always do.'

Saar thrust his fingers into the sand, a curious echo of his actions on leaving the water. This time the movement stemmed from mind-shattering pain. The domed walls wavered in and out of focus. Light dimmed. A sound like rushing wind filled his ears, chased by the rumble of heavy, crashing drums. No . . . not drums. His heartbeat.

Through a misty haze he saw Kazemde drop his cloak on the altar and lift both hands towards the curved ceiling. Gone were the stooped back and rounded shoulders. Instead Kazemde stood tall, his face stretching with a sound like tearing ox hide. His mouth became a long, pointed muzzle and, through his thickening hair, two ears grew. These were tall and upstanding, rectangular and black, covered with short, coarse fur. A tail grew from the base of his spine, curling around his naked knees into a forked tip. His legs lengthened, loud pops signalling a shift in his joints. The feet extended, his ankle flexing to bend like the hindquarters of a desert fox. Fur sprung out all over his body. Between his crooked legs swung the soft length of his manhood.

Saar recognised the hideous shape from temple drawings. The creature with a muzzle and square ears, fighting with the god of the underworld in a battle fuelled by anger and jealousy.

'Set,' he whispered.

'I'm not Set,' Kazemde's voice echoed through the space. 'But I'm permitted to use his form on occasion.'

'You tricked me.'

'I gave you what you asked for.' Thin lips drew back from that terrible muzzle and exposed twin rows of glistening teeth. A pink tongue flopped out and licked the thick black gums. 'Now stand and tell me that you're not stronger than ever before.'

Saar gasped and slumped against the ground, the absence of pain almost as bad as the muscle-twitching agony of moments ago. He drew breath after ragged breath, clutching his head with sandy fingers. He stood. With effort. When his knees buckled, Saar shot out one hand and steadied himself on the edge of the altar.

What he saw upon it made him leap back: dried blood, bright and vibrant. Deep in the cracks of the stone, he saw infinitesimal impurities as clear as the lines on his own hands. Saar looked at these and choked on another embarrassing cry. Through the sand, dried salt and grime, he saw lines and tracks on his palms he'd never noticed before. On his arms, he noticed tiny hairs, pores and imperfections in his colouring that made up the familiar shade of his skin.

Then the sounds came, crowding in from every side. The rush of water, the dry rasp of shifting sand. Snuffles of burrowing creatures and the clicks and rustles of lizards living in dens beneath the earth. He could smell them, dry, musty, reminiscent of snakes.

'What have you done to me?' He swallowed and tasted salt.

Kazemde bared his teeth again. The lift in his voice indicated the gesture might be a smile. 'You're blessed. Protected by Set himself. Touched by his power and strength.'

Saar covered his ears with his hands. Then his eyes. Then his ears again. 'These sounds— the smells— everything crowds in all at once. I'll go mad.'

'Master these new skills or be mastered. If you don't, I'll return to kill you as I did Ramesses.'

'You did this to me.'

Kazemde hopped off the altar. The impact of his feet against the ground exploded in Saar's ears like a clap of thunder.

'Please, stop— the noise— it hurts.'

'Only you can do that.'

'I can't.'

'You can do anything.' Kazemde's laughter filled the small chamber. 'Did Kiya not say so? Your mother? Is their faith in you without due cause? Must I kill you now as I have so many others?' His hand strayed towards the dagger.

Long claws with jagged tips scraped across the stone altar, so loud that Saar screamed. He beat his forehead against the ground.

'Stop moving, I beg you.'

'God-touched men don't beg.'

'Help me!'

The man-shaped creature sighed. 'The most I can do is speed your passing. Set has no love for weak men and he'll withdraw his gift as quickly as he gave it. Then I'll return to Alexandria to dispose of those who may ask for you. Cleopatra. Panya. Kiya.'

Saar sat up. His vision tunnelled to a narrow dot centred on Kazemde's ugly, distorted face. Though his legs shook and his arms trembled, he regained his feet and stepped forward. 'Don't touch them. I'll kill you, I swear it.'

Pain meant nothing now. The sounds died away. The clarity and detail in his sight served only to show Saar how best to destroy the source of his torment. He saw every hair on that sleek black muzzle, every ripple of muscle beneath the wiry fur. He watched the forked tail swish back and forth and felt the tiny motions of the air disrupted by its passage.

'Well done, Saar. I knew you wouldn't disappoint me.'

The moment he stopped to think about the lack of additional sound, Saar heard them again. An owl hooting somewhere above. The gentle swish of a creature crawling through the sand. He focused on his anger again, holding it close to his chest and using it as a shield to block out everything else. Peace returned.

Saar exhaled slowly through his nose. 'I can't do this.'

'You learned to wield a sword before your fifteenth summer. You mastered the bow in the same year. In every battle you've fought since joining Cleopatra's army, you've bested every trial set before you. This is no different. Look at yourself.'

Another deep breath failed to steady his nerves, though it did draw his attention to his body. Saar stretched his spine, and rolled his shoulders. Everything felt . . . normal.

Kazemde grinned. 'Did I not tell you?'

'I was wounded— my back— what happened?'

'Your hand has also healed.'

Saar glanced at the palm he had scraped against the floor of the Pharos lighthouse. No sign of the injury remained. His back, when he twisted to reach it, was smooth.

'Do you believe me now?'

Saar couldn't speak. Instead he clutched the altar again and gazed at the walls. Incredible detail, vibrant colours. Even chisel marks were visible. Faint streaks in the paint, the mark of coarse brushes used to paint temple walls.

'Set is pleased. He welcomes you to his family and looks forward to your future offerings.'

'What offerings?'

'Blood, Saar. Always blood.'

'I don't understand.'

'Marked with blood, by blood. From blood all power comes.' His voice took on a lilting quality as though reciting lines from a long-forgotten prayer. 'Set accepts your gracious sacrifice and in return gives you long life, strength and power. The gift remains so long as you offer regular tribute.'

'I have no tribute. All wealth I give to my mother . . . I have land. Perhaps he will—'

'Are you not listening, Saar?' Kazemde's eyes narrowed above that cruel muzzle. His tail lashed the air. 'Only blood will do.'

'But how?'

'Your Kiya is often keen to give you other parts of herself. Why not blood too? I can help if you wish.'

The veiled threat brought a snarl from Saar's throat. He stood up and, without thinking, without any thought for what might follow, leapt through the air. Kazemde darted aside, dropping the curving dagger. He spun around, tail twitching. Saar faced him, clenching and unclenching his fists.

'Set is a tyrant,' said Saar. 'I want none of his gifts or blessings.'

'Too late. You're bound to him now.'

'No—'

'Yes! You belong to him and will offer regular tribute or suffer a death more painful than anything you can imagine. And I'll ensure you see both Kiya and Panya die before you do.'

With a guttural roar, Saar dived across the floor, snatching up the dagger as he rolled. He came to a low crouch at Kazemde's feet and thrust up with the deadly weapon, driving the blade deep into the space beneath his hairy muzzle.

Kazemde shrieked and struck out with both hands, but Saar swayed clear. Ducking beneath the flailing hands he shoved on the blade hilt until his fingers struck the furry chin.

'If I'm so powerful,' he whispered, 'then I can protect the ones I love.' With one clean slice he opened Kazemde's throat. Blood sprayed out, black and reeking. The other man clawed the air with his broken fingernails, struggling, gurgling, gasping, wheezing. Saar watched the light die in those huge red eyes. A hot river of crimson flooded over his face and chest.

Long moments later the body stopped moving.

Kazemde's tail, muzzle and ears shrank into his body. Fur rolled back as though sucked into his skin, leaving behind a skinny old man with baggy skin, frail limbs and a wide, red smile in his throat.

DAY THREE

Chapter Twenty-Six

Lenina awoke on the living room floor in front of the three-seat sofa. Thorne's body lay close by, arms crossed over his flabby stomach.

Everything ached, from her toes to the tip of her nose.

She just had time to see Jason's face looming above her before her stomach lurched. Rolling left, she retched; dry, throat-searing convulsions that brought tears to her eyes.

'She's awake.' Jason slapped her on the back. Shock and relief mingled in his eyes. 'She's okay. I knew it.'

'Stop hitting me.'

'Sorry. Hold my hand, come on. Stand up.'

As the dry heaves subsided, Lenina allowed Jason to help her up, leaning into his grip.

'How did I get in here?'

'We moved you. Sorry. It wasn't safe in the hallway.' When she didn't answer, Jason licked his lips. 'You were thrashing around. Talking. You kicked the walls a few times before we could move you. Punched me too.'

For the first time she noticed the dark discolouration around his eye line.

'I'm sorry, I didn't know—'

'No, *I'm* sorry. I shouldn't have touched you. It's my fault.'

Still clinging, Lenina grabbed her stomach through the borrowed sweatshirt. The fabric stuck to her skin, peeling away with a faint sucking sound. Beneath it, her skin was smooth.

'You stabbed me.' She looked at Tristen.

He leaned against the wall near the kitchen. Though he still held the wavy dagger, he seemed not to notice it as he spoke. 'It was the only way to know for sure.'

His blank, unfeeling tone cut Lenina to the core. She tightened her grip on the fabric until sticky blood oozed through her fingers. 'You didn't know if I would live or die.'

'Actually I thought you'd die.'

'Don't you care for me at all? How could you do this?'

'I'm a watcher, it's my job.'

Lenina gritted her teeth. 'Your job is to watch me die?'

'All vampires heal after their first tribute,' Jason cut in. 'It's the only power we all get.'

She hesitated.

'Powers. Saar had five different powers and he passed them to us through his blood.'

Mention of the ancient vampire sent a charge fizzing through Lenina's body. She moaned, clutching her head with both hands. Like peeling the fragile shell of a boiled egg, she felt Saar fold back the walls of his mental cage and spring free. He billowed out like a cloud, filling her mind with knowledge she couldn't possibly have.

'*Koach*,' she whispered. '*Shalat, Tzuza, Okhel, Zakar*.' The words tripped off her tongue with ease. 'Xamesh.'

Jason flinched.

Tristen gave her a shrewd look. His eyes narrowed. 'We don't use them any more but those are the old names. Physical strength which includes healing. Mind control. Telekinesis. Sensuality. Blood recall. The Five.'

'I know them all,' she murmured. 'And I know what they do. It's Pauline Lock all over again.'

'So that *was* your kill?' For the first time Tristen displayed open surprise. He chuckled under his breath. 'At least that will be easy to explain to Kallisto.'

'I saw her entire life play out in my head. I was living it.'

Jason tightened his grip on her arm. 'Memories. Knowledge. You're talking about blood recall, gathering memories from the blood you drink. Only Saar could do that.'

Lenina tugged free and faced Tristen. 'Was it really the blood of a god in that bowl?'

Another searching look. His gaze ran up and down her body and Lenina felt the heat of it crawling over her skin. She shuddered. Her feet tingled with the need to run, but she forced them to remain still while she waited.

'No one knows,' he said at last. 'I asked once and he laughed at me.'

'You knew him?'

Tristen gave a bitter chuckle. His hand tightened on the dagger but he didn't speak. That was answer enough.

Lenina reached towards him. 'What did he do to you?'

'None of your business.'

But as he said it, she knew.

She saw.

Saar stepped from the shadows, wiping sweaty palms against his shirt. He felt lightheaded. Breathless. For the first time in seventy years he recognised the presence in his mind that belonged to his first child. His fingertips itched with the need to touch him again. His lips burned with a desire that two thousand years had yet to quench.

Two feet away, a tall, slender man in a fine brown overcoat sprawled on the cobbles. Mud coated his back and shoulders. His cravat and rumpled white shirt boasted several damp spots, a pathetic combination of tears and rainwater from the grimy street. Several feet away, a dented top hat rolled into the gutter.

A second man stood above him, as shabby as the first was fine. He held a dagger, long, with a wavy blade and a pommel studded with blue and white gems. Though his hand obscured it, Saar knew that the hilt was made of silver and gold.

'Please!' The man on the floor wept and wrung his hands. 'You need me. Don't kill me.'

The shabby figure raised his arm. The dagger glinted in the light. 'The others are dead. Only you and I remain. We can weaken him like this.' His voice, so familiar, weakened Saar's knees until he feared he might fall. The thought that this whole scene was simply a means to bring him down made Saar's blood run cold. He rubbed his chest, wishing he could ignore the pain of the old wounds reopening.

'Mosi.' He took another step forward. The scene before him froze.

The man on the ground slumped back into a puddle. His pleading dissolved into desperate, mumbled thanks.

Saar ignored it, focused instead on the first man he'd ever loved. As he took in the long, tangled beard and dirty skin, he felt a pang in his chest. 'What have you done to yourself? You're a disgrace.'

'I much prefer to look a disgrace than be one. I wondered when you would come.'

'You wanted me to, or else the link would be closed.'

'I want? Saar, I want to die. No man should live as long as you or I.' Mosi looked away, his fingers slackening around the dagger hilt.

The man on the ground looked up. Hope bloomed in his eyes. 'Saar? Lord Saar, help me. Please. I'm your servant, I beg you, don't let him kill me.'

Saar glanced down. 'Who are you?'

'Tristen Blake, Master. Please, save me.'

'Why? What are you worth?'

Tristen flinched. His gaze darted back and forth as though seeking answers. 'Mosi killed all his children. I'm the last. He hopes to weaken you before you fight.'

Growling, Saar looked back at Mosi and tried to find the truth. Though the link was there, he felt Mosi form a barrier against him and block the way. Blindly, he groped through the darkness of Mosi's mind. He found no clues.

'Is this true?' he said at last.

'You no longer care for my privacy, I see.' Mosi's lips twisted in a ghost of a smile. 'The years have changed you.'

'Of course they have. But not everything. I still love you. Abandon this foolish plan of sabotage.'

Mosi shook his head. His face, unchanged but for tiny lines about his eyes and lips, was as beautiful as it had been in Gyasi's whorehouse.

'Please.'

'I remember this conversation. Your plans still bring death to those around you— in that you're unchanged. I want no part of it.'

'This time is different.'

'Really? Monsieur Bonaparte won't slaughter hundreds in his quest to conquer?'

Saar sucked in a sharp breath.

'Yes. I know your plans. And like before I'll be on the opposite side. Duke Wellington invited me to join him in laying plans of defence and I was pleased to accept.' He stroked his chin. 'Obviously I'll shave first.'

Tristen Blake crawled across the cobbles. He pawed Saar's boots while blinking sweat and tears from his eyes. 'I told you! He betrays you. Your love for him is legendary and yet he deserts you when you need him most. But I won't. I never will. I'll help. Please! Save me and I'll tell you everything.'

Snarling, Saar jerked his foot away. He snatched the smaller man by the scruff and drove his face into the cobbles, again and again until blood mixed with the puddles.

'I have no time for weaklings.' He spat, releasing the sobbing form with a flick of his wrist. 'It is not my job to save you. If you survive, seek me out. I may have use for you then.'

With a last, lingering glare at Mosi, Saar turned on his heel and stalked away.

Gasping, Lenina jerked free of the memory. She stared at Tristen and shivered as the last traces of Saar's scorn faded. 'It wasn't you. It was Mosi. He wasn't angry with you.'

Tristen bit his bottom lip. In that moment he looked far more like the broken man from Saar's memory. Almost childlike. 'You saw?'

She nodded.

'Then you know. It doesn't matter who he was angry with, you saw how little he cared. Nothing mattered but his own goals. I had no immediate use so he left me to die.'

'But Mosi—'

'—wanted me dead.' Spittle flew from Tristen's mouth. The lost look vanished. The skin around his cheeks and neck reddened. 'He wanted all God-Touched dead. He spent years tracking and killing the others and I was the last of his line. He hunted me down to finish the job.'

Though this insight into Tristen's life was new, Lenina found herself remembering details. Details only Saar and Mosi themselves might know.

'1809, September 29. He took me and made me believe it was what I wanted. Mosi stole everything: my life, my family . . . I had a wife! But he used me to travel around the world, finding his other children while she grew old waiting for me. When they were dead, he turned to me.'

'But you got away. How?'

Tristen's knuckles whitened. Another lost expression crossed his face before he tamped it down. When he looked up again, calm filled his features. He wiped his face with the flat of his hand. 'You don't need to know.'

She closed her eyes. 'I see smoke. Fire. Gunpowder. It's muddy. Guns firing. Men are screaming.'

'Mosi used Wellington to battle Saar just like he did with Octavian. They both died in 1815.' He gave a bitter chuckle. 'Though I'll give Mosi credit for a job well done. He was very good at picking the winning side. Lucky for the rest of us. If Saar had won that day . . .' Sweat glistened on his upper lip. 'I'm glad he's gone. Both of them.'

'You don't mean that.'

'Don't I?' With that, Tristen opened his mind to her.

She felt a space in her mind bend, then give under the force of Tristen's entry. Her legs buckled. Slumping to the floor, she gasped and struggled to think past the sheer weight of his hate. It filled her senses, clogging her throat, stuffing her nose until the air itself became too thick to breathe.

She gagged. 'Stop it!'

'I don't mean it?' Tristen threw back his shoulders. White light filled his eyes again. 'How would you know? What do you know about running for your life? Scared to step outside because someone you love wants to kill you?'

Lenina choked. Clutched her chest. 'How can you do this? I'm not linked to you.'

'Of course we're linked,' he snapped.

And through the gagging sensation of hate, Lenina felt lust. Her fingertips itched with the need to touch his face, and deep between her legs, an answering tingle. Peppermint scented the air. She whimpered and closed her eyes. She shook her head from side to side as the truth became clear. 'That's why you slept with me. You needed a way in.'

'An old trick, but it works. My skill in *Shalat* is unparalleled. If it makes you feel better, you're not the first to fall for it. You're so young; you may as well be human.' Having made his point, Tristen tilted his chin. The white glow faded from his eyes. The weight of crushing hate vanished.

Slumping against the wall, Lenina clutched her chest. As her breathing steadied, she watched his face. She saw the struggle in his eyes as he stared back.

'Two hundred years we've been safe. Red Fang searched but they couldn't find anything.' He pointed at her. 'And now you're in my living room. Tearing the scabs off old wounds.'

'I didn't mean to.'

'Of course not, but this time you're right, it's not your fault. It's in your blood.'

She touched the raw wound on her cheek.

Jason shifted. 'Sorry, Tristen. I know what this means to you but—'

'You don't know! I've always looked after you even if I don't love you. When I Kissed you it was because *you* asked. I'm better than either of them. Mosi Kissed me for money and convenience. Saar did everything he could to find strength and power. You do know Bonaparte was god-touched, don't you?'

His expression said he clearly didn't. Neither did Lenina, though as she lingered on the idea, she saw hazy images of a slim, sandy-haired man in red military uniform licking his blood-caked lips.

'It could still be a mistake,' she murmured.

Tristen glared at her and began to recite, '"The Vessel will be marked with blood, by blood. From blood comes all power. Born from one of The Blood, the Vessel will awaken Saar and guide his children to ultimate glory in the new world". It's not a mistake.'

In her mind's eye, Lenina saw the underground temple again, and Kazemde's twisted, furry body speaking similar damning words. 'I don't want this. It's not fair. Don't I get a say in this?'

'No, you were chosen.'

'By what? Who? Why me? How can you stand there and expect me to just accept this?'

'I don't *expect* anything from you.' His upper lip curled back into a snarl. 'The facts haven't changed. You're the Vessel. From the moment that dagger cut your face.'

'I'm a museum curator.'

'Not any more.'

She sniffed, brushing her eyes as tears threatened to spill forth. 'Please, I don't know anything about blood and God-Touched. My dad's a bus driver. I won't want this.'

'Saar's family were slaves before his mother enlisted him to the army. I grew up on the streets as a filthy street-rat, stealing bread and drinking from gutters to survive. It doesn't mean anything.'

She backed away, groping the air behind her until her fingers touched the dining table. Two long steps put it between herself and Tristen. 'But you hate Saar. What does this mean? What are you going to do?'

A smile. 'Red Fang can't know about you. They can't see you. One look at your face and they'll know who you are and everything we've built since Saar died will be torn down.'

Lenina waited, tensing her muscles.

'Fortunately, I know exactly what to do.' He lifted the dagger.

Chapter Twenty-Seven

Jason moved in a blur of grey streaks. One moment he stood near the door, the next in front of Tristen. 'Wait,' he began. 'Just think—'

Tristen's fangs shot down from his gum line. 'I *am* thinking.'

'But Kallisto! She'll know.'

'How? You?'

'No!'

Despite her shielding, Lenina felt a quick stab of terror to match the colour draining from Jason's face.

'I won't tell her. I've never met any vampire more capable of shielding his thoughts than you, but she's the First Majestic. If she suspects, she'll peel your mind like an onion until she finds the truth.'

'Why should she suspect? She loves me.' Tristen actually smiled. His chest puffed out as he gestured with the dagger.

'Please, Tristen. Lenina *is* the Vessel. You can't kill her.'

'Shut up. You only care about saving your own neck.'

Jason's cheeks reddened. 'Kallisto won't hurt me if she knows I found the Vessel. She'll let me off, but only if we take Lenina to Red Fang. Right now. Before she finds out.'

'She won't find out.' Tristen snarled then touched his mouth, causing his fangs to recede.

Lenina spread her fingers on the table. The adrenalin flooding her body made her skin tingle, but she didn't dare relax. Instead she watched

Tristen's face and the twitch in his eyebrows as he glared at Jason.

'I'll wear make-up,' she whispered. 'Nobody will see the mark. Anyone who does won't know what it means.'

'And Saar?' His gaze snapped to her.

'What about him?'

'Can you hold him back? Stop him taking over?'

She hesitated.

'He's more than two thousand years old. The original recipient of the blessing. No matter how strong you think *I* am, he could swat me like a fly. You *know* that. You think he'll just sit inside you and never come out?'

Lenina licked her lips. 'I'm learning to control it. I'll get better.'

As she spoke the scent of peppermint rolled through the air. It struck her like a physical blanket and smothered everything until she could barely think for the surge of lust heating her body. It came with the memory of Tristen's hands on her body, his lips on her throat, the tickle of his hair against her cheeks, the heat of his breath against her most intimate parts.

Tristen green eyes narrowed. His lips pursed. 'You can't even keep *me* out.'

Her lips trembled. 'I can. Give me a chance.'

'Saar won't give you a chance. All those memories and you still don't get it? He had no mercy or compassion. He trampled weak things and blamed it on Set, but it had nothing to do with any god. It was *him*. He was evil.'

'He didn't start that way.'

'But he *will* come back that way.' Tristen side-stepped Jason and leapt over the table.

Lenina darted around it and sharp pain in her scalp warned her of the near miss. When she looked back, two braids dangled from Tristen's fingers.

'Help me.' She darted glances at Jason.

He dry-washed his hands. 'He's my sire. My link to Set.'

'I don't know what that means.'

'It means he does as he's told,' Tristen snapped. 'Or I'll kill him.'

'Just like that?' The savagery of it caught her off guard.

'It's what Saar taught us. After Mosi he didn't want anybody else thinking they knew better than him.'

'Please, Jason. Please.'

The scruffy man hunched his shoulders. 'If you really are the Vessel, you can protect me, yeah? Helping you is like helping Saar.'

Lenina wavered.

Tristen laughed. 'Yes, admit you're the Vessel and I'll kill you for sure. Deny it and Jason won't help.' More laughter. 'Spoilt and selfish, that's what you are and there's nobody left to bail you out. What now?'

Lenina hesitated. With an angry vengeful vampire on one side and another confused one on the other, allies were hard to come by. She closed her eyes and opened her mind to Jason, breaking down the mental barricade between them. His thoughts and feelings tumbling across the gap like an avalanche. She met the rush head on and ushered him through.

Jason gazed at her and visibly straightened. He pressed his lips into a thin, grim line and gave a curt nod. Even his shoulders lifted and when he moved, the air felt thick with his confidence. Without speaking, he grabbed her arm and shoved her against the wall. Then he turned, put his back to her and faced Tristen with his arms outstretched. 'You leave her be.' His tone resembled steel.

Tristen gave a low, disbelieving chuckle. 'Don't be stupid. You can't fight me.'

'I'm not. I'm *protecting* her.'

'Why? She doesn't care about you.'

'She doesn't have to. It's the right thing, yeah? We promised to look for the Vessel. All of us.'

'Don't do this. You're still of my line.'

'If you believed any of that you would have let Mosi shiv you. You're no better than the rest of us, just looking out for himself. This woman ain't like that.'

Though the words swelled Lenina's chest, they also dropped a lead weight into her belly. His faith in her was startling, a beacon in her mind as bright as a lighthouse. Fascinating. Humbling. Terrifying.

'You know me, Jason.' Tristen pointed with the dagger. 'I won't hesitate. Last chance. Step aside.'

Lenina touched Jason's shoulder. A familiar static charge leapt off his body and he reached back to squeeze her fingers. An instant later his scream splintered the tense silence. Pressing her hands to her ears, Lenina could only watch as Jason fell to his knees. He clutched his head. Blood poured from his nose and ears.

'Stop it!' She stared at Tristen's eerie, glowing eyes. 'Leave him alone!'

The shrieks stopped.

Lenina risked bending down. 'Jason?' He didn't speak, just whimpered.

'I Kissed him, Lenina. The sire-child link is great for keeping people in line. I could do that all day. It costs nothing. If you care about him at all, *you* leave *him* alone.'

Worm-like, Jason writhed in a puddle of his own blood. Though he tried to stand, his limbs shook. His eyes rolled back in his head.

Lenina straightened. 'Leave him. He's only doing it because I asked.'

Tristen snorted. 'He's doing it to save his own skin. You heard him, he wants protection.'

Rolling on the carpet, Jason's grey eyes swivelled to meet hers. The touch of his blood-slicked fingers against her toes made her cringe. 'Help me,' he begged.

'See? It's all about him.'

She looked down again, inched away from the hand groping her foot. The crestfallen look on Jason's face changed to one of wonderment as she positioned herself over his body, standing between him and Tristen. Her hands balled into fists. 'Then I'll protect him.'

Lenina hesitated when Tristen's laughter cut across her bold statement. A coil of warmth took root in her belly and spread through her body. It linked to Tristen and she could smell the mint on his breath, feel the firm pressure of his hands on her hips, his lips slanting across hers.

The power of the sensory memory stole her breath. She stumbled.

'Okay, you made your point. Stop it.'

More laughter.

Eyes closed, she fought off the growing need to throw herself at his body. The burning urge to feel his naked skin beneath her fingers. Gritting her teeth didn't help. Neither did tightening her fists until her nails bit into her palms. Then something hard struck her back. Her eyes flashed open in time to see Jason spring off the floor and tackle Tristen around the middle.

The rush of lust died and she heaved herself to the surface like a drowning man breaching the waves. Both men rolled together, toppling dining chairs as they went. Tristen jerked free, ending the one-sided scuffle as quickly as it began by shoving his dagger into Jason's chest. He leaned on the hilt while Jason screamed and drummed his heels against the floor.

'I warned you,' he muttered.

Jason opened his mouth but no sound came out, just a small bubble of dark blood that burst and slid down his chin. One weak hand fluttered near the dagger hilt. Through the link they shared, Lenina felt it all. Clutching her own chest, she shouldered Tristen aside and knelt near Jason's head.

'You can heal it.' She tried to make the words an order rather than a desperate plea. 'Heal it!'

'He can't. Not the heart. Not after what Mosi did to Saar. That wound weakened every single one of us. Where do you think the stake "through the heart" myth came from?'

Jason gave a wet gurgle, his last attempts to speak. From one trembling hand Lenina saw sand pour from his fingertips. No . . . the sand came from the fingers themselves, and as more hit the floor, she realised his hands were crumbling away.

Her gut twisted like a giant fist had plunged inside to grab a handful of intestines. Liquid fire burned through her veins and every scrap of pain she felt doubled. Tripled. The space Jason inhabited ripped free of her mind with a sound like the wet tearing of flesh from flesh.

'Not again, please!' The voice from her mouth sounded nothing like her own.

Saar's anguish, Saar's fear, Saar's remembered agony rolled through Lenina's head until she could no longer separate them from hers. He watched and felt Kiya die and she joined him.

Jason's presence vanished from her head. As if death had flicked a switch.

Lenina sprawled on the carpet gasping, watching the last ravages of vampire death turn Jason into a pile of sand, packaged in dirty, smelly clothes.

The pain stopped.

Tristen crouched and touched the golden sand. For a moment, Lenina thought that he might feel a hint of remorse, but he simply stood and wiped his hands against his jeans.

'I didn't think it would hurt so much.' He might have meant a paper cut.

'You felt it?'

'He was part of me. His death takes something from me, same as you. But I can handle it.'

His blasé attitude made her want to punch him. 'How? There's a hole where he used to be, like an open wound. Was it like this when Mosi died?'

He stiffened. 'Worse. Then Saar died. I felt that too.'

'How?'

'He was the conduit between Set and the rest of us. Those he made directly got the worst of it. That's why Majestics like Kallisto need him; they think he'll bring back the power they lost.'

'Will it?'

'I don't know. I don't care. I choose weaker, alive and free, over stronger and living in fear. You wouldn't understand.'

But she did. She knew it keenly in that moment because she then felt Tristen's mind touch hers. Like water filling an empty cup, awareness and knowledge of him flooded her mind and filled the space left by Jason.

He gasped.

She shivered. 'What's happening?'

A smile grew on his lips as he gazed at her face. 'Your link is mine now. I didn't know that could happen. Incredible.'

Panic seized her. 'Why? No, please. I don't want you in my head.'

He inhaled, deep and slow, as if consuming her thoughts through his nose. 'You've been holding out on me.'

'What?'

'You know more than you think about Saar. You found a book,' he frowned. 'By Xerxes? I don't know that one, but there's a few. Stupid humans trying to get rich by selling our story. We kill them, obviously.'

Lenina turned her attention to the mental wall, rebuilding it with the same concrete slabs she'd once used with Jason. She'd barely lain the first blocks before Tristen swatted them away, a minor flex of his will.

'Stop. You don't know what you're doing. It's embarrassing.'

'Get out of my head!'

'But I like it here. I can see everything you've been trying to hide. You really did love Nick.' The grin widened. 'But you've got a thing for long hair and green eyes, rather like Saar. Pity . . . for you. No wonder it was so easy. You barely put up a fight.'

Remembering her almost instant attraction to Tristen only made Lenina feel worse. Guilt wormed through her until she saw and felt nothing but her own terrible choices. 'Please don't.'

'Nick suffered by the way. You drained his blood without any hold on his mind. He definitely suffered. It was the perfect tribute.'

Tears burned in Lenina's eyes. 'Stop it!'

Tristen's presence was a physical weight against her skull as he riffled through the storage boxes of her life.

'Your mother looks good for her age. Grace, is it? I can see where you get your looks, certainly not from your father.'

'Don't.'

'Your brother looks more like Ray. I still say he's familiar. Remind me what he does?'

'None of your business.' Hopping from subject to subject was too difficult to keep track of. With each new fact Tristen discovered, Lenina felt him worm a little deeper into her head. His mental probing dug deep, like super-fine needles piercing the very heart of her memories.

'A bus driver. Ex-military. Infantry soldier. Very nice.'

'Leave him alone!' Lenina glared at Tristen and fantasised about hurting him. Imagined plunging her hands into that wide, mocking grin, and tearing it away from his face. Watching his blood fill the air like rain.

The room took on a magnificent level of colour. The edges of the dining chairs and the sofa turned hard and sharp, near-blinding in their brightness. She could smell everything, from Thorne's sweaty body to the dry mustiness of desert sand. She heard low voices from the house next door and the blare of a distant car alarm. Like a river bursting its banks, something barely held in check finally spilled over the sides of her control and ran free.

Saar.

Lenina snarled. Surging off the ground, she dived at Tristen and delivered a sharp jab to his stomach. When he doubled over, huffing with pain and surprise, she swung her left fist into his chin, cracking his teeth together. Saar bellowed in the cavern of her mind. He thrust out, using Lenina's body to pursue the man threatening his family. To destroy him as he'd once destroyed Kazemde. His feelings tangled with hers, but Lenina didn't care. In that moment she was happy to use anything, to let the ancient being wield her body like a puppet if only it would help her escape.

When Tristen backed away, Lenina followed, aiming a kick at his lowered head. Tristen caught her ankle and twisted it. With a cry, she went down, turning into the fall to ease the pressure in her foot. She landed on her back, one leg bent beneath her, the other extended up.

He coughed. A small chip of something hard and white flew from his mouth. 'How did you do that?'

Sweat beaded on her forehead. She felt more of it gather on her skin beneath the over-sized sweatshirt. 'Leave my family out of this.' Her fury ebbed when Tristen twisted her foot, forcing her to flip on to her stomach or suffer a broken ankle.

'How? Lessons from Saar?' Still holding her foot, he crouched over her back. His free hand snagged a handful of braids and dragged her head up, forcing her spine into a painful curve. 'You forget, he taught Mosi. Mosi taught me.'

Lenina laughed. Deep inside, Saar laughed too. His amusement rolled out through her mouth and gave her voice a deep, rumbling edge.

Tristen heard it and paled. 'He's really there. In your eyes.'

She smiled. Saar joined her.

'They avoided each other for nearly a thousand years. You don't think Saar learned a few more tricks in that time?'

Understanding dawned in Tristen's face. He opened his mouth but

Lenina didn't wait. She pressed her palms to the floor and pushed, easing the pressure on her back. With the slack, she extended her leg, shoving the trapped foot deeper into Tristen's body. He reeled back and she rolled with him, leading with her knee to ride his body across the floor. Tristen wrenched his body from side to side. The white glow in his eyes intensified and she felt him hammer her senses, trying to fill her mind with lust. Like swatting a fly, Saar batted it away.

'That won't work,' Lenina muttered. 'He doesn't fancy you.'

Tristen eyes widened. 'If you let him control your body, he'll take over completely.'

'As if you care.'

'I do, I—'

She pressed one hand against his throat. When she spoke Saar's voice came out. 'No. You. Don't.'

He gagged, fighting to swallow past the steady pressure on his Adam's apple. 'He doesn't care about you either. All he wants is power. You think he'll look after your family when Red Fang show up?'

'My family are dead,' she snapped.

Tristen gasped. 'They're not! That's *him* talking.'

Lenina blinked. Shook her head.

In the back of her mind Saar growled and tightened her fingers on Tristen's throat.

<Lies>, he seemed to say. <Only to save himself. We have no one. Only us>

'No,' she rolled her shoulders. 'He's right. Mum and Jordan . . . Dad . . . he's coming here.'

The memory of her frantic phone call with Ray stopped Saar dead.

He considered the images with intense curiosity. <Father?>

'Yes.' Ignoring Tristen's startled looks, Lenina fought to regain control of her body. 'He's coming here.'

Her fingers flexed on Tristen's throat. Shades of red coloured the area about his jaw and nose. His eyes watered and returned to their usual green colour.

Saar roared and Lenina yelped at the sheer weight of his power. She felt him snatch control of her fingers again and squeeze tighter. The muscles of Tristen's neck spasmed under her hand and she heard the frantic flutter of his heart as it begged for oxygen.

'Stop it.' She fought to regain use of her hands.

<Kill him>

'I can't.'

<I can. I will>

'No!' She threw herself backward, rolling off Tristen's body and into the wall. 'Enough killing.'

Wheezing, touching the imprint of fingers at the base of his throat, Tristen sat up. 'I knew it.' His voice trembled. 'We're all going to die.'

'No, I can control him. It's going to be okay.'

'It isn't.' Still coughing, he thrust out one hand. His fingers flexed, aimed at the pile of sand that had once made Jason's body. The dagger, still lying amongst the dirty clothes, leapt into the air and slapped into his palm.

Lenina tensed. Time slowed to a crawl. White noise filled her ears, blocking out everything but the steady thud of her heart.

Feral fury etched deep furrows on Tristen's brow as he lunged, leading with the dagger. His arm arched high, then curved down, a powerful stabbing motion directed at her heart.

As when fighting Jason hours before, Lenina moved with the smooth grace of one with far more experience. She had an impression of incredible speed as she scooped one hand beneath Tristan's advance, closing her fingers on his wrist. Her thumb found a pressure point beneath the heel of his palm, pressing down until his fingers jerked and released the dagger. Her other hand swooped in. Caught it.

Saar roared.

A flick of her fingers flipped the dagger into a reverse grip. Opening Tristen's stance with his trapped hand, Lenina stabbed with the other, driving the blade into his chest.

Time resumed its normal speed.

Tristen stopped. 'I'll heal.' His stare settled on hers, wide and fearful.

'Not the heart,' she whispered, pulling the deadly blade free. Blood oozed free in slow pulses. Tears blurred her vision. 'I'm so, so sorry.'

Saar gave a satisfied purr. <The right thing>

Tristen slumped to the carpet.

Chapter Twenty-Eight

Lenina sat on the floor gazing at her hands. She felt sick and dizzy.

Saar expanded within her, testing the limits of his captivity. His motions brought to mind a cat stretching after a long nap. Or a daisy unfurling its petals to meet the sun. Both analogies were too tame for what she felt: a bulging sensation, like her body held another physical entity.

'Stop. You've done enough.'

Though alone, she heard laughter in the room around her. Saar's voice filled her ears, a soft caress laced with power and hunger. It soothed her, comforted her, frightened her.

<Help each other. You need me. I'm strong>

The ancient god-touched soldier extended the hand of peace and friendship. Companionship. Co-operation. But Lenina knew better. She heard his words and forced herself to feel nothing. She knew his offers were nothing more than veiled threats; the delicate brush of silk over a bed of deadly razor blades.

'Leave me alone. I need to think.'

<Action. Time for doing>

'Shut up!'

A loud crash at the front door made her look up. It was joined by another and the shuffle of urgent footsteps, at least three sets. Lenina leapt to her feet, cramming her hands into her mouth. She glanced at

Tristen's bleeding body and then at Thorne's feet, just visible on the other side of the sofa.

<They come for you. Let me help>

Another crash. Shaking her head, Lenina backed up. She met the wall and pressed her palms to the textured wallpaper, as if to feel something real and solid would steady her nerves.

Crash.

Splintering wood. She held her breath.

<They'll see. They'll know>

Lenina ran. She reached the hallway just as the front door flew inward, admitting three police officers. They stopped when they saw her, their uniforms and hair dotted with diamond droplets of rain.

'Lenina Miller?' The first of the three officers was a thin, wiry Asian man with a dimpled chin and a long, narrow nose.

She nodded, not daring to move.

'Can you speak? Are you hurt?'

For the first time she realised how she must look. 'I—'

'Where's Tristen Blake?'

Her knees buckled. 'Back there, I— I'm so sorry.'

The first officer grunted and shouldered past her, into the room beyond. After him went the second officer, removing her hat and shaking rain from her glasses as she went. Only the third officer remained, a tall black man with dreadlocks, caught back in a thick band. He entered slowly, watching her as if she were a skittish horse.

'It's okay, Miss Miller. I'm PC Shawn Jackson. We're here to help.'

A loud curse came from the back room.

Deep inside, Saar uttered something like a battle cry and surged forward again, claiming control of her legs. He used her body like a familiar tool, driving Lenina back into the living room with her hands balled into fists. She skidded to a stop in the doorway, sliding on a patch of sand. Nausea roiled through her stomach and she pulled her toes out of Jason's remains.

The two officers stood near the sofa, gazing at Brad Thorne's battered body. The first of them spoke into the radio clipped to his shoulder, reeling off the address in a voice that now held an edge of panic.

Lenina's gaze wandered across the overturned chairs and slicks of blood. The pile of smelly clothes by the door. The empty space beside the dining table.

Saar growled and the sound slid through her lips.

Scuffling from somewhere behind made Lenina spin around, guided by Saar's reflexes. Her hand lashed out, fingers pressed together, thumb tucked in, a chopping motion at nose height. PC Jackson avoided injury by slipping on the same patch of sand and landing on his backside at her feet. Lenina's hand struck the door frame, denting the soft wood.

The officer stood slowly, grasping the base of his spine. He seemed not to notice his close shave. Snatching control of her limbs, Lenina turned back to the two officers standing over Thorne.

The female officer gave her a sharp look, one hand drifting towards the speedcuffs clipped to her belt. 'Miss Miller, where's Detective Tristen Blake?'

Looking again at the empty patch of floor beside the dining table, Lenina shook her head and told the absolute truth.

'I don't know.'

This time Lenina rejected the offer of coffee. She wouldn't have been able to drink it anyway, not with her wrists cuffed to the arms of her chair.

On the other side of the table stood a small rat-faced man in a garish pink shirt with the sleeves rolled up. His jacket lay over the arm of another chair, on which he leaned, thrusting his neck forward. Behind him, PC Jackson slouched against the wall, gazing down at his shiny black shoes. The small interview room deadened all exterior sound and the wall clock picking out the seconds sounded flat in the still air.

Lenina twitched her arm, frowning when the extravagant cuffing prevented her from even flexing her wrist. Her nose itched.

'Ms Miller, I want to help you here. I really do, but you're not making it easy.'

She stared at the plain-clothes detective and felt the weight of Saar's anger in her gaze. 'What do you want me to say?'

'I want you to tell me why there's a dead policeman in another policeman's house.'

'I already told you.'

'Yes, Tristen attacked Brad when he tried to take you away. But why, Ms Miller? Why? Tristen Blake was a good, experienced officer. He knew better than to take a witness to his house. Why were you there?'

'I didn't want to go to my friend's house. I thought it would put her in danger.'

'So you asked to go to his house?'

She bristled. '*He* suggested it.'

'Really? Not a hotel? Or one of our safe houses? That would have made more sense.'

Lenina tossed her head and wrenched on the cuffs pinning her to the chair. From the corner of her eye, she saw the plastic cover on the right one crack down the middle.

'I can't tell you what was in his mind. Only what happened.'

The irony of it all almost made her laugh. She would have if not for the intense stare from the detective across the table, and the concentration it took to keep Saar from snapping both sets of cuffs to fight his way free. The old vampire prowled through her mind like a lion in a zoo, looking out through the bars and wishing for freedom. Occasionally he roared and rattled the bars, but Lenina held him at bay with a steady mental image of an impenetrable steel cage with no doors or bolts.

'Fine.' The man wrinkled his nose in an incredibly rodent-like manner and sat down in the opposite chair. He steepled his fingers on the table before him and exhaled long and deep through his thin, moustachioed lips. 'Let's start at the top.'

Saar roared and jerked forward, snatching Lenina's hand off the chair arm. The weakened plastic broke away, revealing the metal bar within that was bent almost in half. At the same moment, the door to the interview suite crashed open and slammed into the adjoining wall.

'Daddy?' Lenina jerked straight, snapping the damaged metal bar.

Her father marched into the room, shaking off the desperate grasp of a community support officer.

'Hey, chuck,' he offered her a brief smile before turning his attention to the man at the table. 'Chief Inspector Hobb?'

Rat-man sat straight. 'You can't be here. We're conducting an interview.'

'No, you're bullying my daughter.'

Hobb stood, stretching his spine to reach his full height of five feet and little else. 'I have one dead detective, another missing, two dead bodies and no answers. No weapon. This woman—'

'Lenina,' Ray cut in.

'Excuse me?'

'Her name is Lenina.'

'Right. This woman—'

'Lenina. Use her name, Chief Hobb.'

Half-hidden behind the door, PC Jackson smirked into his hand.

Hobb wiped his hands down the front of his bright pink shirt. 'Lenina . . . Lenina is involved with two of those three things and I'd like some answers. Now if you'd step outside—'

'Have you been answering the chief's questions, chuck?'

'For an hour,' she muttered.

Ray nodded. 'And do you have anything else to add?'

'No.'

'Then surely you're free to go?' He directed the question at Hobb whose neck had taken on the colour of beetroot.

'I'm not done.'

'Fair enough. I'll just need a second.' Ray tugged a mobile from the front of his leather jacket.

'What are you doing?'

'Calling a solicitor.' He smiled. 'I assume since you're keeping my daughter here, that you've arrested her. She's entitled to legal representation, am I right?'

Hobb's cheeks and forehead coloured to match his neck. 'That isn't necessary, Mr Miller, is it?'

'It is, and by "not necessary" do you mean Lenina isn't under arrest?'

'Yes, but—'

'And she isn't going to be charged?'

'Not at the moment, but I still need—'

'If there's no charges and no arrest, we'll be on our way.'

'I can hold her for twenty four hours, Mr Miller. I don't have to arrest her.'

Ray didn't lower the phone. 'I understand. In that case, if you're going to hold her, I trust you'll be providing her with a counsellor or some other support? My daughter has been through a number of traumas in a short space of time. Did you know her fiancé was murdered less than twelve hours ago? He worked for the local newspaper.'

'Newspaper?' The change to Hobb's face was startling. His gaunt cheeks now resembled the white table on which he suddenly leaned. 'Yes, I . . . I did know that. A terrible, terrible thing.'

'Terrible.' Ray's voice hardened. 'And I'm sure you're all working hard to catch the madman who's clearly been stalking my daughter.'

'We have his description. All officers are on active search.'

'I'm not talking about the homeless man. I mean the detective who was grooming my distraught and vulnerable daughter from the moment he met her.'

Hobb opened his mouth but no words came out. Eventually he managed, 'What do you mean?'

'Did you tell him how he came to the house alone, Chuck? How he gave you his personal number when he thought I wasn't looking? How he touched you?'

Learning that her father had been eavesdropping shouldn't have surprised Lenina at all. She looked at him, watching his face and the sympathy there mingled with frustration and anger.

Hobb's lips twisted as though he'd bitten a lemon 'Did Detective Blake touch you, Miss Miller?'

She hesitated. 'Yes.'

'Inappropriately?'

'He said I was beautiful,' she murmured, skirting around the question. 'He said he would take care of me. I wanted him to— I was so scared. Everything happened so fast.'

'And he came to your house without Inspector Thorne?'

'This morning.' She glanced at the clock. 'Yesterday. He said he wanted to check on me.'

Hobb looked like a man realising he'd lost his winning lottery ticket. 'You never told us about that.'

'You didn't give me a chance.'

Nervous fingers fanned his pink shirt against his chest. 'This changes things somewhat.'

'I don't know what your rules are on victim support,' said Ray, 'but we have every reason to file a list of complaints about the conduct of your officers and your personal handling of this investigation. Fortunately for you, taking my daughter home and looking after my family at a time like this is far more important than embarrassing you or your staff.'

The threat couldn't have been clearer if he'd shouted it. Lenina bit her lip and kept still, trying not to bring attention to the broken cuff dangling from her right wrist.

'Get those things off her.' Hobb jerked his head at the uniformed officer. 'She can go.'

Ray beamed. 'Thank you, Chief. I'm glad we understand each other.'

PC Jackson pushed away from the wall and walked around his boss. Though he kept his gaze averted, Lenina saw the smallest hint of a smile playing over his lips. The left cuff flopped against the chair with a clang and he reached across her for the second. He sucked in a sharp breath.

'What the hell?'

'Maybe it was faulty,' she murmured. 'I didn't want to say anything.'

Saar took the opportunity to lash out with his power, cracking a whip-like line of invisible energy at the officer's head. Jackson shook himself. Swayed. Shot out one hand to grip the back of Lenina's chair. 'Right. Must have been.' His voice was a toneless drone.

She stood. 'Does that mean I can go, Chief Hobb?'

Interrupted from his glaring match, Hobb turned away from her father and rubbed his furry upper lip. 'Not far. I'll need your passport and don't even think about leaving the city. We'll be watching you.'

'She'll be with Ramona Phillips,' Ray cut in. 'I'm sure you remember her from earlier.'

The twist of Hobb's mouth confirmed he did. 'We have her address at the front desk.'

'Good. Come on, chuck.'

Determined to get the last word, Hobb leaned over the table. 'Make sure you get changed before you go, we need those clothes for processing.'

'I'll take care of it,' Ray murmured, leading the way out.

Focused on rubbing her aching wrists, Lenina stumbled and almost fell when Ramona smothered her with a giant hug. Spitting out mouthfuls of curly red hair, she clutched her best friend and felt some of the tension ease from her limbs. Even Saar, though clearly baffled by her reaction, stepped back in her mind and watched with wary curiosity.

'Nina, how awful! What happened? Why did you go to his house? What did he do? Did he touch you?'

Lenina jerked away, afraid the truth of her actions might somehow show on her face or in her words. 'It's my fault.'

'What? No, it's not.' Ramona thumbed her nose. 'You weren't to know what he was like.'

'What?'

'You've not heard, have you?' She lowered her voice and cut a significant glance at the front desk.

Ray stood beside it arguing with a frowning Chief Hobb, pointing at a community support officer.

Lenina tugged her friend to one side. 'What are you talking about?'

'Your dad ended up at my house looking for you. We came here to bust some heads – or so he put it – and found out they were questioning you.'

'I know all that, but—'

'Don't interrupt, I'm setting the scene.' Ramona flicked her hair and pressed on. 'So he goes on this crazy rampage and marches down the hallway, saying he'll knock on every door until he finds you. That guy,' she hooked a thumb at the cringing CSO, 'follows and leaves the desk completely empty. So I wait here, twiddling my thumbs like an idiot and hear these other guys talking about Blake.'

Lenina flinched. She couldn't feel him or hear him, but the faint imprint of his presence lingered in her mind like a stain she couldn't wipe away.

Saar growled. <Should have killed him>

Ignoring him, she waited for more of the story.

Ramona's grin widened. 'They said he was in big trouble for sneaking you away like that. That Chief Hobb suspended him and that's why the other detective was going to get you. They already *knew* that he'd kidnapped you.'

'Kidnapped?'

'What else would you call it? That crazy guy attacks you in your house, kills poor Nick, and runs off. Then this detective comes along and takes you to his house instead of protective custody. I think he saw a chance to play with a new, fragile victim and whisked you away before anybody could help.'

Lenina shook her head.

'And it turns out this isn't the first time he's been in trouble for *fraternising* with witnesses.' She made quote marks with her fingers. 'Before he transferred here, his last force disciplined him for indecent relations with a female officer linked to a murder case. Three weeks later she disappeared.'

Lenina opened her mouth but no sound came out. 'When you say "disappeared"?'

'Those guys said "disappeared" but I guess they meant "transferred". Probably chased out, made to feel slutty for being targeted by a serial womaniser.'

She thought of Tristen's warm fingers on her hips. His lips, his eyes. The cold, smug smile when he spoke of forging a link with her. How she wasn't the first.

'Hey, you're shaking. Come here, hon, it's okay.' Ramona put an arm around her shoulders. Her voice levelled off, as though for the first time she remembered why else they were there. 'Wherever he is, he can't bother you again. And that ginger guy won't find you either. You're coming with me so Verni and I can look after you. You're safe now.'

Safe.

Folding into her friend's embrace, Lenina closed her eyes and wished she could believe that were true.

Epilogue

Lenina woke to an unfamiliar ceiling and sheets smelling strongly of lemons. She sat up, squinting into the shaft of sunlight slicing through the ill-fitting purple curtains.

<Sleep too deep. Unprepared for attack>

She groaned. 'Attack from who?'

<Runt still free>

Though amused at Saar's nickname for Tristen, Lenina had no patience for it. 'After last night he won't come near me. I'm safe.'

<For now>

Swinging her legs out of bed, Lenina rubbed her eyes.

The borrowed nightdress fell three inches short of her knees and she watched the goosebumps prickle into being across her shins and thighs.

She stared at the dresser and the collection of essentials on top: moisturiser, deodorant, cleansing wipes. So small compared to her own. When she would see her own essentials again, let alone her house, was something she didn't want to consider. Memories of the night before crept back slowly, a miserable film reel of events combining to bring her to this lonely moment.

<Lonely is strong. Friends are weak>

'Shut up.'

<Not leaving. Can't. Work together?>

Lenina turned her gaze away from the dresser and over the rest of the room. A cold bowl of porridge stood on the bedside table, complete with a glass of orange juice. A small fly floated on the top.

<Told you, sleep too deep. Many people came in this room>

'You would have dealt with any real danger. Wouldn't you?'

<Yes. Because you are weak>

As if to add weight to his disappointment, the barely healed wound on her left cheek itched.

Soft knocking at the door stole her attention. 'One second.' She knew without looking who it would be. Snatching at Verni's dressing gown, she tugged it on and wrestled it closed.

<Should have borrowed from the other. She has generous bosom, like you>

Lenina rolled her eyes and chose not to give credit to the ancient vampire's fashion advice. When covered enough to suit her sense of modesty, she opened the door.

'Hey, chuck.' Ray spoke in a whisper, his gaze focused on her toes.

She smiled. 'Hi, Dad. You look exhausted. Did you sleep at all?'

'Not really. Too worried about you.' He shuffled his feet, a subtle display of emotion from a man so tall and broad one might expect him to be immune. Lenina knew better. Even without the abilities of a vampire.

'I'm sorry. I should have listened to you.'

'You're my daughter . . . you're not supposed to. How are you feeling?'

She hugged herself. 'Tired. Sore. What time is it?'

'One-thirty.' He nodded at her gasp of surprise. 'Guess you needed the sleep. Lunch is gone, but Ramona won't mind if I make you something. Or I could take you out for a meal?'

'I'm not hungry.'

He nodded, still not meeting her eyes. 'I wish I knew what to say.'

'It's okay.'

'It's not. You're my daughter. My only little girl. But there's nothing I can do to make this better.'

His guilt wrung her heart. 'This isn't your fault.'

Ray gnawed his thumbnail. 'Your mother's coming up with Jordan in a couple of hours. I thought you'd appreciate the extra company.'

'Thanks.' She watched him for a moment longer. 'Actually, Daddy, lunch would be nice.' His smile made the sacrifice worthwhile. 'I'm not promising I'll eat, but I don't want to stay indoors.'

<Indoors safer>

She set her jaw. 'I want to hear people laugh. See people smiling.'

'I understand, Chuck.'

Lenina felt sure he really did. 'I'll get dressed.'

'See you downstairs.' Ray left with a lightness to his step and a lift to his shoulders that hadn't been there a few minutes ago.

After closing the door, Lenina returned to the bed and perched on the end. She shut her eyes, folded her hands in her lap and let her mind drift. Mere seconds passed before she found Tristen. He was far away and moving further, at speed. How she knew, she couldn't be sure, but her awareness of him remained constant. Lenina lifted her hand, pointed through one of the walls and knew with absolute certainty that Tristen lay somewhere in that direction.

<He'll come for you. Wants you dead>

She nodded.

<Must fight back>

'I know.'

<Too weak to fight>

Lenina nodded again and opened her eyes. She imagined closing the lid on a plain wooden box and felt her connection to Tristen click off.

'You'll just have to help me, won't you?'

Though she couldn't see him, Lenina had the distinct impression that Saar was smiling.

A Not-Very-Brief Word From The Author

Hi everyone, Ileandra here ^_^
Thank you so very much for reading. I hope you've enjoyed the story as much as I enjoy the fact that you're holding it.

Silk Over Razor Blades is the first in a trilogy (named Saar's Legacy) which follows the journeys of Lenina and Saar over a period of around twelve months. Yes, Saar too. You didn't think that was all you were going to get, did you?
If you want more, the best way to stay abreast of news regarding the rest of the trilogy is to sign up for my newsletter using this URL:
www.eepurl.com/oyPa1
I send it out once a quarter and keep subscribers well informed of how the *Saar's Legacy* project is progressing. I also give subscribers regular freebies (such as short stories and discount codes) which are unavailable anywhere else.
Sound good? I hope so.

If you have the time, I'd be eternally thankful if you'd write a review. Reviews help me know what you like and what you don't, all the better to make the novels that follow as awesome as they can be.

As additional thanks for joining me on this journey, please enjoy this, the opening chapter of *Walking The Razor's Edge,* second in the *Saar's Legacy* trilogy.
This excerpt is from the advanced review copy and is unavailable anywhere else.

Next in the Saar's Legacy Trilogy:

Walking the Razor's Edge

Lenina Miller leaned against the bedroom door, gazing at her engagement ring. The diamond winked in the morning sunlight streaming through the window. It made her smile, brought her comfort, when all she wanted to do was dive beneath the duvet and hide forever.

<Weakness. Sentiment>

She looked up at the sound of the voice. Though alone in the room she heard it clearly, a whisper in the deepest corner of her mind. 'Leave me alone.' She scratched her left cheek through a layer of medical gauze. 'I don't want to talk to you.'

<Someone approaches>

She wanted to question the voice, to ask how he knew, but before she could, the trill of the doorbell cut off her thoughts.

'How?'

This time smug pride filled the voice. <I know. I see. I hear. You would too, if only you tried>

'I've been a vampire for two days. How about you give me a break?'

<God-Touched> the voice corrected.

Lenina rolled her eyes.

'Chuck, the police are here.' This voice came from downstairs. Unlike the first, this was one Lenina knew and loved: her father.

'Coming.' She wiped her face. Sucked in a few more nerve-steadying breaths. When certain she could do so safely, Lenina left the sanctuary of the bedroom and trudged down the stairs. Rattling the bars of his mental prison, the ancient creature living in her mind paced back and forth, peering out through her eyes to assess the scene in the sitting room.

Tense and straight-backed on the sofa, a short, slender female PC narrowed her eyes when Lenina entered. Her hands twitched towards the speedcuffs she wore on her left hip. Beside her, wearing a watery smile, a male officer sat with his hands in his lap.

When she entered, her father, Raymond Miller, held out his arms. She accepted his hug. Through his clothes she heard the steady rhythm of his heartbeat. His skin smelled of Old Spice, soap and leather.

'You okay, chuck? You don't have to do this now. They can't make you.'

'They can.'

'You've done nothing wrong.'

The presence inside her agreed wholeheartedly. Saar, Egyptian soldier and two-thousand-year-old vampire, crooned to her like a worried parent. <Self-defence. The runt wants you dead. You protected yourself. Me. You saved us>

She pulled away from Ray and addressed the male officer. 'PC Jackson, isn't it?'

'Yes, hello again, Miss Miller.' Shawn Jackson looked much as he had the night before, though now his weary eyes peered out through narrow-framed glasses. Like last night, his dreadlocks were gathered at the nape of his neck, neat and unobtrusive. His gaze touched the bandage on her left cheek. His wince of sympathy seemed an unconscious reflex.

'This is my colleague PC Bristow.' He gestured to the woman. 'I'm sorry we have to bother you so soon after what happened. I hope you understand that we're all incredibly sorry for your loss.'

Lenina cringed. She cut a glance at her engagement ring then turned aside. Guilt and misery crawled through her insides as she broke away from her father to lean next to a low cabinet filled with DVDs. 'Thanks for saying so.'

He nodded, adjusting his glasses across the bridge of his nose. 'I want you to know, in light of what happened to Detectives Blake and Thorne, the Chief Inspector tasked an equally efficient and talented team to find the man you described.'

Lenina bit her lip. They would never find him, she knew that. She had watched him die the night before. After bleeding out from a stab to the heart, Jason's body crumbled away into a pile of soft golden sand, packaged in a pile of filthy grey clothes. A vampire's death.

Ray cleared his throat. 'I hope the men your chief picked are somewhat *more* efficient and talented than the last pair.'

'Excuse me?' PC Jackson cocked his head.

'Well . . . one of them kidnapped my daughter and took advantage of her grief under the pretence of protecting her. He held her in his house then murdered his partner, if rumours are to be believed.'

The younger man fiddled with the collar of his shirt. 'I . . . at this time I'm not at liberty to discuss matters relating to the case, Mr Miller, but I—'

'Look here, Officer,' Ray loaded the word with skewer-sharp sarcasm. '*You* can't tell me anything, but Lenina is right there. I *know* what happened. Tristen Blake is a murderer and a serial womaniser. Brad Thorne was incompetent. Neither of them were up to finding out who killed Nick and I'm sure I'm not alone in hoping that they weren't the best you had.'

'Daddy, please . . .'

Ray's lips snapped closed. His gaze met hers. An instant later his shoulders slumped and his eyes widened as if, for the first time, he realised what he sounded like. 'Tea, anyone?'

'Yes.' Lenina had no intention of drinking anything, but she wanted to give the shaken-looking police officer a chance to recover. 'Two sugars.'

Her father frowned. 'I know how you take your tea, chuck. Anyone else?'

Bristow shook her head. After a pause, Jackson did the same. 'Don't let me trouble you, Mr Miller.'

'It's no trouble. I wouldn't offer if it was.'

'Daddy!'

Muttering under his breath, Ray slouched into the kitchen and shut the door behind him.

Lenina unfurled her fists. 'Sorry about that. He's taking it badly.'

'I understand.'

'No, you don't.' She glared at the officer until he lowered his head.

'You're right. I don't. But I meant what I said before. I wish I could do more, but right now all we can do is follow up on last night with some questions.'

She pressed her hands to the textured wallpaper and slid down to the floor, hugging her knees to her chest. 'I told your chief everything last night. I don't know where Tristen is. He killed Inspector Thorne and . . . took advantage of me. There's nothing to add. I don't see the point in—' The words faded from her lips.

'In . . . ?' PC Jackson stared at her. 'Everything okay?'

She ignored him, focused inward on the lively sensation of irritation pulsing in the back of her mind like a tiny LED.

<Stand. Prepare to fight> Saar's voice filled her head, gritty and hard with command. <Enemies>

She leapt to her feet, a smooth, boneless move. Her heart began a furious triple step in her chest. Every nerve in her body tingled with the sudden rush of nervous energy. 'Where?'

Still staring at her face, PC Jackson frowned. '"Where", what?'

<Outside>

The doorbell rang.

From the corner of her eye she saw PC Bristow tense on the chair, her fingers tugging at the shaft of her asp baton. *She's too slow*, Lenina thought, as she crossed the sitting room. Reflexes like that were of no use against the people waiting on the other side of the front door.

'I need to get that,' she said.

Before she could reach the hallway, Ray returned from the kitchen. He had a steaming mug in one hand and a tea towel in the other. Shoving the former into Lenina's hands, he kept moving past her into the hallway. 'I'll get that,' he said, all brisk and abrupt. 'You finish up with them.'

'No!' She hurried after him, ignoring the startled looks from the two officers.

'I've got this, chuck, don't worry.' Ray reached the door and tugged it open, still looking back over his shoulder. As soon as the lock cleared the hatch, the door swung free of his grip and slammed into the opposite wall. On the other side stood three men, the closest with his arm extended.

He grinned, showing off several gold teeth and a pierced tongue. 'We're looking for Lenina Miller, is she home?'

<Enemies!>

Lenina had no need of Saar's frantic cry to know what these men were. She plunged forward, jerking her father out of the way. With the other hand, she let fly with the tea, mug and all, aimed at Gold Teeth's head. The hot liquid splashed across his face. He screamed, cradling his scalds with fingers covered in gold rings. The mug hit the floor.

Lenina kicked the door shut and bolted it.

'Chuck, what the hell?' Ray stared at her. 'Are you crazy?'

Panic choked off her words. Even if she had been able to speak Lenina had no idea what to say. She grabbed a fistful of shirt and hauled him into the living room. 'You two, stand up,' she snapped.

Bristow leapt to her feet. She snatched her asp from her belt and flicked it once to extend the telescopic shafts. Her upper lip curled back. 'I knew you were trouble the moment we saw you last night. What's going on, Miss Miller?'

Lenina looked past her to the younger officer. 'Seriously, get up, now. They're coming.'

Slowly Jackson did as instructed. The whole time he watched her face, hands raised palm out. 'Just calm down, Miss Miller. Who's coming?'

Lenina felt a tingle down her arms. It came too fast to avoid. Saar's power surged into her limbs and gave the ancient being control of her body. With her hands, he grabbed PC Jackson and hurled him across the room, into the DVD cabinet. While Lenina struggled to reclaim use of her body, Saar picked up the sofa with no effort at all and propped it against the sitting room door on its short edge.

Bristow swore loudly. Ray yelped like a kicked puppy.

<Not strong enough> Saar turned her body towards the kitchen door. <Must leave>

'Give me my body back.' She lowered her voice.

<Leave!>

The tingling itch spread to her toes. Her legs took two steps towards the kitchen.

Sweat popped out on her brow.

'Stop it!'

'Okay, Miss Miller, stop right there.' Bristow pointed with the asp. 'Put your hands on your head and get down on your knees. Right now.'

Saar laughed. The sound burst through Lenina's mouth. From the other side of the barricaded door came the sounds of splintering wood.

Lenina turned her focus inward. The ancient vampire was there, the remnants of the cage she imagined to keep him under control all broken and twisted. He prowled through her mind like a once-trapped beast, marvelling in his sudden freedom. 'Please,' she cried, ignoring the startled looks of those around her. 'Give me my body back.'

<You don't know what they are. They will kill us>

'They won't. I can handle it. Please.'

The tingling stopped. The pressure in her limbs eased off.

<Try then. Try and fail. You're too weak>

A second crash drowned out her answer. Hinges squealed in protest as the door burst open. The sofa shot back three feet and toppled over upside down. Three strangers stalked through, Gold Teeth still shaking tea from his fingers. 'That wasn't very nice,' he murmured.

Their energy crackled through the air, prickly on the skin like coarse fur. Lenina's arms and face ached beneath it.

Though pale and shaky, Ray stepped forward. 'What do you want?' His voice trembled.

Lenina experienced a brief rush of pride before fear rolled in and swallowed it.

'I told you, we're looking for Lenina Miller. I guess that's her.' He inhaled noisily, sucking in air like a vacuum with a punctured nozzle. 'It must be her.'

Groaning, PC Jackson rolled on to his back. An avalanche of DVDs slid from the broken shelves and rained down around him. Their clatter filled the silence.

'What do you want?' Lenina shifted her weight to the balls of her feet. Darted her gaze from side to side. With full control over her body once more, she weighed up the options. Three on one. Not bad odds. Even as a young vampire she should be able to overcome three human men.

Saar snorted but said nothing.

Gold Teeth swaggered forward. 'You're coming with us.'

'Not a chance.'

'The leader of England's Red Fang chapter extends a personal invitation to you. I assume you know what that means.'

Lenina had no idea what it meant, but showing ignorance seemed unwise. She tilted her chin in as arrogant a manner as she could muster. 'I'm not going anywhere. Get out.'

'Don't be stupid. No one says "no" to Red Fang.'

PC Bristow slapped her asp against her thigh. 'You all have five seconds to get down on your knees with your hands on your heads.'

'But why? I'm lovely, me. Wouldn't hurt a fly.' Gold Teeth pressed a hand to his chest, twisting his features into an expression of mock hurt. 'Unless the fly was as annoying as you.' He snarled, a terrible ripple of sound. Yellow seeped across the whites of his eyes, blanking them out until nothing remained but the gleam of lupine gold and a round black pupil.

PC Bristow paled. Her hand lowered. Then, with a shriek, she dived forward, asp baton raised. She cracked the narrow end against Gold Teeth's shoulder and followed with a punch. He caught her fist and jerked it to the side, exposing her chest. His punch met her breastbone with an audible crack.

Her fingers flexed on the asp. Released. Dry, wheezing coughs slipped from her mouth. She fell, clutching her chest.

Gold Teeth released her and stepped over her fallen body.

As silence filled the room he grinned and placed his hands on his out-thrust hips. 'Care to try door number two, Lenina?'

<<<<>>>>

Walking The Razor's Edge, second in the *Saar's Legacy* trilogy
Coming soon

About Ileandra Young

Ileandra Young is one face of the Da Shared Brain who writes erotica and romance under a second pseudonym. Ileandra enjoys writing fantasy (both urban and traditional) and aspires one day to write a piece so long (and therefore thick) that the book would form a good self-defence weapon in the hands of a fan (even been hit by War and Peace? It hurts!).

Her interests include reading large books (see above), roller derby, and gently correcting people who believe that vampires should sparkle.

Discover more about Ileandra on her blog:
www.ileandraxraven.co.uk/about/about1/

or website: www.ileandrayoungsolo.wordpress.com/

Contact Ileandra via email: info@ileandrayoung.co.uk

Find Ileandra on Facebook: www.facebook.com/illyandraven

Stalk Ileandra on Twitter: www.twitter.com/ileandraXraven

Check out Ileandra's Goodreads:
www.goodreads.com/user/show/8564499-ileandra-young

Get Ileandra's quarterly newsletter: www.eepurl.com/oyPa1

www.ingramcontent.com/pod-product-compliance
Lightning Source LLC
Chambersburg PA
CBHW021234130626
46554CB00004B/1480

* 9 7 8 0 9 9 2 6 9 9 5 5 0 *